SLOTBACK RHAPSODY

A NOVEL

CHRISTOPHER HARRIS

ASPHALT
HOUSE

This book is dedicated to Eleanor Krasner

ACKNOWLEDGMENTS

Rachel Vogel, Chris Walsh, Bill Childs, Tony Catania, Craig Clark, Devin McIntyre, Tristan Cockcroft, John Barbaro and my family, thank you for your support and generosity.

THE LINEUP

OFFENSE
QB: Jim Shave
HB: Ezekiel Hoverman
FB: Xavier Toombs
WR: Thaddeus DeNoon
WR: Wendell Vance
TE: Keaton Wallace
LT: Antwan Richards
LG: Dominique Parnell
C: Bill Bettany
RG: Tommy Way
RT: Glover Pendleton
K: Orlando Bolduan

DEFENSE
LDE: Montrae Thomas
DT: Meleki Faafeu
DT: Da'Norris Maynor
RDE: Danny Shugarts
OLB: Chris McIntyre
ILB: Clancy Swift
OLB: Marcellus Blake
RCB: Husseyn Norwell
SS: Ed Scott
FS: Eric Brohammer
LCB: Kevin Hamill
P: Jon Scoggins

Head coach: Starling Fond
Offensive Coordinator: Brian Nugent
Defensive Coordinator: Tom Kolakowski
WR coach: Edward Kitchen
RB coach: Lester Jefferson
Special Teams coach: Mike Geathers
Strength & Conditioning coach: Jay Bedrosian

RESERVES

QB: Butch Hinkler
TE: Marcus Schenk
OL: Ronald Waltz, Ruvell Underwood
LB: Julian Edwards
CB: C.J. Yates
CB: Isaiah Townsel
Long Snapper: Tom Calcaterra
Special Teams: Ahmad Custance, Conrad King,
Nick Morrison

PART I

CHAPTER 1

I'm a minicamp body in 102-degree heat getting screamed at by the only other man my size: a middle-aged receivers coach they call Bow Wow. Gazelles surround me, men whose shoulderpads come up to my forehead. The quarterbacks are dressed in red, like busboys. It feels like Armageddon out here: the sun is perpetually low in the sky and an assassin. There are no onlookers other than the staff—and Coach Fond somewhere above—but the crowd noise they regularly blast through speaker stacks is shuddersome. Every time someone's attention flags, Bow Wow is there to threaten them with something worse than bodily harm: banishment.

It isn't my first rodeo. I was never drafted, but I've been in three camps, have made it as far as early September before the Turk tapped me on the shoulder. I spent two seasons ago on Buffalo's practice squad, hoping for an opportunity to line up on kickoffs and make a projectile of myself. At 27, I'm growing old fast.

*

Minicamp nights are for carbo-loading, offensive meetings and crippling pain. Nobody can raise his arms above his shoulders. My jaw hurts too much to chew gum. Those of us who are new in town stay at Theotokos College. When I sink onto the foam mattress destined to be occupied later in the year by a Catholic woman who couldn't get into Notre Dame, I try chanting *om mani padme hung*, but between my roommate's confusion ("you saying you want a mani/pedi?") and my exhaustion, silence intervenes quickly. When I dream, it's of Bow Wow: all weather and noise.

From the beginning, disaster has loomed in the knee ligaments of our highly paid wideouts. First goes Swinton, a graybeard now but a former All-Pro, during the most innocuous of drills: he yodels his pain and thrashes on FieldTurf while they hold him down. Next comes Barlow, a fourth-round rookie with a fat insurance policy, during private workouts. But the crusher is Desmond Johnson. He's a superstar, a purveyor of the noblest known combination: size and speed, heft and velocity, avoirdupois and flat-out *whoosh*: the two things in life you can't teach, they say. He's a former No. 3 overall draft choice—and thus instantly became a millionaire of about the highest echelon a 22-year-old can attain without narcotics, inheritance or boy-band affiliation— and was three straight years team MVP since, a silky smooth power forward with hands softer than a kitten's belly. They don't make him run in the minicamp heat; Johnson sits unassumingly beneath a modest blue baldachin marked "81" and plays with his phone. And he seems a good, relatively posse-free guy. But physics exempts none of us, and when a driver interrupts Johnson's late-night cardio excursion by cutting him down outside his Bloomfield Hills manse, both his knees suffer catastrophic damage. "Must've been a Chicago fan," someone muses on the radio.

So it is that a knock comes on my dorm door. My roommate, Townsel, looks at me with pure bug-eyed panic.

"Relax," I say. "They don't cut people yet."

It's Bow Wow. He says, "Be catching passes from The Man tomorrow."

"Why coach," I say. "You have a lovely speaking voice. I

don't believe I've ever heard it."

"Swellhead," says Bow Wow. "Nobody likes a swellhead." But something has changed. It's the first time there's even the slightest whiff in the air they need me.

*

The next morning I run with the ones.

No pads, just jerseys and helmets. We stretch in rows far short of military, jiving as the conditioning coach calls out the next calisthenic. Right beside me, middle linebacker Clancy Swift, defensive captain, scratches the inner workings of his big beautiful Afro while yawning. On my other side, Isaiah Townsel—an undrafted free agent trying to get noticed as a reserve corner—tucks his chin into his chest and mutters prayers. Some offensive-line types make a game of trying to land spit blobs on each other's massive bellies. The June heat is excruciating, has already drained sweat into my eyes. An airhorn sounds and I'm standing in the shadow of the starting quarterback, Jim Shave, and some political thing unfolds between Shave and the offensive coordinator: each seems to want the other to call a play. To the coordinator, it's a test of Shave's leadership to get *him* to suggest what play we should practice. Meanwhile Shave is a huge-ticket acquisition with a massive arm who apparently doesn't do head games. He chews gum, waits with his hands on his hips.

"924 F stop swing," the coordinator finally grouches. We line up and the first-string defense is in nickel with the extra defensive back sitting on our flanker, which means I might be the hot read. I have the 2 pattern, the slant: not always the safest route when linebackers are actually allowed to hit you, but a bunny in minicamp. Shave snaps it quick and I dig and push right and the ball is *on* me, a tracer between offensive-line helmets, and it harpoons my hand but I catch it somehow, tuck it away like it's nothing and turn upfield, and Swift hollers at me as I trot back to the huddle: "You *better* go

'Ooh,' little man."

"Did I go 'Ooh'?"

"More like this: *'Eh!'* Sound a 13-year-old girl makes the day she finally gets her period."

"Noted," I say.

Before long we're "running" laps for some perceived misstep, some exhibition in sluggishness the coordinator doesn't like. I limp along behind the toddling left guard, smirk at an equipment kid on the sidelines who on closer inspection turns out not to be a kid, but rather a tall skinny adult with three days' stubble and screw-you wraparound sunglasses. He gives me the finger, but slyly, while furling or unfurling some hose or other. I also run past Bow Wow doing faux military drills with some of the camp's lesser lights.

"You don't go hard now," the coordinator shouts after we reconvene, "you won't go hard when it hurts. You got to grain it into you, you got to teach your fucking body not to listen to your fucking mind. Your fucking mind is your fucking enemy!" It doesn't sound natural when he swears. "Your conditioning is for shit. Look at you! Look at you fatasses!"

"Man," someone says to me just outside the huddle. I don't know all the numbers yet. This is 74, an offensive lineman. "He'd bitch if you hung him with a new rope."

They run a bubble screen for me and Shave zings it too high; I get my hips turned while running on my toes and reach up, dig the ball with my fingernails, my feet drag the sideline by instinct—what a decade of single-mindedness will do—and I fall backwards out of bounds like a southern belle with the vapors. Only someone is standing there facing the other direction, and I mean I *plow* that poor soul: sure, it rattles my teeth a little but my 167 pounds strategically placed can pack a wallop. The other party falls forward, and goes *down.* I hear everyone on the field groan, and when I look up, many of them are hunching their shoulders, covering their eyes, crossing themselves.

I think I've probably killed an off-duty cheerleader or something.

But it's that same middle-finger equipment guy, whose name turns out to be Patrick Gasper. Our heads land beside each other—mine helmeted, his concussed—and we both look at our feet. Something's wrong. Three sets of toes point skyward, but the last goes the opposite way, indicating the road to hell. Well, I count the upturned cleats, one-two, and am ashamed to be relieved.

Team docs stand around and consider Gasper, then a white ambulance marked "Concord" pulls out of the team garage and sleepy EMS techs roll out a stretcher. Gasper is panicked, keeps staring at the back of his dislocated ankle and shouting, "He did it on purpose! He was trying to get me! He did it on purpose!" They roll and drive him away.

"That was nasty," Shave says, spitting out his gum.

"That'd gag a maggot on a gut wagon."

Swift taps a big knuckle on my shoulder. "I once seen a safety's eye pop all the way out, just hanging there by a red piece of string."

"Man," someone else says. "We cursed."

CHAPTER 2

I don't want minicamp to end. I don't want them to have a free month to bolster the receiving corps. The night before the last day, I sit in the dorm with Townsel, who's trying to look at his bare bottom in the mirror.

"Not my butt," he says. "Not my back. Like that little space in-between. It *itches.*"

I pop open my phone, close it. Open, closed. Henny's backlit face grins, darkens, grins, darkens. I'm on the bed, hamstrings screaming.

"Flesh-eating bacteria," I say.

"I can't see what it is," swiveling, contorting, inadvertently fanning out his latissimus dorsi like a flying squirrel. Like a lot of DBs, Townsel is a freakishly well-proportioned athlete: broad-shouldered, tiny-waisted. "Can't see nothing on me. I rash weird, Morrison. Black folk sometimes rash messed-up."

"I don't mean to make you worry," I say. "But I read an article about this. Necrotizing fasciitis. Infection of the deep layers of the skin."

"Bumps. My fingers feel…little bumps. Can't see nothing, but it itches like *heck.*"

"They had occurrences in Cleveland a few years back. Players jumping in the cold tub, getting a fever that night, and their testicles swole up to ten times normal size. Swole?

Swelled? Swelled, I guess."

"I get this stuff at home, whatsitcalled, 'Smoov.' Good stuff for your skin. But maybe you can only get it in Texas."

"It's fatal, is what I'm saying. If you don't catch it early, flesh-eating bacteria is almost always fatal."

"What do you think, Morrison. You think my agent should find me another training camp? You think I'm wasting my time here?"

But I'm dialing the phone. Henny answers.

"I can't believe they made another 9/11 movie," she says by way of hello. "I saw the preview yesterday, and it was like silence. I still don't think people are ready for that. Even though I know it's supposed to be about heroes, I just don't happen to think people are going to want to see it. I was sick to my stomach."

"How goes?" I say.

"It goes." Henny recently moved from New York, where she was a fashion model, to Phoenix. We've darted between friendship and dating for six years; I met her at Middleton College in a Postmodern Literature seminar, with whose professor it turned out she was sleeping. I occasionally paint her as cretinous, but she has a basically generous heart: she's in Phoenix making almost no money trying to ride herd on a charitable foundation that's supposed to give scholarships to poor children. However, before Henny arrived no actual tuitions were disbursed.

"Movies yesterday. What did you do today?"

"I walked around outside part of the day," she says. "I really think a person who lives out here just lives a more active lifestyle, y'know? Oh, man, I think my toes are sunburned!"

"How's Thomas?"

"Shut up." Thomas is the foundation's millionaire benefactor, a disorganized sexagenarian. I've never met him, but imagine him bronze and priapic.

"I'm not implying anything," I say, as Townsel slides on

satin pajama bottoms, swallows at least twenty vitamin supplements, and disappears into the bathroom. "I'm sure his motives are pure as the driven sand."

"You know, I could use a pair of shoes like the ones your mom had. I think they make them in the city. There's this one brand with the toes everyone swears by. Oh, my lips are like peeling off."

"Henny."

"How's camp?" It's to her credit she doesn't excavate much deeper than this, despite the condition I was in the last time she saw me.

"I dunno. Good, I think. What am I gonna do for a month? I was thinking of coming out for a visit."

"Cool. Great."

"No, don't worry. I won't really come."

"I'm not seeing anybody," she says. "I went out with a couple guys from online dating."

"Do you remember that time we went up to Burlington? We went drinking at that cheesy basement Polynesian place and went back to the hotel and listened to music in the middle of the night. I gave you one earbud in bed so we could listen together, remember?"

"I might collapse at the utter too-sweetness."

"And I taught you how to pump gas. You'd never pumped gas once in your life."

She says, "To what do I owe this little trip down something-something?"

"I think that was the same time as Hurricane Katrina, wasn't it? When we got back to Massachusetts everyone was gathered around the television and then I believe you had to run to the grocery store to get some 100% cranberry juice to fight off an impending urinary tract infection."

"This conversation has been awesome. What a charmer you are."

"Well, why does anybody do anything?" I say. "Why does anybody say anything?"

"Because they're lonely in the big wide world. Even in a crowd of millionaire bohunks." She hangs up.

I once wrote a haiku about Henny:

You, the vanquisher,
Leave half-drunk iced tea bottles
Everywhere you go

*

I think about Henny for a few more minutes. The windows are open to capture whatever faint breeze suburban Michigan cares to offer in this ridiculous heat, and down in the courtyard I hear voices: laughter, not the pleasant kind. I can't see much outside three cones of 60-watt light that demarcate concrete from burned-out grass, but then yes, a white t-shirt, somebody's elbow, someone else in boxer shorts.

"What are we gonna do with it?" somebody down there says.

"Quincy will fuck it," I think I hear, and then a beer can fizzing open.

"What are you doing?" I say to myself, gathering up my bathrobe and putting on sneakers. "What are you doing? What are you doing?" down the hallway, down two flights, into the slightly cooler outdoor air feeling my eyes adjust, there aren't all that many guys staying at Theotokos: almost all are a few years younger than I, and everyone's quite a bit bigger.

"Hey, Morrison." It's Billy Quincy, a non-roster linebacker, sprawled on the roof of a car someone's parked here on the grass. Quincy has on shower shoes, underpants and a farmer's tan. "Grab a beer," he tells me. Two other figures loom in the dark, and I think things might be about to get crazy.

"You all are celebrating something," I say.

"End of minicamp," says Quincy. "End of the world. Keep mixing up the two."

"They'll have you back in July."

"What's the point, what's the point, what's the point? You're on the inside or you're on the outside, and I'm definitely on the outside. I'll never make any money doing this, and I'll wind up putting down carpet with my brother. Doesn't seem fair," Quincy says. "Not when I want it so much. I know I'll get cut. It's just a matter of time, right? And then what happens? Nobody screaming for my autograph putting down carpet."

I look around, trying to locate where the others are. I feel them flank me. "You're blowing off steam."

"Boom," Quincy says calmly.

"Why don't we all put on some clothes," I tell him, "and play some two-on-two out here. Touch, tackle, I don't care. I could probably scare up a few other guys, actually."

A different voice, out of the dark, in a direction I hadn't anticipated: "You wanna play without pads, little man? Your spleen'll get broke." And I hear a dog's whimper.

"So you guys have a dog out here," I say. "Nice to see you're helping the league get back in PETA's good graces."

Quincy says, "Walk away."

"Whose dog is it?"

"We're not doing anything," says a third voice, a high-pitched voice I recognize: Brohammer, a reserve safety who made the roster last year. "He's fine." On cue, the dog cries again.

"Don't live up to every expectation," I say. "The world expects us to act like bullies."

"Why the fuck should I care what people think?" says Quincy, and I take a step forward and land a thick-sounding punch against his jaw. He crashes against the car's hood, grinning, and I shake my fingers and duck as someone tries encircling me from behind and I escape thinking sobriety is being awfully good to me, ninja-good, but then something bangs my temple—a bare foot—and I reel against a front tire, Quincy jumps down off the hood and lands his knee on my back and I try rolling into the dark but someone catches me and lands a great, throttling blow across my right cheek. I stay down.

"Gangsta shitbag *fuck*!" says someone.

"Hoooooooo!" someone else shrieks.

"Yeah! Yeah, little bitch! That's one shot! That's one shot!"

And then, their voices receding: "Aw, man. This is my good polo."

I rest in a cloud. The grass feels good on my face. Everything's ringing, everything's fine: I'm in another professional football camp, the thing one side of my brain plainly wants more than is good for the rest of me. And it's cooler down here near the soil. The air is distinctly more breathable.

The dog comes over and rests its muzzle against my cheek like a butcher weighing half-chickens. He breathes rhinoceros breath. I feel his neck for tags or a collar. He's a big, emaciated stray and he kisses me. He's being sweet about it, but he's desperate and knows paths to salvation don't come along often. I might stay here forever, having decided nothing, but a white flash blinds me and it's raining and the dog whimpers and nuzzles me. I get up and limp to the dorm, where nobody tells me I can't bring in a dog. It occurs to me I could've had wild parties all week.

Townsel jumps out of bed to cuddle the dog, sitting directly on the floor and receiving kisses within five seconds of their association. "Who is he?"

"It's your dog," I say. "Gift from me."

"I'm gone to Houston tomorrow night. Can't take a dog with me."

"Explain it to him."

"We got to find him some food!"

So I run some cold water across my face, then drive to a

Meijer and buy a sack of dog food, two raw steaks, and a squeak toy. The dog—he's a mutt with German shepherd and maybe some lab in him—eats slowly, with one eye on me.

"What were they doing to him?" says Townsel.

"The world's work," I say, getting on my bed and liking the jaded way I sound. I put the second steak across my damaged face, like a 1950s movie brawler.

"You keep him for me," Townsel says, "Pick him up when I get back."

"I might be going to Phoenix."

"Keep him for me. Then you got a reason to put in a good word for me, have 'em bring me back for training camp." He picks up his Bible, whose cover looks like it's done over in fake alligator skin, and reads at his too-small desk.

"Yeah," I say, "like I have anything to do with it."

"Everybody know, Morrison. Everybody know you hit your lottery ticket."

"I don't." I pick up my phone again, ignite Henny's picture. She's so pretty it makes my heart thrum. "I don't know what you mean."

Townsel does a white-boy voice: "Hwah-hwah, Huckleberry. I bet by-gosh ya really don't!"

But I don't. It's the underdog in me: the too-smallness, the too-slowness that carves holes in my confidence. I'm not one of those up-at-dawn, power-of-positive-thinking mighty mites who light up a room and make everyone believe anything is possible. Believe me. I don't see trophies in clouds. I see a Wordsworth poem in love with itself. I play football because I play football. I was a hero at a Division III school, carrying around the burden of never being recruited by anyplace bigger. I've memorized the interview I'll probably never give ("I switched to receiver because they told me I was too small to play running back in the pros" "I have to do my best with the body they gave me") and use it as kindling for my fear. Brohammer and Quincy: there's nothing they could do to me, not physically, because I've already signed away my rights to a healthy, normal body. The monsters who'll soon want to crush me in preseason games hold the contract and its dripping ink. I'll be the last to complain about a mangling, and I'll be the last to know anyone really thinks I can do this. Believe me.

I fall asleep for a few minutes, then awake to see Townsel again down on the floor, giving the dog a furious scratching. "Ohh!" he says. "Oh, I love this dog!"

"What are you doing with your teeth there?" I say.

"Can't help it. I get around something this cute, can't help it. I bite down my front teeth, have to like *grit* my teeth. 'Cuz he's so dang *cute*! Aren't you? Aren't you?"

The dog says, "Warrrrrrr!"

CHAPTER 3

In mid-July, with minicamp over and training camp proper a few weeks away, the weather is going crazy. The heat has hung like hot garbage over the Midwest for a few months, leading to drought and farmer suicide. When it rains, there's also hail and ball lightning. People in Detroit already trapped by a horrible economy and no help in sight are casting sideways glances at the sky. It has depth now, it hints at its stratospheric ends and the blackness beyond.

I work out. I work out in preparation for training camp through July's hellish heat with devotion, glad for the focus that hasn't always been easy for me, especially not lately. Oh, as a kid I was always disciplined. In high school and college I never drank alcohol, not because I had some moral issue but because of what someone might say. I ran with track teams, I lifted with wrestlers, I swam while the divers waited for the pool to free up. I wanted to hear people praise me for it. That's the truth: I left no stone unturned so that one afternoon I'd hear a coach or a parent or a friend raise my name to the rafters. When I tired, I imagined some middle-aged woman—attractive in a just-shy-of-matronly way, maybe someone's mother, perhaps a teacher—watching me, rooting for me to endure another lap, another set, another rep. Isn't acclaim our God? Isn't it what we dream of when we speak into our pre-teen hairbrushes and give our Hall of Fame acceptance? Don't we always pause for the crowd's roar? I'm probably just the kind of guy you'd expect would play for no adulation, in the middle of an empty stadium. Just the kind of high-effort waterbug. Oh, maybe I would. Maybe I would.

Anyway, I work out six hours a day, *hard*. I run with weights on my ankles. I vomit on hilltops. I double my lifting time in the gym. I eat hundreds of thousands of calories and torch them all with the white heat of a supernova monk. Every day has a pleasant blankness, despite or perhaps because of the heat. I could be in Palm Desert or Tupelo or Guam. The challenge is to view my actual being, my physical protuberance into the universe, as a creature of the mechanical age to be fueled and ignited, every day. I don't hurt as much as I bleed into my gauges' danger readings. People speak of a runner's high, but this is more pneumatic: a dissolution of the mind and a defeat of the body that leaves…either nothing or something worthwhile.

I don't go to Phoenix. I stay in the Detroit suburbs, in a chain hotel suite two miles from the team compound. The rooms are sterile but big, and the place allows dogs.

*

It's a week before training camp and this morning I run ten miles into Redford through River Rouge Park. Nobody is playing tennis, nobody is mountain biking, and only zombies are golfing. There are blown-out restroom buildings that look like haunted houses, picnic shelters with crashed-through ceilings and scorched tables, no glass on the light-pole fixtures; the park is watched by abandoned brick apartment buildings and tiny row houses with nobody stirring in them, and is flanked by liquor stores and a high number of suspiciously idle postal cars. The park grass is so burned out as to be unrecognizable as grass, and rather resembles Henny's spiked blond hair after a faux-punk photo shoot. Things are better once I reach Redford: the houses are still mostly ranch-style but the lawns are healthy and trimmed and the trees aren't dead. I run past a sign that says "Berwyn Pond: No Skating After Dark" but there's no water, just ferns in a deep basin.

I stop at a small brick house like all the small brick houses around it, except for a gruesome gargoyle-looking statue slumped on the lawn, surrounded by white-painted rocks. The gargoyle's face is twisted in pain, and he appears to be wearing a football helmet. This is Patrick Gasper's house.

He hobbles outside on crutches to meet me. "That's a pretty long run," he says. "You apologized just fine over the phone."

"I wanted to see if there's anything I can do." I'm saturated in sweat. I look like I've been swimming in team-logo t-shirt and shorts. "I feel really guilty."

"I'm getting a nice little worker's comp thing in the mail soon," says Gasper.

"I didn't mean to. You were yelling I ran into you on purpose."

He raises his hand. "Fuck. I don't think people should be held accountable for things they say when they get their ankle dislocated. It's one of the mottoes I tend to live by."

"How long have you worked for the team?"

He looks at the stirrup boot on his lower leg. He's in his early forties, tall, thin and red-haired, with a patchy strawberry-blond beard. "I know you can't partake," he says, "but I'm going to go inside where it's air conditioned and get really, just stupefyingly high. C'mon get some water or something."

His house's interior is a four-square of rooms decorated in Early Ataxia. Strewn food is absent but nothing else is: couch segments, books, lecterns, headphones, dumbbells, golf balls and much more are scattered around this place. He rolls me a tattered executive chair and prods a few buttons on a laptop. "The latest thing I'm working on," he says, "well,

I'm not working…it's a computer buddy of mine. There's a lot of people with a lot of free time on their hands at this exact moment in history. So we did this:" and he clicks something, I hear an automated voice mumbling gravelly nonsense.

"That's truly amazing," I say.

"Wiseass. Tell me something. Something totally random." He lifts a glass bong and his sky-blue plastic lighter, but holds steady for a moment. "How old are you? You're a fucking baby."

"This is the part where you straighten me out, make me question all my assumptions. Do me the biggest favor of my misbegotten life with your wisdom."

He types with one hand, and the gravelly robot says, "'My misbegotten life.'"

"I don't get it."

"It's Kurt Cobain, man. My buddy got every dipthong, glottal stop, sibilant and labial off his recordings, and wrote a program. You can have the mighty K.C. talk to you. We're thinking of having him make a new CD for us."

"Who's Kurt Cobain?"

Gasper blinks. "You're fucking with me."

"I am, yes."

"I get it. I'm old."

"You are."

"It used to be 'I can.' Now it's 'I still can.' You'll get there someday."

I say, "It doesn't really sound like him," and he lights up.

It strikes me lives are like this: so self-contained. Here in this house, on this street, people have routines of which they're weary, but of which I know nothing. It seems wonderful that a person could come here, stay on Gasper's book- and electrical-cord-covered couch, do a whole different set of activities that would be pressure-free and escape-worthy, except no vacation is ever permanent and pressure always finds you. I'll probably live in a place like this if and when the team cuts me from camp. "Who the fuck are you, anyway?" says Gasper. "I have to worry about drafting you in my fantasy league? You're a receiver."

"I was a running back in college. As you can tell, it was a pretty small college."

"Don't let the bastards grind you down," he says. "I once heard an interview with a famous rusher and everyone told him he was too small. 'I'm a small piece of leather well put-together,' is what he said."

"That works in theory, until someone literally more than twice my weight gets in a good shot. But hey, anyone you want to talk to down there."

"Oh, sure. Got the GM on speed-dial. No-ho, I'm on the PUP list. Say, make sure you're not getting any of this smoke, right? Sometimes it's a clam bake in here. Well, you got the world by the balls, Morrison. The world is yodeling at your command because it knows you'll squeeze if you have to."

"What's the prognosis on your foot? That was…." I pull a face.

"I get a walking boot soon. The pins out in another month or two. The worst part? Let me tell you the worst part, buddy-boy. Ice massage. Four times a day. Jesus fucking. You get a big Styrofoam cup, freeze water in it, tear off the bottom. Then put it all up and down the ankle, really knead it in there. Feels great for a minute. Hurts so bad by the end I could stick a fork in my eye."

"Sorry."

"I'm a native of Austin, Texas, even though I don't sound like a Texan. Things that cold don't sit right with my central nervous system. You get a quarter-inch of snow on the highway in Austin, people are skidding off into ravines, flipping over thirty times. But *God* I'm a colorful bastard with a little weed in me. You're asking yourself: did I sit around and get high like this before you fucked up my ankle? And if I wanted to torture you a little bit, I'd say no. But that'd be a lie. You don't seem like a dumbshit, by the way. You got that going for you."

"Thanks."

"Oh," he says, "I'm sure you have a big sweet spongy center same as any jock who's had his knob polished from the time he was five. But you got a half-a-vocabulary on you, at least. You ever read this?" He picks a paperback off the floor and flings it my way. But I drop it.

"Books? Oh, gosh no. No reading allowed. It's bad for the athlete's eyesight."

"Ha. Two years, by the way. I've had the gig two years."

"What'd you do before that?"

"Time," Gasper says. "Time-time-time-time-time. But everyone in jail is innocent, remember."

"I'll remember."

"Hey, don't take it personal I gave you the finger. I give everyone the finger at some point. It's a rite of passage. Anyway, I'm a nonviolent offender, don't you worry." The window unit humming in the corner drips. "And my plan," he says, "is to go on and keep being offensive."

I scratch my head, and feel the sheet of sweat loitering in my crewcut. He does make me feel young. In a profession where everything seems designed to do the opposite, it's not an unpleasant sensation.

CHAPTER 4

Training camp begins with a tattoo contest. Offensive linemen peel up their t-shirts to reveal flaming skulls and Challenger II main battle tanks; linebackers display new sleeves of laser-shooting octopi, dynamite sticks, mushroom clouds and the requisite judgment day crucifixes; our #1 draft pick—a cornerback out of Rutgers named Husseyn Norwell—has the team logo across his shoulderblades, for which he's mocked mercilessly (nobody else is so callow to believe they'll spend their entire pro careers with the same franchise); someone has a hyper-detailed Resident Evil zombie on his calf; but the winner has to be a reserve tight end, Marcus Schenk, who on the back of his shaved skull has M.C. Escher's "Hand with Reflecting Sphere," a total screw-with-your-mind effect where the hand coming up out of Schenk's neck seems simultaneously to be holding the reflecting sphere *and* Schenk's head, and the reflected old man seems to be happily residing there in Schenk's brainpan.

This contest happens in the facility's biggest meeting room, where eighty players and various staff sit in inclined rows while we wait for Coach Fond to enter below and address us. I'm not in the contest; I sit beside Townsel and watch, smiling. My only tattoo is on the inside of my right ankle: a tiny monochromatic Che Guevera acquired roaming the Vegas Strip the summer before college, in effort to appear deep. Truthfully, I'm kind of hazy on what Che Guevera actually did. Someone shouts, "Sugar Tits!" and star defensive end, mulleted Danny Shugarts, sits on my left after bumping potatoes with several other veterans. He offers to bump my fist, too.

"I'm Dan," he says.

"Hey there."

"You're Morrison?"

"Yup."

He puts his gym bag on the floor between our chairs, rests his hamhock forearms on the desk. His ginger goatee sparkles with a just-finished shower, and his red nose is a fullback charging into the open field. "Well, I heard about you," he says. "Welcome to the Show." And I can't help it: I get goosebumps.

At nine o'clock on the dot, Starling Fond steps into the room. His baseball cap is down tight over his face, his white shirt is pressed, and the tendons on his forearms and elbows stand out naturally, in the way of athletes entering their seventh decade of life. "I know you-all were disappointed with last season," he says in a soft baritone. It only takes a few seconds for the room to get intensely quiet. "Now, I was too. So what w'gonna do, w'gonna work you-all harder. There's a thing in this country they call the work ethic. I can tell you in my experience the team that works hardest wins ninety percent of the time." His feet are rooted to the blue carpet, and he gestures minimally. I can't see his eyes. "So we go' block. We go' tackle. We go' hit. What I want you-all thinking about is precision, men. Be precise. We go' work. Most important thing: we go' focus. We go' focus to the exclusion of all else. Some of you-all may have heard that my young son has contracted acute lymphoblastic leukemia. Well, he go' focus, too. Let's get out there this morning and focus." Coach Fond steps aside, and someone has turned on the overhead projector, which displays that single word in stark military lettering: FOCUS. When I look back down, coach has disappeared.

The practice locker room is big but not luxurious, with an island of towel bins and two refrigerators of Gatorade, an electronic scale that in another life might've been used at a truck weigh station, and sickly fluorescent light. The close-together locker stalls are a bone of contention with some veterans, who loudly grouse to nobody in particular about not having enough room to get dressed. I was #89 in minicamp but now I find a #84 jersey waiting in my locker, the same number I tried to make Buffalo with two years ago. I've spent the last month visualizing myself as 89. It doesn't matter.

We clack to the practice fields. I'm forever amazed the way it comes together: so many men—millionaires, iconoclasts, gangsters, rednecks—converging into the same space, the same clothing, to do the bidding of old men half their size. Maybe it shouldn't seem like such a miracle; there are teams in all walks of life. But here it somehow seems the equation should be different. Oh, sure, maybe football players are bodies looking for someone to tell them what to do. Still, you think so much about the stars on your team, the guys like Jim Shave and Desmond Johnson and Clancy Swift and Danny Shugarts, and they're so much bigger in your head, you can't imagine them all fitting in the same place at the same time.

They fired the old coordinator, and the new guy, Brian Nugent, is regarded as a bright young mind in the game. He gathers the offense for a few minutes and says, "None of your jobs are safe. I watched film on every one of you shitheads from last year, and you should be ashamed. Listen to what your position coaches tell you. You have to want it. Do your job and worry about nothing else. That will be all I'll ever tell you. Do your job. Focus! Focus! Focus!"

In the morning session, we do nothing but hit. It's a welcome development. It isn't always good for us, but most football players love contact. Match us up against someone roughly our size and let us smash one another. I remember thirsting for these drills at the lowest levels, in my Pop Warner days. I couldn't understand why all the kids didn't treasure these moments: lined up three yards away, three-point stance, cleats dug in, waiting for the whistle. Look at a man's belt, they teach you, but I couldn't help it: I always stared at his eyes, trying to find fear. On this team nobody fears the little man, but as I pound into running backs and wide receivers I aim to wipe the relieved confidence out of their expressions. I'm a blitzing corner bent on getting around a backfield block and by *God* I'll let them know I'm here; I'll use leverage and what strength I have, I'll get in their kitchens, I'll expend everything. Now I'm the blocker drawn in from my slot position and I'll deliver the blow before I receive it, I'll break fingers if I can, I'll make them toss me aside before I give ground. You hear that sound replicated a hundredfold: that click of helmets colliding, that meat-and-plastic percussion of pads giving and taking. Whistles screech all over the field, and you hear the requisite, "Hoo!" from onlooking players admiring a particularly vicious blow.

They line us up for Oklahoma drills. One man on offense, one on defense, in a narrow space (confined by a corridor of blocking bags). One ball carrier, one tackler, get through the corridor. It's a first-day tradition in many camps; it "sets the tone." You can't hide in an Oklahoma drill. The proven veterans rarely partake, but everyone watches. Everyone roots. Some place wagers. It's a vicious, bloodthirsty practice. Nugent demonstrates for the rookies: he blows the whistle and goes half-speed, walking forward as everyone laughs because the man opposite him is Meleki Faafeu, a 350-pound defensive tackle. Faafeu puts his arms out wide and the offensive coordinator is engulfed by him in a pretend-throttle. Then they quickly put in Tommy Way, our young right guard, and they give him a ball and the whistle sounds and he runs screaming forward with no hint of evasion and Faafeu absolutely decks him: one shoulder, square to the chin and down goes Way. He gets up clapping and pats Faafeu on the butt, and as he stumbles off I hear him saying to himself, "Finer than frog hair split four ways."

When my turn comes, I make a discovery. This is it for me. This is my last training camp. I'm 27, I've trained, I've studied. This is the last, because it's too hard on me. Break my bones, tear off my limbs, but everything between my ears is invested in this, and it's too much to give. I don't know why this revelation comes right now, especially after the past year I've had. But there it is. I take the dirt-smeared football from Nugent and tuck it under my arm with six points of pressure and wait with my eyes on Husseyn Norwell's belt and for the first time I can remember there's *something else*, something other than anticipation of the pure moment of athletic expression when I'll crush or be crushed: there's anxiety that investing so much emotional energy in something destined to end in heartbreak is truly damaging. You see, I know how this movie ends. I wind up cut, then despairing, then emotionally comatose.

The whistle blows and I charge at the #7 overall pick in April's draft, I give him the slightest leg-drag hesitation to get his weight going the wrong way and then barrel into him—he's got six inches and 30 pounds on me—and he is (in the parlance) *blown up* and falls backwards as I streak past and I discover that I'm crying.

Bow Wow brings the receivers into the end zone and we practice toe taps in the back corner. He throws fades and posts, intentionally too high and too far, and we go up and get the ball, and try to get both feet down in the field of play. Bow Wow screams at us: "You terrible! You terrible! What the fuck you think? You think every ball come in room-service? This is pro-fesh-shun-al football! They wanna kill yo' fucking quarterback! You gonna die for him? You gonna die for him?"

Actually, maybe he's saying, 'You gonna *dive* for him?' I can't tell.

"Watch this, little man," #88 says to me, and he runs a corner and stretches himself beautifully and the catch is good.

"Nice," I say.

"Go do it your own damn self," he says. I try, but Bow Wow's pass is too tall. "That's all right," says #88. "Good look. Good look."

They record everything at every practice. There are cameras all over the two exterior practice fields, and the one field inside our practice bubble. The coaches spend hours digesting everything they see, even body language, and then show us highlights in meetings. I didn't know this my first camp. I'd laugh and joke with other guys, guys whose job I was nominally threatening. I'd go down on one knee to catch my breath. But what message does that send some poor assistant coach or assistant's assistant, who has to sit there and chart every moment of a half-dozen cameras' worth of video? He's working hard, and I'm not? I need that guy's approval. I can't give him a reason. So today it's all business. I have a plan for every instant out here.

*

At lunch I sit with Townsel at a six-man table otherwise occupied only by defensive players, a group which includes Norwell. We exchange a quick look of hatred, but then he remembers he's a millionaire and asks me where I went to school.

"I went to Middleton, up in Massachusetts," I say. "But I'm not a rookie."

"Oh. Cool, man. Cool." He has two racks of ribs on his plate and squirts a half-bottle of hot sauce on them. Everyone's jaws are moving like biceps. I'm not hungry, but need propellant for the second session.

"So Rutgers," I say. "Know the fight song?"

"Shit, yeah. I'm ready."

Townsel says, "Nobody knows the place I went to.

When they make me sing it, I could make up the words."

"Do it!" says Norwell. "Off the chain!"

"Man," says a guy at the table's other end, "I don't feel too good," and he throws up the half-chewed contents of his stomach all over the floor and himself, and the room erupts in masculine banging and applause.

"Dang," Townsel says.

"Oh, shit," says Norwell. "You know what that shit mean. Free pass. First clown to puke, he safe from the Turk first time he come around."

"Really? Morrison, is that true?"

"No," I say. Norwell looks at me. "Maybe."

"Naw, they probably take his playbook right now," Norwell says.

"'Son,'" says Townsel in his Old Man Fond voice, "'We-all don't got any use for weak stomachs 'round heah.'" Everybody breaks up laughing, then he says, "But that dude's a genius. It's an honor to have him as my coach."

Norwell looks around. "Where he at anyway? I know coaches don't eat in here, but I ain't seen him since this morning."

"He likes to watch upstairs," I say. "He doesn't come down and mingle much. If you'd signed your contract in time for OTAs, maybe you'd know that."

"Shit," Norwell says, smiling, "man's gotta make his bank while he can."

After position meetings, all newcomers to the organization—rookies and free agents alike—attend an additional "orientation" session hosted by beefy Jay Bedrosian, the strength-and-conditioning coach. "You know, don't do any drugs, because you'll get caught. Don't get in trouble with the law. Don't gamble. I mean, nobody gives a shit if you fill out a college hoops bracket. But don't bet on football. What else?" I've only ever seen Bedrosian with his neck tendons puffed out and his face three shades of purple. Now he wears reading glasses and a scholarly frown. "The vets know this, but for fuck's sake you kids, don't spend all your money at once. The average lifespan in this league is three-and-a-half years. Don't be a truck driver when this thing is over."

On the way back out onto the practice fields, somebody pats my shoulder. It's Zeke Hoverman, the former second-string running back promoted by default to the top job this winter. Last year's starter left in free agency, and there are doubts about Hoverman, a career underachiever. He's a physical specimen and has some potent-looking dreadlocks, but he's never done much in the league. "Yo," he says. "Carry these." He hands me his helmet and shoulderpads.

"I'm not a rookie," I say again.

"Tell it to the fucking union."

*

We hit more. I run past Shave and say hello, and he says, "Hot enough for you?" The quarterbacks are in a row, first-, second- and third-string, taking simultaneous snaps with three different footballs, dropping back in lockstep, executing the same fakes and tosses with perfect synchrony. Nugent is here, nodding. The quarterbacks coach is shouting, "The Mike is blitzing! What do you do now! The Mike is blitzing! What's your checkdown!" Somewhere off to the side, a punter shanks one and it comes inches from thumping into the quarterbacks coach's head. Shave says, "I'd have paid good American coin for contact."

"Throw to me after practice?" I say.

"Sorry," he answers, grunting a little on another laser throw, "photo shoot."

I sprint to where the defensive linemen are driving blocking sleds like donkeys in the insane summer sun. Bow Wow is about to summon us back for more drills. Danny Shugarts gets to the end of his rep and waves at me. "Mighty Mouse!" he says. "What's up, Mighty Mouse?"

I shout, "What's up with you, Sugar Tits?"

The placekicker, Orlando Bolduan, steps over (even he's got an inch or so on me) and says, "Pretty brave, calling him that from way over here."

"Do I know you?" I say.

"I'm Bolduan. I'm the kicker."

"*I'm* the kicker," I say. "I'm the new kicker."

"You're wearing 84."

"I guess they ran out of numbers. I guess we're in competition together."

"They didn't tell me," Bolduan says. "Nobody told me this."

"Sorry to be the one to deliver this news. Let's make it a clean one, right? I know you've got a lot of experience, and I really respect that. I'll have you know I'm here to win the job. I've been training at high altitude, in Buenos Aires. I made three straight from 74 yards out, but it might've been the thin air."

"Oh," says Bolduan.

Bow Wow blows his whistle and I sprint, thinking, *None of that, none of that, none of that.* If this is it, don't give them a reason.

Sure enough, as I approach him Bow Wow says, "You got a great future, Morrison! You got a great future right beside me! You gonna be a coach, Morrison! Someday you gonna make a great fucking coach!"

CHAPTER 5

Public admission begins our second day, and a tiny kid wearing matching camouflage pants and shirt stops me and hands me an autograph book, which I dutifully sign and give back, only to hear the kid say, "Who? I don't want *yours*!"

I line up holding a football, waiting for the whistle. I sprint forward and they bombard me with fire hoses: I'm nearly knocked to one knee but stay balanced, unable to see, the turf is mush and I keep my legs going, my helmet feels like a portable aquarium, I look for the tackling dummy at drill's end but wind up simply launching myself at something blue. I hit the padding, sluice to the ground, still holding the ball.

I watch others partake of the hose drill. #88 is here: Wendell Vance. I come up to his chin.

"There you go, Morrison! There you go!"

"Whoo!" I say.

"Bring it! Bring it!" With his gloved hand, he thwaps the side of my helmet, hard.

"Yeah! Yeah!"

We hold our first scrimmage for the fans, just one play at a time. I'm on the sidelines with many others, as the starters endure long hands-on-hips interludes of animated coaching punctuated by moments of frantic violence. The crowd of perhaps five hundred onlookers cheers on every hit. The defense is dominating, and a reserve offensive lineman named Ronald Waltz says to nobody, "That's all right. That's all right. The defense is supposed to be ahead of the offense at this point. At this particular *juncture*."

"You sure?" says Townsel, who's staying in the hotel suite next to mine, though so far I've retained ownership of Agamemnon the dog. "Maybe you thinking of baseball?"

"Naw," says Waltz, "naw. It's easier to destroy something than build something. It takes a…it takes a finer hand. Anybody can just run into a room and break something. We got to train ourselves on offense to make something. We got to."

"Or maybe," Townsel says, "you all are just real bad at football."

I shield my eyes and look up at the one-way windows that overlook the field, where Coach Fond is presumably evaluating the obvious first cuts, allowing his assistants to do the grunt work out here. I've had disappointments in my life. Failure to earn a big-school scholarship offer. The first time I looked at the Dean's List and didn't see my name. (I got used to it). When Henny came smirking out her front door trying to block my view of a hairy leg reclining on her couch. But each time the Turk has called my name, especially two years ago in Buffalo, well, it's a physical thing, a coldness that washes you out, a rejection so thorough it feels like there's no coming back. But of course, you have to thank the assistant coach who has the distasteful task of cutting you, you have to ask him for constructive criticism, you have to promise him you'll try harder and be back next season.

"Don't spin! You fucking one-hole friction whistle! Don't fucking spin! Hit the hole! Hit the fucking hole!" This is Nugent, the offensive coordinator, with everybody stopped around him: he walks past the receivers, through the offensive line, and pokes his finger into Zeke Hoverman's chest. "I watched you! We all watched your film! You know what I see? I see a guy afraid to get hit!" Looking down at

Nugent, Hoverman says something I can't hear. "Then fucking play like it! Hit the fucking hole!"

They run Red Right 30 Pull Trap and Hoverman dervishes upfield behind Tommy Way and gains 25 yards, bouncing up from the tackle and shrieking his excitement, but Nugent stands with his arms folded, holding his laminated play sheet, looking pained. He doesn't say anything. After a couple pass plays, he calls Ace Big 16 Power—a simple short-yardage buck—but Hoverman seems to feel the hole closing on him and bounces out wide, gaining another dozen yards. Nugent blows his whistle, and keeps blowing, storming over to Hoverman, blowing, blowing, blowing, so the tailback stops slapping five and puts his hands back on his hips.

"Locker room!" the coordinator shouts, through his fussy little mouth that looks like a flower petal. Hoverman removes his helmet, gently places it on the field, and walks off, un-Velcroing equipment and looking to the horizon, at nothing.

Geathers, the special teams coach, fills the silence, yelling for the punt return and coverage units to line up. Right now I'm second-string on returns. They punt once and Brohammer makes a couple shifty moves, then they line it up again and I'm out there counting teammates, finding the sun, wiggling my fingers. When I hear that thump, when the ball's in the air: it's the exquisite torture of Christmas Eve or being tickled so hard I can't breathe. I am trained to look away from the charging bulls. There is only the oblong object spiraling like a child's charm. And something will happen next: something is coming. When I look down again maybe there'll be an alley worth weaving through. Maybe all options will be exhausted. The fear makes it twisted. It is *fun*. I get lucky on this punt: it's a boomer that sends me backwards, but this gives me more time than usual to assess the field. I get a great block and turn it up, I suddenly see no color but green before me, the punter has no interest in tackling me during a drill, and I'm gone. The fans, such as they are, roar.

*

After this scrimmage Tom Calcaterra, the long snapper, has his feet in a bucket of ice and he says to me, "You know what I saw on TV last night? A show about the times America almost nuked itself."

I'm out of my shoulderpads but in my uniform pants, which are still soaked. The locker room is quarter-filled by those of us who've made quick work of the midday meal. Most everyone else in here is listening to music through ear buds, but someone hidden from view way down the room's other end is playing hiphop aloud and trying in bass monotone to sing along. Everyone I can see looks exhausted and bored.

"One time was in the Korean War," says Calcaterra. "A B-29 bomber crashed in California. It was transporting nuclear bombs to Guam just in case we were gonna hit Korea with one. Another time was Idaho Falls, which isn't that far from Jackson, Wyoming, where I'm from. Somebody did something wrong with some cooling system and the thing melted down, the only time somebody ever died directly from nukes in U.S. history. They found one worker's body pinned to the ceiling by an exploded control rod, and they all had to be buried in lead coffins, they were that radioactive."

"Man," I say. Calcaterra has a squarely handsome face and comically rounded eyebrows, and is probably 35: a hanger-on in a league that can never find enough long snappers. He smiles most of the time and takes naps in the equipment room.

He says, "And I think they said there was a nuclear incident here in Detroit. I was falling asleep by then, though."

*

That night, Gasper has on a blue chef's hat for some reason. We're in the back of a Hamtramck saloon, a dive next door to a Polish League of American Veterans outpost. The streets outside are broad and dotted with squat buildings. I'm so sore and wasted from the day's camp and it's so hot in this back room, where the bar's owner has taken Gasper and me, I fear I'll drift off. But I listen: the conversation begins with drugs, moves seamlessly to my ineligibility to partake, then on to the question of how easily I could sneak clean urine into a screening.

"Really," Gasper says, "you don't understand. They *watch* you piss."

"Just take a Visine bottle with clean pee," says his friend Sumon, the owner. "Hold it in your hand when you go. I beat it just like this one time."

"No way," from Gasper. "Trust me, I've been there. This isn't You Get To Duck Into A Private Stall For The Actual Pissing. This is Let Me See Your Hands While You Do That. They look at your dong. No Drano under the fingernails. No bleeding into the sample. They flat out look at it, to make sure it's you."

"A catheter," Sumon suggests. We're sitting on a couple overstuffed couches, hearing Sumon's clientele laugh and whistle just on the other side of this beaverboard partition. A stack of unlit incense sticks are on a table before me, and there's a red-felt cutout of a human heart on the wall just here by my head, on which are written Arabic letters. I wonder what they mean.

"And what? Surgically implant a bag of clean piss under his skin?"

Sumon scratches his chin and then snaps his fingers. "Inject the clean pee into his bladder."

"Ding-ding-ding. Right answer. But his bladder's got to be completely empty, and his clean-pee source has to be the same every time. Plus he has to not mind the turkey baster up the old drainpipe and the possibility of infection."

All this ignores the fact that I've only smoked marijuana twice in my life: once I coughed too hard to feel anything, the second time I was hell-bent on actually getting stoned and overdid it, becoming so irredeemably high I reportedly spoke in a Yiddish accent then raced to vomit in the toilet.

Gasper is handling some sleek-looking gray disk with more Arabic writing on it, writing that goes around in a circle. Absently, he passes it from hand to hand, laughing at Sumon's jokes, then he leans forward to say something and lets the disk fall; I find myself straining to catch it, but it bounces off the couch cushion and somehow back up into Gasper's waiting hand, though he isn't even looking. He says, "I have a buddy with a cabin up on Houghton Lake. We can use it any time. After I get the pins out of my foot, let's…. What's the squad's bye week, Nick?"

"No idea," I say. "Never yet made a team."

"If it's early October, that'd work. Yeah. Maybe something special along for the trip. High-resin and delicious."

"No no no," says Sumon. "This is not time for a vacation. Some of us have a family, you scalawag."

"We'll get Hamilton to come. And the Kinseys. Is Zbigniew still living up in Gladwin?"

"You do not listen, my friend. I most certainly cannot leave my business in these times."

"You know the only thing worse than Detroit 'in these times'? *Talking* about Detroit 'in these times.' Fuck, man, the new biggest export of our fair city is heartbreaking thought pieces. Did self-pitying tears put the rust in the Rust Belt? Yeah, the jobs suck, the money's gone. It's bad. It's really bad. Do we need to make ourselves feel like shit *talking* about it every minute of every day?"

Sumon's eyes are bugged out as though he's horrified, then he laughs a throaty, baritone laugh.

We hit a few other Hamtramck dives, and chef-hatted Gasper sees many more friends whom he greets with modesty and delighted smiles. In Frenchy's Old Fashioned, we meet a drunk named Cliffy who tells us he's 62 and has wasted half his life in this relatively quiet bar. "That's what makes the young'uns here love me," he says. "They only wasted a couple years so far." I'm not drinking much because there are more two-a-days ahead. But I'm having a good time, laughing and grousing with all the characters. Everyone talks to Gasper about unemployment, or layoffs, or crime, but they do it with heads cocked to the side, palms up, eyebrows raised, smiles wry. In my experience happiness is rarely so obviously mixed in with sadness, and maybe it appeals to me. Nobody here feels the need to act artificially overjoyed. There seems to be a love of tragedy in this place: or maybe that's overstating it, but at least maybe this group takes droll pride in its helplessness. The world will deliver what it will deliver.

*

Nugent stands next to me as I stretch. He's stooped over, hands on knees, and his whistle keeps tapping him on the shoulder as he tries to keep our conversation private. He says to me, "You know Slant Left 787."

"Yes, sir," I say to his upside-down visage. "I go to the post."

He thinks for a minute, and in this position his face goes a little purple. "You know Green Right Near 60 Trap."

"I think there's a tight end in on that one, sir, not me."

"So what I'm getting at here is: do you know more than just the slot routes on these plays? You know what the fullback does on Green Right Near 60 Trap?"

"Yes, sir."

"I want you to show me. You know what we look like in Fullback East Right?"

"Yes, sir."

His mouth is a scrunched-up little bowtie. He straightens and dons his team-logo visor. "Show me," he says louder.

"Show me."

We're scrimmaging with real referees now. I'm in with the first-team offense. I look around the huddle and see the faces of the offensive linemen, looking youthful and squished in their helmets, like five sumo wrestlers. Hoverman is in here, too, and I watch his rockinghorse eyes. We're in Fullback East Right and I'm set half-a-step back from the line with the mammoth tight end, Wallace, and the even more mammoth right tackle, Pendleton, on either side of me. By all outward appearances, it's a small change from where I've been lining up since minicamp. But it's a huge difference: being inside the tight end puts me in the suck. I run a decisive little slant and Shave zings it to me, whereupon I'm flattened by an inside linebacker who says, resting for a moment on top of me, "Eek. A mouse."

Three plays, four plays, five…I'm still playing with the ones. Nugent comes over and says, "Morrison plays half on this one. Hoverman, you're full." Hoverman doesn't say anything.

We line up. This is about to be my first professional carry. We're in Brown Left, I'm offset to the right. Hoverman lunges forward and dings a linebacker, I run behind Shave, parallel to the line, and feel the football pounded into my stomach in the old familiar way and I follow Hoverman—he gets a good block! he's a good man!—and I break through the defense's first level and take a crunching hit from a safety. The crowd's murmurs tell me it was a good-looking run. My shoulder feels sticky from the contact but the most important thing I'll ever do is not let the discomfort show. I flip the ball refward and step quickly back to the huddle.

CHAPTER 6

You'd think the pain of camp would abate after several days, but no: in a Secretary of State branch office I sit on a hard wooden bench and feel stinging in my lower back, my calves, my ribs. There's a television here with the news on but the sound off. Nobody here looks up. We all stare willfully at our knees.

I phone Arizona.

"Where are you?" says Henny.

"DMV, or whatever they call it here."

"Ugh. God. Don't they have *people* who can take care of—? Wait a minute. Why are you there? You have a New York license. I remember talking to you, what, last year? You were waiting in line just last year."

"I moved, didn't I?"

"So what? Nobody changes their license until the expiration date. It's a right of citizenship."

"That's not true. You actually have thirty days."

"Boy scouts make me nauseous."

"I never made it that far. I was in Cub Scouts, though."

"This is what you do with a morning off? It seems somehow…metaphorical."

It's Henny's broad contention that I habitually cut off my nose to spite my face, something I don't necessarily agree with. I believe I have as strong a grasp on the big picture as the next person. In this case, the truth is more twisted. I love licenses and ID cards, shopping advantage memberships and even old-fashioned bankbooks. I've moved from New York to Massachusetts to California to Ohio and each time I've taken patient joy in anchoring myself, have made certain to destroy defunct cards and licenses. I'm eminently trackable. My phone wedged under my chin, I look through my wallet and find: library cards from four different towns; a gym membership from my parents' club; a video rental card; two credit cards; a gas card; an ATM card; a picture-ID-cum-magnetic-stripe for the team facility; three restaurant gift cards; and advantage cards for a supermarket chain, a pharmacy chain, a haircutting chain, an electronics chain, a bookstore chain, a discount shoe chain, a pet food chain (lately acquired), and a sporting goods chain. There are no photos in my wallet. I can't exactly explain why all these registrations and memberships are such a comfort, but they are. One dirty secret: sometimes if I can't sleep I walk to my kitchenette and spread all this plastic on the countertop and feel soothed by the notion of the transactions that have put them all here.

"What number are you?"

"C-52," I say. "They're on C-14."

"And how do you feel?"

"Good. Great. I mean, I'm okay."

"Remind me again why you're doing this to yourself?"

"I hate when you say stuff like that, Henny. What, I'm tilting at windmills? It's impossible, what I'm trying to do?"

"No. Jesus. Why do you twist things around? Instead of, 'She cares about me,' you hear, 'She thinks I suck.' I just meant wanting something that's so hard, right? You're not a casual wanter."

"I'm not?"

"I'll be crystal clear. I think your outsides are super capable of making this team. It's your insides I worry about."

I watch a middle-aged lady whose nametag reads Yolanda. She's patiently explaining something to an over-tattooed kid in a ripped t-shirt and oversized work boots. He stabs his finger against the countertop, but she keeps cool.

"Anyway," Henny says. "Are you…coming out to see me?"

"Uh-oh. What happened?"

"Everything's really good. It's a hundred million degrees and I keep getting colds from sweating in the a/c. I got up early yesterday and went golfing with this guy, he owns this biometric workout place or something. I really need to go to the driving range." I imagine she's looking at herself in the mirror. She says, "Remember Gould's Victorian Lit class? Remember the first day? He walked in with a cardboard box, and he told us to pass it around and look at what was inside."

"I remember that."

"It had like a mirror, some rocks, an action figure, a ruler. We passed it all around and put it all back in the box, and he took a long look at us and said, 'All right. Do the first reading and have a three-page paper done by Tuesday.' We were all like, *what*? Did you know I talked to him about that on the last day?"

"No."

"I asked him, 'What was up with that stuff in the box?' And he was like, 'I have no idea what I was doing. I just made it up. It was just something to do.'"

"Henny."

"I made such a mistake."

"With Thomas."

"Yes."

I don't want to have this conversation, but I do. My heart aches groundlessly but there is pleasure—biting a painfully sour candy—dropping into another of her personal cataclysms.

"His wife caught us. Nothing really happened. But she saw what she saw."

I want to say, *You're dallying with a married guy easily old enough to be your father, it goes bad, and you want me to fly out there and massage your shoulders and feed you bellinis until our clothes are off, and* then *you can decide whether you really want me.* But it's no time for indignation. There's no insight here: we mean different things to one another. I'm the type of foal to which she attaches herself, I'm her developmental bet. She's inspected me, trained me, and I've taken great pride in the quality of the saddle. Imagine if I didn't have any saddle at all! I know it: Henny has always recognized me as a type, but she's recognized me.

"Do you still have your job?" I say.

"I don't know yet."

"Worry not, fair maiden. You're a good person."

"Oh, I know it. I know I am. I wasn't looking confirmation of *that.*"

But this isn't true.

*

I'm in a running backs meeting. There are eight of us here, nine counting Lester Jefferson, who coaches the rushers. Jefferson is lately retired after three seasons of trying to come back from a neck injury; unlike our other ex-player coaches, he's still in the general vicinity of his playing weight, and his pectorals still protrude further forward than his gut. He wants to be our buddy.

"Yawl can do this," he says, using a tiny remote device to advance and rewind a recording of this morning's practice, so the Clydesdale offensive linemen jerk into motion then improbably take long backwards strides and swan beautifully back into perfect formation. "Yawl just gotta think a little bit, right? Come on, gahs. Come *on.* Yawl gotta read. Yawl know how to *read!* Every last one a yawl went to college! If they run a stunt here, yawl's job is read the end. Sugar Tits come around thoo the middle, he's yawl's guy. Block his ass. Sugar

Tits back off play cover, yawl find the linebacker. It's just *readin'*, gahs."

Coach Jefferson will one day learn this isn't the best approach. We are better motivated by fear. Nobody here is sleeping or doodling, but we've lapsed into the classroom passivity that probably defined all our academic careers. Nobody is learning anything. I've been careful not to sit in the front row of these meetings, not wanting to seem the teacher's pet. But really, I do know all this stuff. None of the mistakes Jefferson shows are mine. Instead I'm studying necks: the furrowed, skin-flapped, tree-trunk necks all around me. Necks that have no doubt had weights swung from them and have supported millions of trapezius raises, but necks that are also naturally among the world's knottiest, a veritable genetic convention of cervical outliers. For some reason, this is mildly upsetting. I try to think about other things—a photograph I remember of acolytes in saffron robes listening to a guru at Bodhgaya—but I keep coming back to the corrugated, shiny flesh of these beastly napes, flickering in the TV light. Oh, my own mother-of-pearl debutante's! Well, maybe this is simply yet another club to which I'll never belong.

We finish and I walk out with the fullback, Toombs. His goatee is beautifully manicured and his hair is cut in a mohawk. He says, "My kids comin' today. Off from summer camp, gonna watch daddy bust a few heads."

"How old?" I ask him.

"Six, five and four. Three little men. Sign my first contract, wife start shootin' them out. Some people get the signal from God to have kids when they get married. Us, we start when the check cleared. They gonna like you, rook. You 'bout their size."

"I'm not a rookie."

He pats my shoulder. "I know it, Mouse. I know it."

Getting back into pads, one practice session bleeding into another, the day of the week impossible to know, my hips and ankles throbbing like tiny dance clubs, Hoverman sits down two chairs over, in front of someone else's stall. He's making a production of hooking and unhooking his pads, tightening and buckling. The tips of his dreads have lately been dyed orange, giving him a sun-tinged aspect. He looks at me, looks away, fidgets more with his equipment. The second-year backup quarterback, Butch Hinkler, comes over and says:

"What have we here? What. Have. We. *Heah?*"

"Hey, Hinkler."

"Check it out," he says, "I'm trying out new nicknames. 'Hurricane Hink.'"

"Uh-huh."

"'Bringin' the weather,' baby."

"Hink, we were just taking note," I say, "of what a good sport you've been about all this. Me and Zeke were just commenting to each other."

"About all what?" says Hinkler.

"This Wildcat stuff. These new packages. They'll be taking Shave off the field, oh, ten or fifteen plays a game, putting Zeke here under center."

"They are?"

"I guess it means they might keep only one quarterback active on game days."

"They can't do that," says Hinkler. His cleft chin twitches. "I think it's in my contract they can't do that. I gotta talk to Nugent."

I smile at him.

"You dick," he says, and saunters away.

I try not to look at Hoverman, but can't help myself. He knows I'm looking, and almost suppresses a smirk. He says, "You make that running back room just a little more *fundamental.*"

"Ah, right," I say. "And worse-jumping."

He slips on his jersey, turns his chair in my direction. "Help me with something. I've got you in San Diego. Then

Cleveland. Then Buffalo a couple years ago, and you were on their practice squad."

"This is very flattering."

"But nothing last year."

"No."

"What do they say? Your star is rising. The public will want to know how their new hero came out of nowhere."

I feel a little sick, and it has nothing to do with exhaustion. It's true. Last year I was, as they say, "out of football."

Hoverman sees me squirm, and exhales big. He has a roll of tape and tears away little strips with which to individually cover each joint of each finger. It's work of high concentration. He says, "We're the same age, you know that? But I feel like I'm maybe fifty. My toe hurts like fuck. I move around my ankles when I sleep, and the noise sometimes wakes me up, man. I think it's somebody setting off firecrackers. I'm not used to this shit. My elevator has always gone up, you know what I mean? All of a sudden, maybe my elevator isn't going up anymore."

"You're saying that's my fault."

He's still tearing and taping, tearing and taping. "No. It's the asshole coordinator. Looking for a reason to shitcan my ass. My wife says to ask for a trade, get the fuck away from him."

"I don't really even have that many plays, do I?"

"It's not you, man." His dreads sway. "Not you."

So the truth. The truth is I didn't try and make a roster last summer because I was still, as the saying goes, sulking in my tent. I really thought I'd make the Buffalo roster, and failed to get off the mat when I didn't. I also wasn't eating much, and every time my mother came to my childhood bedroom to order me around—take out the trash, for example, or do a load of laundry—I smiled sweetly and fluttered my eyes. At my therapist's office, I was charming with anecdotes from my aborted pro football career, soulfully aware of the worry I was causing my parents, a model patient in all regards and obviously (to the therapist as well as myself) preoccupied with how I came across. It became a familiar exchange:

"What do you think would happen if you let your guard down?" he'd say.

"I don't know what you mean. I don't know if I even *have* a guard. Maybe that's part of my problem. Maybe we should work on that."

"Tell me what you *feel* right now."

"What I feel? I feel frustrated that you won't listen to my suggestions."

"Is there anything I could do or say that could make you feel sad? That could make you experience sadness right here, right now, in this room?"

"What's there to be sad about?"

"You tell me, Nick. You're the one who's in his mid-twenties and doesn't have a job, you're the one who doesn't leave home much. These are things you say you want, yes?"

"Yes."

"But you're not sad about them."

"Not really."

"Hence: your guard is up."

It went around and around, me trying to pinion this kindly man with instances where he violated his own logic rather than try and understand my hermetic act. Well, I was a little jerk. All because the universe dared deny me my dreams? I didn't know. My father brought me to blood specialists to see if my condition was physical, but they found nothing other than mild anemia. After last Christmas I visited Henny in the city and one morning while she was in the shower I wept over her discarded pajama bottoms: their cotton-soft dilapidation, the way they looked slung low on her hips. She brought me to parties just shy of trendy but filled by people who *wanted* to be trendy, and I said cutting things afterward. I begged her to stay in bed with me all day, tried too hard to bring her to previously unimagined orgasmic heights, sulked watching television when she left for a photo shoot, then had vivid dreams in which she left me for good, again and again, in all manner of emasculating ways. The final fateful afternoon, I had maybe half-a-glass of vodka and set fire to her telephone book, which I believed to be a devastating gesture, except the book turned out to be from 2006, and also nobody really uses phone books anymore.

"What is *wrong* with you?" she said. "You didn't used to be like this."

"I know it."

"Either keep trying or give up, Nick. You have two choices. You can't invent a third. Go teach high school English or something. Just stop acting like a…little bitch!"

"It takes it out of me, Henny," I said. "I can't even explain how much it takes it out of me."

"What does?"

"The rejection."

"Then just stop. Nobody will blame you. People grow up. They want to be astronauts and firemen when they're nine years old, and then they grow up and realize being an adult is hard and you have to do the best with what you've got."

"Said the fashion model."

"And when I get old, or when somebody throws acid on my face, I'll do something else! It's not such a tragedy! It's not such a disaster!"

"But I was so close," I said. "I wanted to get up and work out last winter, I kept meaning to, but then another week would go by and I hadn't done it. I didn't really even wonder why. Then it was May and I was out of shape and it was too late."

"Nick."

"I know I'm not supposed to care so much what they think. But they're the ones holding the keys to everything. How can I not care? And how can you not be on my side?"

Now, in the locker room, I tell Hoverman, "You don't really care what I think."

He says, "No, I do."

"Well. I think nothing's guaranteed, especially not in this world, in here, and you're a former first-round draft pick and a physical marvel and you should remember that and not get too high or too low based on what somebody else says." By God, I feel good. It is certainly the good of hypocrisy and some degree of *schadenfreude*, but it's a soaring high that makes me magnanimous.

He has the slumped-over posture of a movie cowboy riddled with bullets, smoking his final cigarette. His pads demarcate armored ridges under his jersey, and his exposed biceps are dark and dramatic, adorned by a chamfered omega branded onto his skin. "Elevator up, man," he says softly.

CHAPTER 7

Two nights before our first exhibition game, we gather at the team facility. It's a road trip down to Texas, and weather is a big issue for our flight. Cold temperatures in the desert have made the Grand Canyon into a foundry for record winds, which have expanded into the Midwest and are making air travel thoroughly unpleasant. Heavy rain is also expected in the morning.

"Here's what we doing," Bow Wow says in a receivers meeting. "Don't drive to the airport tomorrow. Drive back here. We all park our cars here, and the team got a bus to take us out to DTW. That way, nobody needs to break they necks driving."

Wendell Vance raises his hand. "Coach, what time does the plane leave?"

"It don't matter, Wendell. Come here by 10 a.m., park your car, and we'll all go over together."

Vance raises his hand again. "Coach, what time does the plane leave?"

"You ain't hearing me, son. Rain and wind gonna be bad tomorrow, so instead of putting everybody out there on the road in the mess during rush hour, getting somebody in an accident or what-say-you, we all drive to DTW *together*. Don't matter what time the plane is. Be *here* by 10 a.m."

Vance puts up his hand again and says, "But coach, what

time does the plane leave?"

Next morning, the heat is gone and the rain is literally horizontal. Power lines are down all over, and whatever few traffic signals are still in operation flash red. I drop Aggie at a kennel and receive from him several distressed kisses and yowls: Townsel's June departure doomed him to second fiddle in the dog's eyes, and now Aggie has very much become a daddy's boy. I try and tell him I'll be back tomorrow, but as we're commiserating the lights go out.

Three coach buses wait at the team complex, catching blast after blast of rainwater with bovine obduracy. Players run in from the parking lot holding carry-ons and sweatshirts against their faces, umbrellas unusable with the wind. Everyone gets on a bus grinning stupidly, showing the whites of their eyes. Interns and quality control assistants run back and forth between the buses carrying laminated lists, getting a head count. Word surfaces that we're one man short: Wendell Vance.

We wait for what seems like an hour. A couple times the engine starts roaring and it seems we'll leave, and finally, surprisingly, we do. We're off to the airport in a convoy, most everyone listening to music on earphones. The buses go straight onto the tarmac, right up to the charter, and we stagger down the stairs, through the wind, up the stairs, and take our seats on the airplane.

But Vance still isn't here.

I can see Coach Fond in a porkpie hat with a red feather on the side, wearing a clear-plastic rain slicker over his suit, whisper-barking a few words into Nugent's ear. Vance's phone is apparently off. It's only a preseason game and despite the fact that he's our most proven receiving commodity, I start to believe we're going to leave him behind, and this is exciting: maybe I'll play even more. It's impossible to see the ground from my window; the rain makes an abstract painting out of reality. The air in here is hot and close. Players fidget with their consumer electronics.

And finally, after all this waiting, here comes Vance.

He's wearing a soaking-wet, full-length fur coat and sunglasses, and is carrying a box of fried chicken. He smiles, sits and starts eating, and we're off.

*

I fair-catch one punt in Houston and play zero snaps on offense, even long after the first team has come off the field. Hoverman has a big first quarter and Shugarts scores a defensive touchdown. On the flight back, Nugent tells me he doesn't want me on game film just yet, and I shouldn't worry.

*

We're downtown in Campus Martius: Gasper, Aggie and I. Nominally I'm looking for neighborhoods where I might rent, in case I make the team. Actually, we're looking at women.

It's noon on a Monday, hot beyond reason once again, and hundreds of people are out here in the park with brown-bag lunches. Aggie pants madly and wants to trot into the fountain. Gasper, looking to prove a point, crutches over to the first woman we see eating by herself—she wears a floral-print dress with sneakers—and begins his patter. The woman shakes his hand, then shields her eyes to look in my direction. I wave with the leash.

Gasper returns with her number, carefully not making a big deal out of it.

"Something I can never do," I say.

"I told her you're a professional football player," says Gasper. "She called me Cyrano and John Smith in the course of thirty seconds, and my heart melted."

"I didn't get a girlfriend for the first time until college," I say.

"Oh, you can't out-virgin me. I lost it at 24."

I say, "I remember sitting around with a friend in high school, talking about a girl I liked. It went without saying that I'd never ask her out. My friend had a girlfriend, really nice, and I remember I said, 'Hey, did you ever get the feeling that all women are basically the same?' And he said, 'No! Not at all!' It was the first time I understood I was missing something."

"You were on the football team, right? Jesus, you should've been waist-deep. I was the same height I am now, but I weighed a hundred and ten pounds. I played Dungeons & Dragons. *Passionately.* And suddenly after college, I realized women are actually people. It was quite a discovery. That they liked to be talked to just like anybody else, that sometimes they were lonely. And even if they weren't, it was okay. If they didn't want to talk, it didn't have to be embarrassing. The heavens opened up."

"I tried online dating last year," I say. "In some ways it was much easier." We begin another lap of the park, which rests in the eye of an endless traffic whorl. "It was easy to spend a long time working on my profile, getting it to be the right balance of poignant and clever. And easy to sort through all those women, pick out the pretty ones and the smart ones. Eventually I even screwed up the courage to email some of them. But it's tough when they don't get back to you. I'd kind of fall in love with one, and craft this very enticing email and wouldn't hear anything back. Then I'd fall in love with another one, start picturing our kids, and then nothing back. I never met one in real life."

They're out in abundance: young graphic designers and software engineers and personal assistants sunning themselves and representing the Midwest in high style. They all seem tall and gap-toothed and big-butted and lovely, wearing the types of shoes Henny and her friends gave up as passé six months ago. Where do they all go at night? Where do they meet their men? Some wear wedding rings, some are sweetly absorbed in a paperback or with texting, some pick blades of grass as they chat with one another. Aggie prances to the prettiest of them, a tall brunette on a bench eating a cup of yogurt, and he sits beside her patiently, as though waiting with her for a bus.

"Sorry," I say.

"He's adorable," says this wide-featured, common-looking-yet-gorgeous woman.

"He only has seven days to live," says Gasper.

"That's terrible! What's wrong with him!"

"Oh, I didn't mean the dog," Gasper says. "I meant this shambling excuse for a human being. He's dying of loneliness."

"Oh, my God," she says. "Really? What a line. That is just total cheesebag."

"I know," says Gasper. "It totally is. I'm Patrick, and this is Nick, and I'm going to take the dog right over there where it looks like there's some very interesting garbage he can make himself sick on." I make a show of reluctantly handing over the leash, and am left alone with the brunette woman.

"Hwell," she says. "Are you the quiet one of the group? Need your buddy to set 'em up so you can knock 'em down? I have a boyfriend, Nick. Sorry to bust open your hopes."

I say, "No no no."

"I tell you, this is just disgusting." She looks down at her yogurt. "It's so hot out, you can't keep anything cold for more than a minute."

She extends the half-empty cup and I dunk it into a trash bin. I say, "What's the proper protocol for not seeming stalker-ish, but just curious? Am I allowed to ask what you do around here?"

She says, "I'm a glorified librarian. An archivist. Over there," and she points to a 40-story Beaux Arts skyscraper.

"Were you an English major?" I say.

"No. Polysci. I fell into what I'm doing now, like everyone I know. That is, everyone lucky enough to have a job. But I guess the ones who don't have one fell into that, too. What do you do, Nick?" I tell her, and she scrunches up her nose. "Sorry, I don't watch football. But I bet a lot of girls are really impressed."

"In my experience, the ones I like? They tend not to be."

This makes her smile, and she has seven hundred perfectly aligned teeth. "They call that a paradox, don't they? Well hell, son. I'm sure you do fine for yourself. Are you rich?" Her eyes glimmer; she's enjoying the conversation's chaffing tone.

"Only in hopes and dreams," I say.

"And bullcrap!"

"I've been thinking of giving it all up to become a bike messenger. Would that make me more attractive?"

"Absolutely! Two things I like in life are powerful quads and lots of scars." We laugh. "Well, I shorely have to be getting back. It was nice to talk to you Nick."

"Wait."

"Sorry, buddy. I really am seeing somebody."

"Archivist, right over there. Got it."

"Now that *is* a little stalker-ish. No means no, buster." But she's grinning, teasing, she doesn't mind the interest at all, and of course I know I won't follow up, I know I'll never go sniffing around that Beaux Arts building trying to uncover which businesses might have need of an archivist, because this has been perfect, the entire winsome exchange has been from a dream and I'm glad just to have *it*, no need to mess it up with anything more. She walks away, turns her head, waves like she learned to do from the movies.

"Ah, Junior!" Gasper says, before I have a chance to relay anything. "What's it like to be young and strong and perched atop the crumbling catacombs!"

*

So what finally changed this past winter? How did I get from there to here?

I put my Chappaqua Public Library card to work and spent January and February sealed away in the stacks of my childhood. I stood for hours reading bits of old Joseph Wambaugh and Len Deighton novels trying to soak away thoughts of myself. One day, mixed in with my typically middlebrow fare, I found a wonderful book called *The Heart Treasure of the Enlightened Ones* by Dilgo Khyentse. And I started meditating.

In an undergrad class I wrote a paper on Wallace Stevens, and I remembered a poem of his called "The World As Meditation," particularly these lines:

> *She has composed, so long, a self with which to welcome him,*
> *Companion to his self for her, which she imagined,*
> *Two in a deep-founded sheltering, friend and dear friend.*

which just shattered me at the time, that bit about composing a self. But that poem was all I'd ever really thought about meditation, until Dilgo Khyentse, whose kindness and gentleness was much better. As soon as I had that mantra, the one about the jewel-lotus (*om mani padme hung*), suddenly I was able to sleep and to run, to lift, to swim, to build. My discovery was of course not really a discovery at all: that extreme physical exertion and spiritual meditation are, if not two sides of the same coin, at least two endpoints on a near-completed circle. The deep concentration I'm supposed to be looking for—the *jhana*—is a state where they say the five physical sense doors fade and mental defilements are suppressed. Maybe being exhausted is a way to that kind of deep awareness. I tried not to question it. I looked down and saw my arms and legs working. I repeated the *om mani padme hung* and breathed deeply. I phoned Dave Blum, who was nominally my agent, and asked if he would call around the league.

I've never read *The Heart Treasure of the Enlightened Ones* a second time. I don't want to ruin it.

*

Today I absently soak my ankles, and Calcaterra reads something aloud from the newspaper: "'A super-typhoon is nearing landfall in the Philippines. Its winds are 125 miles per hour, waves are 45 feet high.' And look at this, there's a picture from the International Space Station. Complete white cloud cover seen from outer space, except for a hole in the middle, a hundred miles across: the eye."

CHAPTER 8

On camp goes. It's late August. Roland Waltz breaks his leg one practice. Apiyo Omdat tears up a knee in the second preseason game, a circumstance which promotes Brohammer to starting free safety. Shave gets mildly concussed in that same contest and won't play again until the regular season starts. First cuts are coming two days after the third game, and I still haven't played a down. Nugent's soothing tone doesn't calm my nerves: why wouldn't they want to put me on game film unless they were going to try and sneak me through waivers? I don't think I could spend another season of drudgery on a practice squad, pining for teammate injuries.

This afternoon, Coach Fond visits field level to address us. We assume the universal posture of gridiron repose: down on one knee, opposite hand atop grounded helmet. I see Townsel chewing the side of his mouthpiece, listening eagerly, trying to communicate to anyone watching him just how important he considers the head coach's thoughts.

"That outfit we go' play Friday, they mean sonsabitches, boys. It's the preseason, so they ain't go' scheme, and we ain't go' scheme. Nobody go' show anybody nothing. You know what that comes down to: hate. You got to muster up all the hate you got. Defense, you go' smash somebody. Offense, you go' bring the fight to them. Don't sit back. Don't wait. Now, I know you-all are thinking about what's go' happen

Sunday night. The Turk, right boys? A visit from our friend Pot Roast, who's a good man, he's a good man. Hell, it's just human nature. But for sixty minutes Friday, you go' put it out of your minds. 'For Moses had said, Consecrate yourselves today to the LORD, even every man upon his son, and upon his brother; that he may bestow upon you a blessing this day.' Hear that? 'Today.' 'This day.' There ain't nothing else, boys. You go' put it out of your mind, you go' win."

"Coach," Sugar Tits says. "Tell us how your son is doing?"

"Well now, he's doing just fine. Just fine, Danny. I do thank you for asking. But I hope I can rely on all of you-all not to say anything about my little boy's cancer to any reporters. His mother would be just sick to read anything about it. But I'll tell you-all something: this is a five-year-old boy, and he'd be mighty pleased to have a win. You can bet he go' be watching. He surely will."

To get ready for our dome, we scrimmage under the practice bubble. It's testy. Marcellus Blake, one of our outside linebackers, wrenches Pendleton's facemask and doesn't let go after the whistle, and soon these two giant men are wailing away at one another's helmets with their free arms and also kicking one another, snorting and spitting and finally Pendleton falls down over on top of Blake and a few defensive players are halfheartedly trying to break it up but the coaches are staying conspicuously out of it, understanding this is what grown children do when they're freaked out. Hoverman makes a play-action fake and blocks Meleki Faafeu viciously low, which starts another scuffle, with Tommy Way grabbing Faafeu by the horsecollar and flinging him down backwards; Husseyn Norwell uses the opportunity to steam in my direction and flatten me, and Wendell Vance rushes to my defense and bum-rushes Norwell. Coach Fond or maybe Nugent signals for the artificial crowd noise to cut out, and the defensive coordinator, Kolakowski, shouts, "Huddle up, gentlemen!" and the fighting stops. The knuckles on my left hand are bleeding.

The night before the game, I lie in bed with Aggie's muzzle across my chest and visualize the route tree, what it looks like against every defense I can imagine. And in my (I'm quite certain) bastardized notion of what it means to visualize in a spiritual way, I picture myself as a Buddha, in the name of giving external form to my internal illumination. And part of this project as I understand it is also to visualize the football world around me as pure and sacred, as opposed to defiled and dirty. So I am a Buddha and the defense's chaotically exotic alignments are sacred and the point of this isn't necessarily to make me a better player (though that would be nice), but rather to reveal gradually that our *entire* experience of the world is actually visualization, that "reality" is actually a multifarious intersection of our own and other people's visualizations of "what things are." This is a cool idea. But I get bogged down a bit in the literalism of it: I am a chubby man in sandals stumbling on FieldTurf to run a post-corner, and the safety may want to tear off my head with a throttling blow, but he's also pure and sacred? I find myself muttering unconsciously, eyes closed, and Aggie gives me a kiss on the cheek.

*

San Francisco wins the toss and defers. Norwell returns the kick to our 33 and Nugent gives me a shove out onto the field.

No big deal. I've done preseason games before. The blue-clad home crowd—impressive-sized despite 3-13 last year—is appropriately respectful of our offense, and hushes a bit. Yet Hinkler calls out a play and I don't hear him. I mean, I can tell he's saying something. The words just bounce off my helmet's earholes.

I try to ask Hoverman, but he's busy running out wide and lining up at flanker. This is an unusual spot for him, and should be a clue. But I have no idea where to go.

Hinkler looks over the defense, doing his quarterback voodoo psych-out thing while trying to establish what formation they're trying, then he gets under center and takes a cursory glance at our alignment, and starts gesturing wildly at me to get on the strong side. I run over there but it's too late: Hurricane Hink has to burn a timeout.

I hide in the huddle, studying the fascinating texture of my cleats. Hinkler returns squinting at me. Way says, "Easy, rook," and it isn't the time to correct him.

*

The speed is ridiculous. I feel like the slowest man on the field. I feel like the middle-aged umpire could juke me out of my jock. There's a trans-dimensional sense to every play: people are over there and then *they are over here*, and it's bedlam. The utter pandemonium. I mean, it makes you paranoid. I am in my body, I am in my bubble, and these other creatures are in and out of my awareness, three hundred and sixty degrees of danger, intersections of mass, the artificial floor and the artificial ceiling pressing and squeezing and the swell of sound contributing to a cloistered sensation of no escape, so notions of duty and self-preservation forever conflict: run where I'm supposed to run but simultaneously find the tiny empty spaces where it's momentarily safe, both for my survival and for Hinkler to sling a pass at me, and this is the game: can I do both? Robotic route running doesn't work, but neither does going fetal and praying.

The loudspeaker says, "Hinkler pass complete to Morrison," which is how (in a manner of speaking) I realize I've made a catch.

Later I grab a screen on third-and-long and turn upfield, my head is pleasantly blank and the moment calls less for hard cuts, more for a looping burst where I accept a glancing blow and overstuffed arms around my midsection, but use the tackler's momentum to keep propelling me, his legs swinging behind me in sympathetic testament to Newtonian physics. For a moment I'm a mule whose plow is barely unstuck and as I topple forward I *reach*…. The ball slams down just beyond the midfield stripe and bounces up out of my hands and the crowd groans, but I'm clearly down. Plus I've made the yardage. The very next play, San Francisco is in their 4-3 with the safeties pulled way forward and I'm in the tight end's spot; I run a simple stick-nod-go route and Hinkler hits me perfectly, I run and run until a corner catches me from behind and I topple forward like an escaped fugitive in a western, shot by the last desperado in range. It's a gain of 34.

*

"Sure," says Gasper late that night, in some dive. "You know Kai. Good guitar player. He's the one with the novelty moustache. Squeaky little voice. He's kind of my archenemy, but I don't think he knows it."

"He's the one dating your ex-girlfriend?" I say.

"Maybe I was stretching it with 'ex-girlfriend.' We threw a frisbee once. He's probably a nice guy, but he sits around all day writing songs about 'How many sides does a woodpile have?' That's really one of his songs. 'How many sides does a woodpile have?' Does it have two? Does it have four? It wraps up with the song proclaiming it has infinity sides. Really profound."

"Yeah, I hate him already."

"Laugh it up, superstar. He's like you. Preoccupied with insignificant crap because he was born without fear. That's the thing about people my age: we still thought about the bomb every day of our childhoods. We had *The Day After* and Soviets and shit. Despite how unstable the world actually is, you little fucks can still somehow pretend none of that ever happened. Oh, sure, maybe you figure someone out there'll set off a suitcase nuke, but not anyplace your Eurail pass goes. I wonder what it's like. You're like dogs: completely oblivious of death until it's perched on your shoulder."

"I really zoned out during the game tonight," I say. "For a little while there at the beginning, I was just gone. Really punctured my gestalt."

"Punctured your…. See, but you pull shit like *that* out of your ass, how can I not be your friend?"

*

Saturday morning, Townsel is silent with worry. He's either sixth or seventh on the cornerback depth chart, and only saw action in the fourth quarter last night. We drive to the old pancake place on 8 Mile and try not to look at one another across our booth. He eats four scrambled eggs, four pancakes and ten strips of bacon. I eat two orders of French toast and three orders of home fries, perhaps flirting with vegetarianism as well as gluttony. We're logy and leaden on the ride back to our hotel.

"I know all there is: you try again," he says. "Ain't the end of the world."

"Don't let's talk about it."

"Making me crazy. It's out of my hands, man. I'm supposed to be okay with things out of my hands. God know what I got inside, He testing me. Sometimes I wonder: why not take those…supplements? If they got something make me faster, jump higher, work out better, shouldn't I do it? God don't like a cheater, I know. But if it's the only way to make it? I get cut tomorrow, why shouldn't I go out and get me something? If it's the only way?"

The sun is doing its thing: staying strangely low in the sky even as noon approaches. I squint: quarter-blinded, sore, overheated and bewildered. I'm afraid he's going to ask me if I know where to find PEDs. I've never taken your nandrolone or THC (which everyone realizes will show up in tests) or human-growth hormone (I'm less clear whether they can test for that), mostly because I'm terrified of getting caught, getting stained. In theory, if there was something I could take that would guarantee I make a pro roster and never be detected?

"You shouldn't wear thigh pads," says Townsel. "Nobody wear thigh pads plays receiver, man. Makes you slow."

"I like my thighs," I say. "They're my most attractive quality."

I'm in the passenger's seat, spellbound by the rushing-past scenery. A shocking afternoon squalor makes itself known: junky yards behind chewed-up fences; a half dozen Caterpillar land-movers trackless and abandoned in a lot; shiny pickup trucks parked in front of rotting barns and corrugated shacks; broken glass everywhere; bashed-in former liquor stores and video rental places and a place proclaiming "Urban Outsider Art!" whose roof has collapsed. Detroit has nicer areas, of course—yuppified suburbs and reclaimed neighborhoods congratulating themselves for sanctioned funkiness—but to get anywhere you have to drive past the tattoo shops and diaper-strewn lawns.

I comment on this neighborhood's sad state, and Townsel tells me about growing up in Houston's Third Ward: "We lived in a shotgun shack, four kids and my grandma and a whole 'nother family. We had one bedroom for five of us, man. Vacant lot just outside the window with dolla boys hanging around all day, every day, so grandma nailed up some wood over the window. Power lines with like a dozen crack tennies, just like that," he points out a pair of sneakers tied together by the laces dangling above the street, "it was LTP turf for a while then it was Crips. My grandma, she walked us to and from school every day, man. Every day. She made us promise to try. Always try. I got a doctor and a lawyer in my family and now a sister studying to be a professor, and I'm the baby, right? So that's why I got to make it in the league."

He accelerates up past a supermarket and a brightly lit stripmall. "No, I don't see nothing in the D I ain't seen a hundred times growing up."

"Maybe we're doing our part," I say. "Rooting for a team makes people happy, maybe makes them forget for a little while."

"Yeah," says Townsel, "but soon enough the rain start dripping on you while you sleep. You remember real quick then."

We pull into the hotel and walk around back. I follow Townsel to his room, acting as though I can't find my keycard. He ribs me, chuckling at my absentmindedness, and opens his front door. Aggie barks and comes running.

Townsel says, "What the!" and stoops over to accept the dog's welcome. "What are you doing in here, boy?" He steps inside and gets the full effect: I've had a couple teammates lay newspaper down all over his floor and bring in a petting zoo's worth of animals: bunnies, a baby sheep, chicks, piglets and a sleepy-looking goat. Townsel says, "Oh! Oh, man!"

"Pretty cute, right?" I say. "Cute enough to grit?"

"I'm gritting," he says, bending down, his incisors clamped together. He lets one of the rabbits sniff his finger, whereupon it toddles over onto his lap. "So cute! Oh, my gosh! My jaw hurts!"

*

Sunday morning I drive in alone, my mind on pursuit drills. I feel no special tension walking into the air conditioning, nodding to security, taking the right turn down the long hallway to the locker room. Another day older. The vesicle separating me from everything else firmly in place. Then I see a very fat man in too-short shorts: an old-time defensive tackle nicknamed Pot Roast. He's our team's Turk. If he lets you pass by, you've survived. If he doesn't, you bring your playbook to the second floor.

Pot Roast is one of the grizzled hangers-on many of us hope we'll never be in thirty years. He knows everyone by name: the rookies, the street free agents, the lately acquired and the soon to depart. As players filter to the locker room—there are a few who've arrived just before me—each has a heart-stopping moment where Pot Roast says his name by way of hello. And so it is that when he says, "Morrison," I fear the worst has happened, but realize he's just being friendly.

Then I feel his hand on my arm.

Very softly, he says, "They need to see you upstairs. Go get your playbook, okay, and please go on upstairs."

PART II

CHAPTER 9

How can I say it? Hanging out around Gasper is like being the mayor's claviger: the absent-minded old fellow who walks around with a massive key ring, not quite sure what he'll be able to open next.

Because I've got nothing to do with myself, because I've failed to make a pro roster *yet again*, the September days bead together. Gasper gets the pins out of his ankle and we play long games of stationary catch on the street in front of his Redford house—it'll still be a couple months before he's allowed to run—each of us with multiple beer bottles scattered in convenient locales. I read in the afternoons: long idylls on a hammock in his tiny back yard, swaying while Aggie pants beneath me. Nights, we hit the bars, almost always in a new neighborhood. We watch the frat-boy pratfalls of backward-baseball-cap-wearing twentysomethings as they yell and scam and take offense and shove each other, jaws tight. Eventually, Gasper's phone rings and we're invited to a poker game, a house party, a TV viewing bash, a nighttime basketball tournament. At first I suspected that Gasper is a dealer and these friendly hundreds his clients, but surely there'd be evidence at his house and I've seen none.

I admit, one reason we get along well is I'm willing to listen. Gasper can talk. By his own reckoning, he has America figured out: the pressure-release valve culturally installed in all our chests that makes us happiest at a middlebrow movie and electing morons to political office, the lack of intensity that characterizes the nation (and the subtle ostracism of those considered overly excitable), the tapioca practically dripping from our veins. "You watch," he said once, "I'll get on a roll about how nobody reads anymore and what an utter travesty it is that tax breaks are so important to the upper crust that we can't afford to teach kids music in school, and everyone around us will turn their eyeballs up and *endure* me, and then later on get shitfaced and talk about what a prescriptive, hyperactive prick I am. But you, young Nicholas, you at least put up with my bullshit until I talk myself out, now don't you?"

So you can't say he doesn't know himself at least a bit.

Despite Gasper's claims to the contrary, however, the effect of all his talk is variable. Many of his friends listen patiently for a time, then grip his freckly neck and shake him. But he has a few groupies—I guess maybe I'm one of them—who take him seriously. Some dare to contradict him, and to these people Gasper is inclusive and kind as he destroys them with logic but never humiliates. He's in it, we know, for the fun of hearing words, and this is rare: that a person cares less about how his manner is perceived than about jabbing needles in the air on the off chance one will pierce the nature of reality and manna will start pouring through.

I'm not equipped for debates with Gasper. I have to take his word for the esoteric things he says, and sometimes suspect he's making stuff up. But I've spent my life grunting and sweating and this is the cost. One cost.

Lately I've had a popular song called "Mountain Man" stuck in my head, so badly that I downloaded it and now play it constantly, twenty times a day. I've learned all the words (*whoa, straight out on a headwall; whoa, turned into a freefall!*) and sing—complete with handclaps—no matter where I am, compulsively. This happens to me occasionally with a new song. To Gasper, I say, "I literally can't stop listening to it. In the process of loving it, it's like I need to take it apart, learn every sound, every second. There can be no surprises."

"Mm-hm," says Gasper.

"Don't you think that's disturbed? This song made me so happy when I first heard it. It gave me chills. But it's like something in my brain is saying, 'We can't have this! Listen to it again and again, so the effect wears off!' Why do I need to completely wring magic from things?"

Gasper, moderately high, says, "Well. Better to get something out of it and touch those exalted feelings as many times as you can, right? Better that than walk around with no pulse. There's always more songs." I'm out of the hotel and crashing in his house, on his couch.

I'm mostly numb and waiting for true pain to collapse in on me. I walk around feeling I could tumble to pieces at any moment. I don't know what comes next. I read more, I meditate a little. It's easy to fall into transience with Gasper and his friends, but sometimes I wake in the night with tears on my cheeks. I felt so close. I believed the offensive coordinator. What a fool I was: I didn't even make it past the Turk once. That life goes on, one frivolous day at a time, is humiliating. Mostly I do a good job playing along with Gasper, keeping a stiff upper lip as though I'm untroubled, but sometimes I catch him looking at me as though he expects me to detonate. I guess I'm the mental patient nobody wants to excite.

Gasper says, "I'm reading Freud. Look at the size of this book. *Civilization and Its Discontents.* I wish I could read German. Civilization as our protector and at the same time a tormentor because of the conformity it requires? That's heavy. You should try some of this," holding out a joint. "No reason not to anymore."

I think, *ouch.* I type on his keyboard laptop, press enter, and hear demi-Kurt-Cobain sing, "Nobody likes a swellhead!"

*

I'm shirtless in the bathroom, watching myself in the mirror. My shoulders are still thick. My forearms are still distended. But my stomach is podgier than it was. Skin bulges like leavening dough at my waistband; nothing horrible yet, but I'm trying hard not to lie to myself now. Knee-jerk, my thoughts are of more training, of getting back on the wagon. I'm not doing much of anything with myself, other than rendering a glorious portrayal of a shattered man being brave. Why not go back to the summer's fervor and discipline? Any time I emerge from meditation, I feel certain I've played my last football game; it's only when the larger world intervenes that I wish to crawl back inside the athlete's armor, and start yet again.

I find my phone in Gasper's living room and call Townsel, who was also cut but made the team's practice squad. He answers on the first ring and says, "Yo, Morrison. How you doing, man?"

"Hey! How's life in the big leagues?" I hate the way I sound.

"Winless and touchy, dude. Everybody running around looking over they shoulder. Kolakowski going on rampages, tearing off everybody's head. Shoot, you didn't call me back, Morrison. I left a bunch of messages. You all right? Where you at?"

"I'm still here. I'm in Detroit."

"Come on, man. I thought you must've gone home to New York. How come we don't hang out?"

"I wanted to, Townsel. I guess I haven't taken it very well, man."

"Everybody know you can play, Morrison. The way we losing, nobody here thinks they any good. You just got to stick with it. You still working out, right?"

I'm sitting on the couch, squeezing the bridge of my nose. "Not much, man. Not really. I think I've lost interest."

"You don't mean that. I can tell just by listening to your voice you don't mean it."

"No?"

"Everybody feel that way sometimes. You just got to picture what it'll be like when you win. Hey, what do you got going on tonight?"

"Oh," I say. "I mean…maybe I'm not ready, man. I appreciate it. Let me get back to you, all right?"

"You feeling sorry for yourself," says Townsel. "You got a faith problem."

"Do I? Faith in what?"

I hear him chuckle. "You expected me to say God. But naw, man. I dunno. Maybe you just too smart. Me, I'm dumb enough so I don't know what I don't know. So I just keep banging my head."

I say, "Kick Norwell's tail for me in practice, will you?"

"All right, Morrison. Hey, you keep working. And gimme a call, too."

*

A few days later, I come home from a dogwalk and find Gasper sitting in his rolling chair, grinning at me.

"What?" I say.

His eyebrows arch. His smile gets toothier.

A voice from the kitchen says: "So then I went up to Canyon de Chelly, and they don't let you go on the canyon floor unless you're on one of those *authorized* tours, but I talked to the guy and he was this really nice guy, and he said, 'Okay, you can go.' And I got to camp like right *under* Spider Rock!" She walks into the room bearing a glass pitcher spangled with sweat. It's Henny.

"Omigosh, Nick!" she says.

"Omigosh," says Gasper, looking at me still.

She's brown as a berry, her gold hair is light, she wears an ankle-length sun dress the color of pocket change and her feet are already bare, her toenails unpainted. She places the pitcher on a table, steps over some of the miscellaneous living room junk, and glides into my arms for a chaste hug.

"Surprise!" she says, and then to Aggie: "Ah! The young squire!" The dog eyes her suspiciously and sits back into a corner. "Wait. I've got something for you, doggy-daddy." She retreats to the bedroom and I hear rummaging. She comes back with a book: *Meditation for Dummies.* "I know. It looks a little lame. But I started to read it in the bookstore, and it's not! It's kind of sweet and pretty smart about it. I thought you might be able to use it, since you're going through a rough time and I know you've been meditating."

"It's great," I say. "Thank you."

"Nicholas, my friend," says Gasper. "You have outdone your station in life. You have, as they say, out-kicked your coverage."

"He's so sweet," Henny says, holding me around my middle and looking down at seated Gasper. "I was just telling him about desert life. I was in this friend's pool yesterday, and there were *scorpions* in the trees. I guess my friend has gotten used to it, but I kept one eye up there. I really didn't need a scorpion falling on me the day before my plane ticket."

She's a picture-book blonde princess. Women who look like Henny are the reason most men do anything. It's funny just to watch her walk around, the notice that gets taken, the calculus between *them* (trying not to stare, but staring, smiling, believing that she might be for them) and *her* (gamely trying to imagine men are taking her seriously, that she can just *be*). She was born and raised in Memphis but only when she's drunk does Dixie start coming out of her mouth. She was a soap model at six, a makeup model at fifteen, but also—to the vexation of some, including her family—quite scholastically inclined, at least to the point where private tutors had to be upgraded at regular intervals. It helped that daddy was a Middleton alum, but I bet she'd have gotten in on her own. She took a four-year break from being a woman in New York to be a kid in western Massachusetts, but her disfigurement (that incredible, sophistic beauty) still marked her. I met her early in our sophomore years while I was almost dating a Math major and Henny was dating a not-insubstantial portion of the male faculty. The first time I saw her outside the classroom, she was stepping from a professor's BMW holding an armful of books, looking like old pictures of Grace Kelly. She said to me, "Hey! You scored three touchdowns last week," and I was lost.

We were casual friends for a year and then she came to a party at the house on High Street a few teammates and I rented, sat on the kitchen counter with a bottle of Maker's Mark and listened to everyone spin stories about how dumb all this college stuff was and how what they all really wanted to do was travel in Europe or disappear to Hollywood or infiltrate the highest levels of Wall Street, all things Henny had—either literally or in a manner of speaking—already done while of high school age. But she said nothing, blinked her olive-colored eyes and drank bourbon from the bottle. Later she was too drunk to go home and so I installed her on a basement couch and when she hugged me goodnight I was helpless: I knew what she wanted, and I knew I was powerless. In the blinding, chilly morning she climbed into my bed and I felt her skinny body, her big breasts, her strength, her softness.

I don't believe I'm the jealous type by nature, but obviously Henny gave me cause. We had wonderful times. She's much smarter than anyone (even she) gives her credit for. But I was never her one-true. She could be generous with her time, but then not. She shied away from drama, because drama was the thing *models* did. She loved, but she loved too much or too well: too many people fascinated her, too many risks seemed worth taking. That face. Tennessee may hold her birth certificate, but that face is pure southern California. She's the eternal image of the surf bunny, all the more so now that the desert sun has done its work. She's dark-skinned and slightly freckled with twin showers of gold falling from a middle part, she's smiling that white detonation of a smile, she's holding me tight and turning up the charm, turning Gasper to mush.

All of which means: trouble lies ahead.

CHAPTER 10

"What a nightmare at the airport," she says, letting go of me and turning her attention back to the sangria she's just made. "I thought security was bad in New York. My God, what do they think's going to happen in Phoenix? And even the lines when I was getting off in Detroit!"

"Well," says Gasper, "Rome *is* burning."

"You're preaching to the choir, Patrick. This lady once I was *on* the plane? First of all, there are kids in front of us, and whatever, I mean, kids have to go see their grandparents. But the minute this woman sees kids, she gets all conspiracy with me, rolling her eyes, cursing our fate. Later on she pays for the snack and it's sitting on the table in front of her and she sneezes. Right *on* the food. I mean, stuff gets sprayed *all over* the place. She doesn't think I noticed and she starts wiping down her food with a napkin and she *eats* it. People are just animals."

We fall to drinking, chewing fruit as we go. Gasper is quieter than usual, acting awed by the clever young couple before him. At least, I think it's an act. Anyway, Henny takes the lead with stories about the desert, where neither Gasper nor I have ever been. Apparently they go through 400 million gallons of tap water every summer day in Phoenix, which I admit sounds like a lot, though I don't have a frame of reference. There was also a 69-car pileup on a freeway out there just a week ago, which Henny attributes to elderly retirees who drive like it's the Wild West all over again. "Such as it is," Henny says, "the city goes on forever. It'll stretch to Tucson before long, just one long highway with a hundred Applebee's stacked side by side."

"Sounds heavenly," I say.

"Easy there, champ," she answers, suddenly in the big, hearty Great Smokey Mountains version of her voice. "I mean, y'all ended up in *Detroit*."

*

We cab across the Ambassador Bridge through customs and into Windsor, Ontario, and hit dance clubs just across the river. Henny and I sweat and jump while Gasper sits and drinks. I wonder what he thinks: if he thinks I knew she was coming for a visit, and was hiding it from him.

In the streets of Windsor, police SUVs spin their siren lights, stretch limos idle, and a cataract of young, dressed-up-for-the-Midwest people is angling to look in windows, check out lines, share whatever pills their neighbors are taking, hoot, squeal, fluff hair, trip on clunky shoes, hoist strapless dresses, curse at the night sky and otherwise fulfill the mandate of acting American Young (because most everyone here right now, Gasper assures us, *is* American). We do not stand apart ironically from this mess. We wait in line for half an hour to get into a crowded strip club, going "woooo!" every time someone on Wyandotte honks. Inside, Gasper and I grow shy while Henny pulls out a sheaf of twenties and pays a series of dead-eyed women to waggle their breasts in her face. I expect Gasper to know someone here, to have some connection who'll get us free drinks in the Champagne Room and sit with us smoking Nat Shermans and telling us bawdy stories. But he just quietly turns maroon.

A very young dude wearing a checked raglan coat and fawn-colored kid boots taps Henny on the shoulder and shouts, "Are you an off-duty dancer!" and she says, "I'm never off duty!"

My God, the women. The light here is amber and selective, across the room the bottles shine at the bar, our booth is stretched tight with some manner of opulent vinyl, the floor is black and reflective: all in anticipation of the women. Our waitress is redheaded and clothed, barely, and seems to like the fact that we're here with Henny, an escaped kinswoman back among the beautiful with news of the outside world. One dancer is naked upon a table, showering. A stockier, more athletic woman—she has a stud in her nose and glitter painted across her body—does the subequatorial-floss move with some guy's proffered t-shirt. A black woman accepts Henny's cash and plants her spherical bottom on Gasper's lap, then wiggles. He scratches the bald spot at the top of his head.

I say to Henny, "Do you really like places like this!" but she pretends she can't hear me, gets up to use the ladies room. I look back to grimacing Gasper and feel words bumbling out of me: "I need your help!"

"What?"

"It wouldn't commit me to trying again! It could be just in case! For when I actually decide!"

"Dude, am I supposed to understand what you're telling me, or is this idle drunken chatter?"

"I'm drunk!" I say over the music. "But it's not idle!"

"Um."

"I've never been good at asking for help! I'm looking for something to make me…you know! Stronger!"

Gasper blinks at me, tries a dismissive grin, checks my eyes again. The calliope around us coils tighter, the sequined skin and hooting would-be paramours. Why is it tempting to view places like this as a microcosm of larger forces? Gasper stands, grabs my shoulder, and walks me to the club's quietest corner.

He says, "I can probably get it for you. Have you really

made up your mind to do this? It's serious shit."

Of course I don't know. I don't feel as though my mind is even involved in the process.

"Even if you wind up back on a team," he says, "you wouldn't get caught. It's a blood test, and it isn't part of collective bargaining, and besides, the test they use is so unreliable, it would never stand up in court. Maybe half the players use HGH, from what I've been told."

"Then why shouldn't I?"

"Because you're not them. You wouldn't be able to live with yourself."

I think about this. "You make me sound noble or something. What makes me so different?"

He smiles in that charming Gasper way, and a little flare of recognition goes off, how subject I am to other people's charisma. "That's a good question," he says.

*

Later, after we've gotten bottle service and the Maker's Mark is mostly gone, Gasper is someplace else and I'm kissing Henny, we're wrapped around each other in a booth and every so often a kid in a bowler hat or novelty tie will slap our table, and I'll see the kid giving me the thumbs-up, or peeling off a five-dollar bill and donating to my cause. Henny's hand is high on my leg and I'm drunkenly paranoid everyone can see this, and I'm thinking, *Great Caesar's ghost! We're back together! We're really back together!* and the universe can obviously be very cruel but maybe it delivers us something to keep us going just when we really need it.

Later, back out on the sidewalk of a busy street, I hold her neck tight in the crook of my arm as a safeguard against the hammer of disappointment that must fall: everyone has had this moment of disbelief that things could possibly be so good. The raglan-coated kid from inside asks if he can bum a cigarette and we tell him we have none. He says, "Then I guess I'll take your wallets then."

"The fuck you will," says Henny. The boy menacingly pats the waistband of his retro-gabardine pants. "The *fuck* you will," she repeats.

"Rein in your woman," the kid says.

"'Rein'?" says Henny. "'Rein'? What kind of mugger says 'rein'? He's a little college kid with a thesaurus."

"So you guys are willing to get dead for a couple bucks?"

"Show me," she says. "Show me your weapon." I've been regaled with a dozen stories of men doing Henny violence: her dentist once angled himself so that as her hand lowered, it lowered upon his rigid member; she's been groped by a skycap and kissed by a woebegone bartender; as a teen she once woke on a Greyhound bus with her shirt pulled up and a lawyer from Murfreesboro kissing her navel. I'm quite drunk, but take comfort in her experience and evident incredulity. Her hands are backwards on her hips and she leans forward, a taunting posture.

Then the kid takes something out of his pants and I see a flash of metal, Henny spins around and there's something cold on my neck and I'm walking, we're all walking into an alley. The kid shoves me into a brick wall and my ersatz girlfriend stands me up straight. I feel a dumb grin on my face, and I see an automatic pistol in the kid's hand.

"Dude, don't date strippers," he says. "Nothing but bad news." He has absolutely tiny front teeth, a true and very odd deformity.

"This can't be happening," says Henny.

"Shut up," says the kid.

"Take the money," I say.

"I think I want something else now."

"You want," I say. "You want. I should beat your head in. You think anyone in the world cares what you want? No, seriously. You think the planets lumber around all for you? A butterfly in Asia flaps his wings and a typhoon hits your bank account? I mean, is the little devil on your shoulder whispering that things are supposed to be *fair?*"

Henny gives me a look that reads: *Not the best time for this.*

"Bitch," says the mugger, "unless you want me to shut him up forever…." And he comes close and I smell gin and cucumbers on him. He raises the gun and presses its muzzle against my lips, forcing my teeth apart. His own tiny little stalagmite teeth are bared in a happy wince.

Henny sighs, and one of her raised hands slowly reaches down to her knees and then way up under her sun dress, grapples with some equipment up in there, and then she stoops over, takes a couple steps in place, and stands back up holding her underpants looped over thumb and forefinger. She wears a veteran's expression: one eye cocked, smiling with half her face. The gun is out of my mouth; the kid and I both have slack jaws. We look at her silver-lamé underwear, and at one another. Then there's a metal reverberation and a fleshy thump, I feel a vibration across my chest and shoulders, and the mugger falls face-first into me and then crumples to the alley floor.

Tall, gawky Gasper is holding a steel trashcan lid that he's just smashed into the kid's head. Henny saw him coming.

CHAPTER 11

We wait sobering up for hours in a sterile courthouse antechamber, believing Gasper will be released any moment based on our testimony. But the mugger is concussed and trying to counter-press charges for assault, and Gasper has a record. So blind justice torques us well into the small hours. Occasionally Henny tries the alternate strategies of eye-batting and righteous indignation, and the on-duty constable isn't without sympathy. But I'm a little stressed Aggie hasn't been walked in half-a-day, and also wonder how Gasper knew the gun wouldn't go off near my face when he made his swing. Finally we get word he'll be held overnight and well into tomorrow, and call for a cab to pick us up near the Detroit-Windsor Tunnel.

Back home (which is to say: Gasper's home), the sky is almost light and we prepare for bed (which is to say: Gasper's bed). Henny has on a black nightie that's cut dramatically low in front, and busies herself with organizing pillows and topsheets. She can charm the rest of the world with that face and that body, but the two of us know: the bowstrings of Henny's heart play most captivatingly when she's teetering above the jaws of calamity. She sees a look in my face and drops the bedclothes, gets up a sleepy/seductive expression and begins to crawl across the bed to touch me.

I say, "Henny."

This arrests her approach. Up close, I see the twin parentheses just outside the corners of her mouth: they're deeper now, and serve only to enhance her beauty, but I imagine she hates them, spends thousands on products designed to eradicate them. She inspects me anew, then draws her elbows over her breasts, looking away, turning away, sliding beneath the sheet and coming to rest with her back facing me. I click off Gasper's bedroom light, but with the new day I can still see everything.

"I probably can't stay in Phoenix," she says to the wall. "I don't know what I was thinking going out there in the first place."

"Did things get resolved with Thomas?"

"If by 'resolved' you mean 'getting fired.' His wife made him. She was right."

"I mean, Henny. He's *old* isn't he? A pop-psychologist would say you're out looking for romantic father figures, but I happen to know your dad is a sweetheart retired lawyer who plays video games all day."

"'Pop' psychologist? Ha. I get it."

"Seriously, are you heading back to New York?"

"I like this new you. So concerned with my well-being, too busy with it to fall apart yourself."

"Henny."

I've gotten in bed beside her, studiously not touching her. She rolls partway in my direction, so I can see her face. "What the hell are *you* doing *here?*"

"What, Detroit?"

"Detroit. This house. Hanging out with ex-cons. Name it. Is this another breakdown? What do *your* parents think?"

"I told them I'm on the practice squad again. I don't think they do much daily reviewing of the league transaction wires."

"I mean, what is it, Nick? Why'd you even bother trying again, knowing it could end like this? I don't want to be the bitch who says these things, but I mean, you have to decide what you want to do with the rest of your life."

"First of all, I don't think it's very charitable of you to call last winter a breakdown. I was with you, trying to make it work with you." This is a mistruth; my face heats. Softer, I say, "What else do I have?"

She turns all the way over, facing me now, and a tan hand with a white palm strokes my cheek. "Part of me just wants to tell you to suck it up again, but who the hell am I to do that? Look at the two of us. Total messes, in our little bubbles, right? I don't even read the news anymore. I'm just woe is me. Going to Phoenix was so stupid. I didn't know anybody and the whole foundation thing was basically just a crock. And I had other job offers but mostly from guys on the make. Plus you know how other women are to me. I just went for walks in the desert and went to the gym. I got so lonely."

"What are you going to do?"

"What are *you* going to do?"

"I'm thinking of becoming a vegetarian. Gasper is."

"I know," she says. "He told me."

"There's a line from this book I read, something like: 'If you look hard, you see nothing, not even a single atom, has a verifiable existence.'"

"What will you do for protein?"

"This time I tried to approach it like this: I want to do this, I want to play pro football and make a team not because my happiness depends on it, not because of any of the material things it brings. I tried to give up my love of the *belief* that these things will make me happy. And just do it to be happy doing it. But there are coaches grinding you down. And cameras trained on you all the time. The offensive coordinator who holds your fate in his hands. So I tried. I really did try."

"But here you are," she says, and I finally start to cry a little. She scooches close, and I know Henny doesn't exactly walk the path of Buddha herself, despite her intrinsic goodness that I see much better than she does, and I know that this Redford house is but a way station on a journey to her next baroque drama. But she holds me now like maybe I could free her from the frenzy that's infected the soles of her feet since adolescence, and all I can do is kiss her. After a long while, just as I'm drifting into sleep, she says, "So what's up with this Patrick guy, anyway? He's a schemer."

*

Early on a Sunday afternoon. Gasper is passed out on the couch, hugging a pillow dearly. Henny's in the bedroom. She's an awful sleeper: prone to dreams of ugliness and icy abandonment. In college, she would do anything not to go to bed. We played double solitaire and pad-and-paper games of hangman, we watched *I Love Lucy* at 4 a.m., we searched Internet real estate for farmhouses up and down the Pioneer Valley, spinning yarns about how we'd fix one up after graduation, grow organic Romano beans and zephyr squash, and read each other Chateaubriand. Some of the most adventurous sex times we ever had happened because Henny didn't want to go to sleep. So now I won't take the chance of waking her. Instead, freshly walked Aggie and I step out to the tiny, sunken sun porch and I tune the old cathode-ray television to football.

It's raining in Miami. No, not just raining: the drops amount to a wall of water, and the way they ricochet off the field and the players makes the whole scene appear lost in fog. The TV producers can't use their long-distance cameras, so they stick with close-ups and field-level action shots, along with lots of extreme-slow-motion, and the results are utterly beautiful. Oh, you wouldn't call the game itself an aesthetic victory: the players fall down and slide in mud puddles, forward passing is impractical, kickers lose traction on field goal attempts and flop on their behinds. But each time a replay lingers on a downfield heave—the receiver and defensive back straining to sprint down the sidelines while remaining upright, the raindrops themselves ticking diagonally into the players like some fanciful science-fiction explanation of how gamma rays work—I find myself holding my breath. The cartoon chins poking beneath facemasks. The obligatory dopey shirtless fan howling at America. The end-zone paint rubbing off onto fat lineman elbows and uniform pants. I remember waking up at six a.m. on childhood autumn Sundays, unable to believe I had to wait seven hours for football to begin. My parents didn't do church. I raked leaves then tossed long Nerf passes to myself, diving into leaf piles to make acrobatic catches.

Detroit scores a touchdown—Shave hands to Hoverman who stumbles through his waterlogged assaulters and splashes to paydirt—and a muscle above my right eyebrow twitches.

They're finally going to win one.

I hear car tires squeal in the street outside. I hear pop-pop-popping noises, loud, like someone setting off fireworks. I don't think much of it. This isn't a terrible neighborhood, but neither is it free from teenage mischief.

Later, as we're all gathering ourselves to go out for a late lunch, Henny shows me a strange hole in the front closet door. Then we find another. And another. Gasper clambers outside into the heat. There are burnout marks on the pavement out here, and we inspect a stretch of aluminum siding between the living room window and the little-used front door. Three corresponding holes. It's impossible to reach any other conclusion: they're bullet holes. Gasper calls the police, who do some protracted forensic work but seem resigned to the case's unsolvability. I watch Gasper answering questions, shrugging his shoulders.

*

A week or so later, I take a shower, towel myself off, and shoot myself with a hypodermic needle in the pinched flesh beside my navel.

CHAPTER 12

The first Sunday in October, we drive three hours north in Gasper's Jeep. The highways are humpbacked and worn gray, the wind bears no hint of autumn. Henny and I listen to Gasper shout tall tales of catching bluegill and largemouth bass when he first moved to Michigan, before he decided meat is murder. It's been widely disproved, Gasper says, that Adolf Hitler was a vegetarian, but Albert Einstein definitively was. "So were Tolstoy and Lord Byron! Plato and Ovid! Cesar Chavez and Lisa Simpson!"

The cabin is narrow but deep: a blue A-frame with a big front deck covered by a narrower roof. There's a detached red garage around one side with a basketball hoop nailed above the retractable door, a doghouse for Aggie in the shadow of a pine forest, a chemical toilet set a ways into the backyard, and directly across the dirt road sparkles Houghton Lake. A few other cars are already here. We step inside and take off our sunglasses to find a charming cottage setup, basically one big room with many beds. Sumon is here with his wife and children, as are some new folks.

The cabin air is stifling so everyone steps out back where, despite the heat, men are trying to build a campfire out of maple-oak and white pine logs. Gasper takes over the construction, has specific ideas about how the wood should be arranged. Everyone cracks open beer from a variety of coolers and soon enough the fire roars. Then comes the meat, scads of it: hamburgers piled high, plus venison steaks and yellow perch filets, a massacre of delectability but I stick with Gasper and huddle around a frozen box of veggie burgers, and everyone is cool about it.

A wife of one of Gasper's stadium friends tells me, "These two rugrats are mine," indicating small boys who've lately been swimming. "Your girlfriend is so beautiful!"

"Thank you," I say.

"Pat," she says to Gasper, "we haven't been out here since Tip-Up-Town in January. Oh, that's an ice-fishing thing they have, it's really fun! It was their diamond anniversary last year. And what do you do?" she asks me.

I smile and open my mouth, then Henny makes herself known slapping up behind us in flip-flops and she says, "He does me!" and there's a moment where we all check if this middle-aged lady's Midwestern hoot-owl face will take offense but she puts a hand on her forehead and laughs like a mad cowboy. Henny grabs me from behind and plants a tough kiss on my neck: we're about the same height.

When everyone is good and lubricated, when the pop-culture references and madcap vacation stories are exhausted, I sit back and drift into a private haze, trying to decide whether it's to my credit or shame that I read Dilgo Khyentse's book only once. Why don't I dig further, learn more, hear teachings, go on pilgrimages, immerse myself? It's not like I don't have the time. The calm I feel when repeating the meditation sound—the *om mani padme hung*—was the key to this summer's training camp, and now surely it's the key to settling myself down for whatever comes next. With fire on my face I make myself hear that sound again, hoping to feel the fabric of what I guess we call reality fall to tatters.

Voices rouse me. The sun is low and I hear Gasper say, "How can we not think about Trotsky in times like these?" This is certainly an interesting sentence by which to emerge from a funk. Many of the others have gone swimming; now near the fire it's just Gasper, Sumon, Henny and me, slouched in plastic lawn chairs. "Trotsky was a great man," says Gasper. "He was an intellectual. He may have founded the Red Army, but when he was at the front defeating Denikin at Orel, he was reading great French novels. Of course I know the Russian Revolution didn't fully work. But Trotsky was still onto something."

"Murder," Henny says, lazily watching the flames. "They were all pretty much onto mass murder."

"America is the bourgeois end game," says Gasper, "the place where the proletariat mindset went to die. *Everyone* is bourgeois. Most people don't have the means to be bourgeois, but they are anyway. And permanent revolution— that was Trotsky's idea—seems more necessary and less possible than ever." He crackles up out of his chair. "I'm hot and I need a smoke."

"Maybe I think politics and campfires do not mix very well," says Sumon. "And maybe I think Gasper really wants to check out the scores of his precious football games."

Retreating, Gasper says, "Ha. Maybe."

Henny takes my hand and we sit linked like this for a while. Eventually Sumon's wife calls him away. The sky is on the verge of twilight. I say, "I forgot there was football even going on. Maybe that's a pretty good sign."

"I have to say, one thing I didn't expect this weekend was a bunch of kids." Henny skims her fingers into that wild golden thicket of her hair.

"Why not? I told you Sumon has a family."

"Hm. You remember Nathan Boyd? He was the year before us. I was always really impressed. If you went someplace with Nathan, you were *in*. No matter where you went, minimum five people came up to him and bumped fists, like, he was a cool guy and he remembered people's names, and everyone just *loved* him. Free slices at Antonio's. Free drinks at the Bitter End. Guys like Patrick, who it seems like they know everybody? Just call me suspicious.

Remember? It turned out Nathan was a dealer."

"Gasper's not a dealer."

She smiles. "If you say so."

"I hate it when you play the jaded sophistication card."

"Hey, I can't help it if you're a bumpkin. But oh, phoo. Look at me, over here by myself in a chair big enough for two." I get up and join her. We kiss, and I feel her hand inching down my stomach. "Well hello there," she says. "Who's your friend?"

"I'm sure I'm no Nathan Boyd."

"Don't sulk. You'll do fine." She bites my ear and works her hand, and I'm quiet for a while. Eventually she whispers, "Are you close?"

"Jesus, yes."

She slows down, and it's torture. "You like how I look," she says.

"Of course I do. I can't get enough of you."

"You like my breasts, right?"

"Jesus. Henny."

"They're not getting flat yet?" We've had many conversations of this kind, me asked to approve this or that body part. One militant stance of hers: she will remain childless, like Emily Brontë without the tuberculosis. "Look at you," she says. "All whiskers and muscle. You should walk around with your shirt off all day."

For a moment, I think about the injections. Then I whisper, "Don't stop."

"This is relatively scandalous behavior for you. I thought for sure you'd make some noise about how the kids are nearby, and it isn't decent. I guess everybody changes."

"…"

"I like you scandalous."

"…"

"Have you really changed, Nick?"

I see stars: the kind of nothing everybody knows. For these few seconds it's possible to believe I'm not a failure.

Then Henny's shoulder disappears, I feel her grip depart and her body moves away and something nearly weightless covers my lap. She says, "Hey, Patrick. How's it going?"

Gasper says, "Not nearly as well out there as it is over here," and I look up: he's got his arms folded and his mouth scrunched up. He looks at my waist and I do, too; I'm holding a bloody cellophane tray over my crotch, the remnants of hamburger packaging.

"Would this be a good time," Henny says, "to ask you why the fuck people *really* shot bullets at your house?"

*

On the edge of an Edward Hopper dusk, we play basketball: the driveway is loosely packed dirt and there are seven players a side, but it's great fun. We are hippies and housewives, immigrants in too-tight corduroys and one gold-haired nut running around in bare feet hooting and clapping for her teammates. Gasper sits beside someone's elderly mother, cheering and drinking gin and tonics. Sumon is breathing hard and his face turns gray, so the two of us take it easy guarding one another and laugh watching everyone else, including that middle-aged hoot-owl mom who insists on shooting underhand no matter where she is on the court; we crack up when she makes three ludicrous bank shots in a row, and lose it even further when Sumon's tiny seven-year-old daughter rejects the next attempt and then strikes a menacing, arms-folded pose. I'm taking secret sips from Gasper, and truthfully have lost track of the teams. It's bedlam with players backlit by sunset, unselfishly passing the ball to anyone who seems to want it, occasionally shooting a jumper over the garage roof forcing one of the kids to go chase into the backyard. Then Henny says, "Bet you didn't know Nick can dunk!" and they egg me on until I'm alone with a car's headlights illuminating the driveway and dust swirling around my ankles like dry ice. I take four big strides, palm the ball (my hands are just big enough), and send it down hard, cracking my forearm on the rim. Everyone whoops and hollers and slaps my back.

Gasper told us to meet him across the road after dark, down at the lake. But when we arrive, the dock is empty. In the moonlight, Henny sits Indian-style and stares expectantly up at me. Crickets do whistling verses to a chorus that never comes.

Gasper and Sumon crunch down this macadam path in Tommy Bahama shirts that shine like flags in the dark. Gasper takes up a spot at the end of the dock, with his back to the water, and says, "Sorry for this clandestine shit. It's nothing, guys." He looks at Sumon. "I happen to owe a little bit of money, is all."

Henny says, "Information that might've been useful before we almost got shot sitting in your house."

"I know it looks bad. But seriously, I don't know for sure the two things are even related."

"Okay, so one thing you might not have learned about me yet," says Henny. "Our friend Nick here is a trusting soul. It's a major part of his charm. You could be planning a Brinks truck robbery directly under his nose, and he'd ask about the chemical properties of tear gas. But I've had business managers rob me blind and security guys corner me in a dressing room." She taps her retroussé nose. "It's helped me develop one hell of a bullshit detector."

"Start over," I say. "What do you owe money for?"

Gasper grins wryly and puts his interlocked fingers behind his neck. Sumon says, "For thinking he is smarter than the linesmakers."

"Gambling," says Henny.

"Listen," Gasper says. "It's fine. I'm not asking for anything. I don't want anyone else to know about this, is why I didn't want to talk about it back at the cabin."

"Jesus Christ," I say.

Henny says, "You assholes are under attack from the

fucking Mafia?"

"Not me!" says Sumon. "I have nothing to do with this! I am his bartender only!"

"The Mafia?" says Gasper, laughing. "No. C'mon. No. It's one guy. And I don't even know for sure he's the one who…you know. Shot the house."

"How much is it?" I say.

"It's nothing. It's down to practically nothing. I had a good day today. Whenever the local team loses big, it's usually pretty good for me." Gasper looks out across the black water, rubbing a wrist against his cheek. "Oh, come on. Nothing's gonna happen. You know me: I'm a sweetheart."

"Well." Henny stands. "I'll tell you three things. One: Nick is moving the fuck out of your goddamn shooting gallery. Two: stay the fuck away from him, because I don't want him around when you get your fool head blown off. And three…." She takes off her shirt and unzips her shorts, revealing a two-piece suit, then dives into the water and swims out into the darkness.

Gasper watches her go and says, "This is crazy. This is stupid. Nick, did I say I'm sorry? I really am."

"This weekend," I say. "What, you're hiding out? A couple hundred miles out of town where nobody can find you?"

"Dude," he says. "No. We've been planning this trip for months. Seriously, this is blown way out of proportion. This isn't anything. This guy, Ronnie the K, he's an okay guy. A bunch of his clients are *on the team*."

Sumon smiles and shakes his head. "I have seen this man also. I have met several of the players with him."

"Pretty weak sauce," I say. I disrobe and jump in.

*

I can see flashes of Henny in the moonlight, swimming far out into the lake. I turn around treading water and see the dock from whence we've come: the pinpricks of lights and outlines of trees are frighteningly small. I listen for voices, but even if Gasper and Sumon are still over there, it's too far to hear. Henny has stopped at a floating platform and is dangling from its sun-worn wood edge. I charge in and grab her around the middle, hoping to get a squeak out of her. But Henny's in roughneck mode and sets her jaw, spins around, splashes my face.

I press against her and kiss the place on her neck she can't resist. We're kicking to stay afloat, her hips arch forward to press mine, I push my nose behind her ear and she sighs. Sometimes her exhalations sound too emphatic to be real, and I think she's doing a burlesque of the excited woman. Maybe it's hard for me to imagine a Henny who relinquishes control, but anyway, it always surprises me. She kisses me hard on the mouth; we each have one hand on the platform and one hand doing furious work underwater.

"Get up there," she says.

"Are you sure it's a good idea?"

"Really sure."

So my naked butt is pressed against wood slats and Henny perches atop me, riding wetly, and I raise my arms searching for her, continually misplacing her as she alternately leans forward and then arches back. She comes hard, laughing down at me.

We spend a great while listening to the platform creak, smelling faint mud and natural gas odors. I slide my wet underpants back on and feel like a teenager. Henny says, "Let's buy a house here," but she says it in a mocking, puncturing way.

"What if we stayed out here all night?" I say. "You wouldn't have your eyeliner for hours."

"Don't tease me. You know I always have to have the upper hand."

"Oh, I think that's all about convenience. Who doesn't like to have the upper hand?" I place a knuckle on her thigh.

"We both know who wears the pants."

"My God. What total bullshit."

"Oh?"

"I'm at this lake because of you. I'm at that house. I'm in Michigan. I hate when you make it sound like it's just you putting up with the supermodel's moods."

"You're super all right."

"Did you ever bother to ask what Patrick went to jail *for*? I mean, why don't you join up with the crime syndicate in there? My God, at least you'd be doing fucking *some*thing."

"I don't want to get into a thing," I say.

"Of course you don't. You wouldn't."

"Henny, why are you picking on me all of a sudden?"

She sits up, and I see she's somehow already back in her bikini. "Go ahead," she says. "Tell me you love me."

"You hate it when I say that. You tell me not to say it. I love you. How's that?"

She smiles fixedly at me. "Tell me how committed you are, tell me you want to marry me. No? Nothing?"

"What's this all about, Henny?"

"I don't *know*. I try to imagine what it would be like with you, in the future, but I can never see what you're *doing*. I can't imagine you doing anything. You're too *good*." She leans back on her elbows. "You're too good for everyone. It's a little bit exhausting. You're so misunderstood."

My reflex is to be angry with her, to lash out with all the selfish things she's ever done to me. But that's how our arguments usually go. I think about attachments. What if she's right? What am I attached to that paralyzes me this way? I sit up and pull my knees under my chin; my lake-whitened toes practically glow in the dark. Well, it's true that Henny has always made me dislike myself at least a little. But I suppose that merely makes her a member of a rather large club.

Her voice kinder, she says, "Remember you stayed over my house that time, and it snowed like crazy overnight? We didn't know about the parking bans."

"I remember."

"We walked outside holding hands in the blinding sun, feeling all grown up, and there were no cars on the street."

"The towing fee was 150 bucks," I say. "Plus waiting 45 minutes for a cab to come in Middleton on a Saturday morning. I threw snowballs while we waited and you thought I was so ticked off."

"I didn't, though," says Henny. "I knew you weren't. At first I expected you to freak out, maybe because everyone in my family would've gone ballistic and started pelting me with garbage for not knowing the parking rules. But I could tell you weren't mad. That always stuck with me."

I don't know what she's getting at. We pass a while listening to wavelets slurp against the platform, and those distant tin-pan tweets of a million crickets.

She says, "Things have been better the past couple weeks. You've noticed, haven't you? I barely look at myself in the mirror at all."

I envision what would've happened if I'd made the 53-man roster, and I know Henny would've liked me more. These doubts of hers would've vanished. "Maybe I'll be a gym teacher," I say. "I've been thinking of that."

"You have not. You came up with that just this minute."

"Well, now, that's true."

"Would you really get a job like that, Nick?"

"Yes. I guess I would."

"I could go back to school and get a masters in social work."

"I can't see you," I say. "I can't tell if you're being sarcastic."

"God. You're such a fucking romantic. I feel like everything's gone to shit. I thought getting out of New York would be the answer. At least you've got something to strive for. I look at that passion, and I just feel so jealous."

"But you see what it's come to," I say. "Better to be even-keeled."

"I'm sorry for what I said. I know you don't mean to walk around with a chip on your shoulder." I hear her breathe deeply. "And I know you really do love me."

But there it is, so carefully phrased to ring with generosity but not reciprocity. It's her art and instinct. A friend would tell me I should pick a profession and a woman where much less is so constantly unresolved, where less is in such perpetual doubt. But what friends do I have, really? "So maybe we should get married," I tell her in the dark, feeling as though someone else is saying the words.

She agrees and kisses me.

*

I run. Everyone else is sleeping back at the cabin. I stabbed my stomach and injected human growth hormone, my daily dose, and now I run. These moonlit lake roads yield secrets. I listen to tree frogs and cicadas who are unaccustomed to 3 a.m. interruptions and stop their singing as I pass. The air is remarkably still and so the trees are quiet. The occasional streetlight is battered only by soft-winged moths. Yet I receive the information. My skin melts to nothing and I'm released to the sultry air, I list the six virtues—generosity, ethics, patience, diligence, concentration and wisdom—and feel integration flutter my way. It's all right if there's purpose or no purpose. It's all right to be wanted or not wanted. It's all right to be aware or unaware. I run faster and barely feel it.

CHAPTER 13

But a day later, Henny's gone. Having driven back to the city, Aggie and I follow Gasper to a physical therapy appointment, and when we return, she and her bag have vanished. I call her cell, but it rolls over directly to voicemail.

Gasper nods and frowns as I hold forth. "She's right. I know she's untrustworthy, but that doesn't mean she's not right. Look at me. It's either I focus only on football—and we see where that got me—or I get blurry and sulky. What kind of choice is that? I don't roll with the punches. When the world has the gall to inject reality into my perfect little fantasies, I can't hack it. I mean, can't you just picture me in ten years, still training like a madman all winter because someone said Kansas City might need a slot receiver? Not listening to anyone, not paying attention to anything else, hoping against hope that someone will finally come to realize how *special* I am."

"She's fucking cold-blooded, man," says Gasper. "I think she might be part lizard."

"She's only as selfish as I am."

"Hey," he says. "The great ones focus. That's how they get great. How many times have you heard some idiot superstar giving an interview?" He pats my shoulder. "You have to be a little selfish to be good."

"Come on."

"Well. I mean who isn't selfish, Nick?"

I'm a zombie. I shift back out onto Gasper's couch, relinquishing the bedroom. I don't expect her to call.

Life keeps happening. It hurts when I inhale, my stomach is a dead balloon. I hold Aggie against me in a spooning position. Aggie is so good. He's streetwise where I'm moronic. He knows which neighbors are friendly; I have no idea. He stores rawhide bones beneath blankets and behind couch cushions; I can't find the remote. Actually, in subtle ways, I find myself resenting my dog. I know this is insane. But here he is, this street urchin who by luck and guile chose a soft landing place. When we first found each other, I imagined Aggie and I shared a dedicated, ardent personality, but now it occurs to me he's much more pliable and manipulative, like Henny. Still, he hasn't run away. He stays with me, and to be honest, I don't walk him or play with him as much as I could. I have fever dreams in which I can't find him.

I drive over to Royal Oak and visit the zoo: the red pandas and Amur tigers wear expressions of deep concern, the river otters' busyness is an affront, the seals are dog-faced and stoic like veteran actresses performing despite dire personal prognoses. Each habitat has its own weather and light and is thereby comforting; it's only the walking between that sets my teeth on edge. Seeing anyone with long blonde hair—even crones with bad dye jobs, even hippie boys—is excruciating.

*

We're at Sumon's bar in Hamtramck, which is half-filled. It's a week since Henny decamped. Gasper's attention shifts between the TV and the front door, while he absently chats up an older lady who's eating chicken wings: he tells the story of his injured ankle and incidentally mentions how most chickens have their beaks ripped off their faces at a young age so they can be kept in tiny boxes without pecking one another to death. The lady nods and keeps eating, stacking bones high, like Jenga.

Gasper has placed just one bet today, but it's an important one.

"I'm giving thirteen points," he tells me. "Use your psychic powers, kid, and get that sorry excuse for a football team who cut your ass, get them to fuck up by at least a couple touchdowns, all right?" Gasper's bet is double-or-nothing on the remainder of what he owes. Ronnie the K will reportedly arrive at four o'clock one way or the other.

Sports gamblers. I've known my share. At Middleton our sophomore starting quarterback McManus got booted from school for running an enormous football pool; the injustice of his expulsion became a momentary cause among the undergraduate student body, until the college president himself strolled into our locker room and showed us McManus's bank statements. This was my senior year and I was offensive co-captain, and I took it upon myself to visit McManus at his apartment. He was charming and dismissive, demonstrating the kind of fracture with reality that can make a fine on-field leader when the chips are down. Maybe all quarterbacks are sociopathic. Anyway, with great eloquence he swore that it was all an administrative mistake, and that his reinstatement was days away. Eventually he skipped out on FBI charges, and we lost our final four games.

When Gasper hits the men's room, I say to Sumon, "It's like watching a car crash in slow motion."

"I have known him for six years," says Sumon. "He is a good man. You know this. He will do anything for a friend. If I had the money, I would give it to him myself. But he always comes out okay in the end."

"To me, it just sounds like a six-year car crash." I don't know if I mean it. Sumon doesn't smile. He steps behind the bar to polish fixtures.

Early in the second quarter, New York is up by ten and

driving. Gasper is giddy. He chats with everyone, he bets a friend twenty dollars he can't walk from one side of the bar to the other on his hands, and he pays up when the friend pulls off the trick. I scan the room and most everyone's looking at Gasper, and smiling. Then Husseyn Norwell picks off a pass and takes it back for a touchdown. Patrons who don't know better start cheering and high-fiving. The TV announcers are B-list and effusive: Detroit is showing signs. Detroit has a ton of young talent. Never mind that they're 1-3. Watch out, Gotham.

On the barstool next to mine, Gasper taps me on the arm and quietly says, "There's this great line from an old movie. 'The farther north you go, the more things can eat your horse.'"

It's a funny way to watch a game, and I've never liked it. Who wins doesn't matter much; it's all about the point spread. Plus maybe now I see there's something flat and lifeless witnessing the whole affair on TV. Maybe being on the field has finally spoiled me. At halftime I step outside onto Holbrook and wonder if I should just go home. A few guys shuffle around smoking cigarettes in the heat.

"Your buddy from New York?" says one of them.

"Texas," I say.

"Ah. Then how many points did he give?"

It's October, but it's still so humid out here my hands have that strange over-inflated feeling, and I make fists. "You'd have to ask him." In a market parking lot across the street, beleaguered parents and gangster teens march by, arms full of prizes, everyone looking scrubbed and sympathetic.

"He's sure got the look," another guy says. "There's caring, and there's caring."

I say, "Do you guys know Ronnie the K?"

The first two shake their heads, but the third smoker, a squat blond guy with a baseball cap and a dead tooth, says, "I know Ronnie."

"He's my friend's bookie, I think."

The blond guy shrugs and inhales down to the filter, holds the smoke in his lungs and squints like a wise guy.

"What's he like?" I ask.

"Well," underhanding the butt onto Holbrook, "I'd say he's ten pounds of shit in a five-pound bag." The guy walks back toward Sumon's. "Except I'm not sure the bag's even that big."

*

Watching football in a bar almost always devolves into a contest of cool. Knowledge of minutia is crucial, but it must be delivered at the most crushing times, and in the most casually irrefutable tones. Many of Sumon's patrons merely grip their pint glasses and cheer. But the experts nominate themselves, eschewing obvious moments for celebration and instead paying tribute to technicalities like blitz pickups and substitution patterns.

"Oh, come on!" a jersey-clad fan shouts as the second half begins. "You can't run that route out of bounds! That's just a terrible mistake by Vance, and it costs us a sack! Watch him! Watch him step out!"

"Holding! They're holding!" cries an overweight goateed guy, keeping his eyes glued to the screen so we know he's serious, and not doing this for attention. "Pretty hard for Wallace to get open with the linebacker draped over his back!"

"It's not Wallace," another expert says dismissively. "It's Schenk."

"Well, maybe Wallace should be in there! Maybe Wallace gets that fucking call!"

"Don't worry about the first down! You need five yards to get in field goal range! Don't go deep here! Don't go deep!"

"Look at the left side! It's just caving in! How can you keep calling seven-step drops and draws to the left with

Richards blocking like shit!"

"God! Hoverman sucks! One hand on him and he goes down! They miss Collins so bad!"

"Dude, Collins is averaging like 3.1 yards a carry in Denver, and Hoverman's up over four. Plus Collins is out this week with a bad toe."

Gasper doesn't partake. Now his elbows are on the bar, his face is in his hands, and he watches the fourth quarter through splayed fingers. New York is marching the ball up and down the field, but the lead is still only seven points. I'll bet Gasper can fit more statistics inside his brain than all these geniuses combined, but his torment holds his tongue.

"At first I kind of wanted you to lose today," I tell him. "But seeing you like this, I know it's serious."

"I forgive you," he says. "Depressed people want everyone to be depressed."

Funny. Until just now, for the first time in a week, I wasn't thinking of Henny.

New York's young quarterback is suffering through a five-turnover day, but he's got his offense in the red zone again and a camera captures him tight at the line of scrimmage, his handsome face barking pre-snap signals. He drops back and his eyes go big.

"Come on," I say.

What does he see? In this moment the game does its magic and goes Technicolor in my eyes, the two-dimensional figures slow down, I see the offensive right side clear out and the quarterback rolls that way, tucking the ball, baiting a safety. These reads-and-reactions happen every week, in every game, ad infinitum, a void filled, a mistake punished. But they're beautiful. At the last possible instant, the QB pulls up, I feel Gasper absently grab my t-shirt sleeve, the pass lofts, a receiver double-taps behind the Detroit corner (it's Kevin Hamill), touchdown, and this time Gasper doesn't erupt, he accepts a low-five from Sumon and sags into a puddle of fandom. The thought crosses my mind how his employer might feel about bets placed against them.

"Goddamn it," he says. "Six more fucking minutes."

"Ah. That's the life of a fish. Can never enjoy the good times." A short, shaven-skulled black man steps between our barstools. He's a middle-aged guy turned out in a suede shearling coat and Cuban heels, a ludicrous outfit in this heat. Ronnie the K. "Patrick, your taste in companions is getting better. This is Nick Morrison. It's a great pleasure to meet you, young man." I shake his hand, which is smaller than mine and swathed in rings. "You were a star those first couple weeks of training camp, Nick. I'll never understand what they were thinking."

Gasper says, "You're early, Ronnie."

"Nick, I have to say I'm glad to see you've stayed in our fair city," Ronnie says in his gravelly voice. "It's making a comeback. The media won't tell you this, but money is pumping into the D. To say nothing of the fine cold cash Mr. Gasper will be paying me in, oh, about six minutes. Don't worry, Patrick. I'll be putting it to good use, to stimulate the economy."

We watch the kickoff. Brohammer takes it out to his own 30. Loudly I say, "Were you the one who fired a gun at Gasper's house?"

Ronnie looks around. "What?" As he smiles, his thick goatee spreads wide. "Nick, what kind of businessman do you think I am? How counterproductive would that be? No, I don't know what kind of other trouble Mr. Gasper gets himself into, but I assure you violence isn't part of my bag."

It's third down. Shave steps under center in hurry-up mode, barking a command. He fires one across the middle to Thaddeus DeNoon, but it ricochets off DeNoon's pads and is intercepted. Gasper covertly pumps a fist, and some of Sumon's patrons begin to drink up and leave.

"Funny thing, violence," says Ronnie the K. "That game up there, Nick, your game. They say it's the most violent thing around. Giant men trying to crush one another, a dozen collisions on every play. Bones break and ligaments shred." He looks at Gasper. "But then on the other hand you have actual war. I guess maybe war puts a different face on the discussion. Sort of puts the topic of violence in a whole new perspective."

Gasper's jaw is tight. New York is killing the clock, running doomed bucks directly into a stacked defense. They take it down to the two-minute warning, then bring out the field goal team. It's good. The lead is seventeen.

"What I want you to do," Gasper says, "and I want you to be really clear about this, Ronnie. I want you to go fuck yourself. Take the whole afternoon. Really get in there, clear things out. Use, I dunno, a bottle or a lead pipe or your fist, but just make sure you do the job right."

"Tut-tut. Such foul talk." Ronnie smiles magnanimously. "I'm not sure this is the lifestyle for you, Patrick, if you're going to get so worked up. Sumon? How are you doing today, my friend?" Sumon shakes his head and smiles. Ronnie says, "It's quite a sizable amount of money you were on the hook for, Patrick. You hit a winning streak at the right time. I have no doubt in the world I'll be speaking to you again real soon." He walks to the door. "And Nick, it was an honor to meet you. You're a talented young man. I know I'll be hearing big things from you." Gasper turns around and gives the middle-finger salute, and Ronnie the K is gone.

"So," says Sumon. "The warning shots. Do you really think he did it?"

Gasper shakes loose his shoulders, does neck stretches, straightens his arms above his head. "Normally I'd say no, man." He bites his lip, smiling. "But it really was a lot of money."

Sumon puts three shot glasses in front of us, reaches beneath the bar and comes up with a bottle of Johnny Walker Gold. These are my friends, and things are all right. It's possible to believe life will get better.

Then Brohammer returns the ensuing kickoff 98 yards

for a touchdown, to precious little on-field celebration. After all, it doesn't affect the outcome. New York still wins by ten.

*

It's a hung-over Monday and I sleep past noon, briefly regaining consciousness twice to vomit. My phone, scrupulously plugged into the wall, wakes me up for good.

"Hello?" I say.

"I could sell you some story," says Henny, "about how you'd always resent me, because I'd be the one who made you give up your dream. But that wouldn't do it, Nick. It wouldn't be enough. We'd be right back at it again in six months."

"Where are you?"

"So instead I figured out the truth. The truth is, when I'm around you neither one of us will ever make a damn decision. We'll just sit around all *burdened* by the possibilities, or else so secretly dissatisfied with one another that we'll never let ourselves or the other person make any actual steps. We'd rather sit around and worry and complain. But you know what? It's not 'us.' It's 'you.' I'm not like that when I'm not around you. I can be in the world. I know I can. The problem is you. You invent these…*stories* about yourself as a way to button yourself up, box yourself in. It makes you feel so good about yourself, Nick, but it also makes you so fucking small."

I'm careful not to say anything inflammatory, because there's still a possibility of salvaging things with her. Don't let go with both barrels.

She says, "I don't know what makes me such a fuckup, Nick, but I know being with you will never work. You're trapped in these pictures you have of the way every little thing should be, and my God, everybody around you just ends up feeling so judged. But what if I'm not a good person today? What if I feel like telling a lie, or ignoring the phone, or gossiping behind someone's back? Does that make me a failure, because I couldn't live up to standards? I mean, fuck, if I'm gonna be a failure anyway, why not have fun and not be so hard on myself?"

"All right," I say. "I get it."

"I know what you think of me. But I want somebody who doesn't judge me just by breathing. Do you remember when I told you I had an abortion? It was senior year, I remember like it was yesterday, I told you I had one when I was 16, and do you remember what you said?"

"I don't."

"You said: 'Jesus Christ, you were just a child.' You were so condescending!"

"I probably meant your manager was committing statutory rape with you. I wasn't blaming *you*. Have you left Detroit yet? Can I come see you?"

"I had to call you up and tell you it was really over. I figured if I told you what I really think of you, you finally wouldn't keep crawling back."

I say nothing. I can see her beautiful face, her hands, the lines of her inner thigh.

"I'm in L.A.," she says. "I have a photo shoot tomorrow."

My head feels filled with mercury. "What could I do differently, Henny?"

"Nothing. You could take care of yourself. You could be kinder to yourself. Just, you know. It takes a toll, being around you. Not everyone was born to be a monk."

*

I lie on the couch opening and closing each eye, feeling my scalp tighten and loosen as my body processes alcohol. I can't reassume verticality without throwing up again. Aggie must need to pee badly, but he's on the floor, carelessly snoring alongside my drooping hand.

The phone rings again, and I don't look at the number,

wanting to believe she's calling back with her regrets, surging with pride that I didn't torch the bridge between us with the truth.

"Nick?" It's a man's voice.

"Yes."

"It's Dave Blum."

I say nothing.

"I just got off the phone with Brian Nugent. Are you sitting down? He wants you back on the squad, man. You're still in Detroit, right? Are you there? Hey?"

PART III

CHAPTER 14

"I always wanted you," Nugent tells me.

The team is 1-4 and going into its bye week, a respite that gives the coaching staff an opportunity to reevaluate personnel. *Nothing else is working,* I imagine them saying, *so let's try something ridiculous. Let's try the midget.* Next up is a home game against Minnesota, a division rival who's 3-3. There are placards around the complex about how much everyone is supposed to hate Minnesota and their star running back Darquavis Greylock, and his celebrated post-touchdown Inferno Dance (in which he mimes flames shooting up from the end-zone turf). Nobody takes special note when I enter the building for the first time in two months: Pot Roast is here jiving with security and I think he must be waiting for me, but I walk past uncommented upon.

Townsel texts me to meet him in the trainer's room, and we bro-hug and smile. Everyone else around here has his head down.

Oh, they always wanted me. Quarterback Jim Shave was no doubt pounding Coach Fond's door shouting his demands. Running back Zeke Hoverman couldn't concentrate without me in the backfield. Wide receiver Wendell Vance held up every form of transportation he was supposed to be on in passive-aggressive protest. Well, now I'm jaded on top of my jadedness which of course is a way of saying I've been suckered back in telling myself stories regarding my wisdom and savvy, how my eyes have been pried eternally open. I once listened to a teacher lecture on the transcendentalists and copied down a note from Emerson's journals: "To fill the hour—that is happiness; to fill the hour and leave no crevice for a repentance or an approval." Oh, yes! But my heart will melt the first time someone gets rah-rah with me. Two years ago in Buffalo friends around the building nicknamed me Professor. Around here, I'm Mouse.

"We're going spread," says Nugent. "I want you to be a big part of that." There are dozens of new plays, and two weeks of extra practice sessions featuring seven-on-seven drills well into the evenings. "Everyone's starting fresh," Nugent says. "You're not behind anyone. Nobody's job is safe." There are grumblings around the locker room that Nugent is angling for the job when and if Starling Fond gets canned.

I move out of Gasper's house. He's mum on the subject of his debt, deflects all inquiries. "No, this is your day, young squire." He limps around the place making sure I've got all my t-shirts and sticky wideout gloves, and Aggie's toys. His burning cheer makes this feel like a defection. He says, "You are an iconoclast. Bring something new to the savages."

"Why, whatever do you suggest?"

"A rakish insouciance. A whiff of superiority, and the sense you're somehow above it all. You don't give a fuck about any of 'em, because now you're sure they don't really give a fuck about you. The history of the universe is a history of the advancing of consciousness, so be the furthest-along citizen you can be." I'm shown back into the same hotel room I lived in during camp; when I walk in, I'm struck by the odor of non-occupancy. Townsel is still next door.

*

"Shave's our problem," Hoverman tells me. "Putting more pre-snap decisions in his hands is a fucking disaster. In Chicago, we all see a blitz coming on the left side. It's not like they're disguising it or anything. It's really rudimentary stuff, just check to a sprint draw right. Shave can't do it. I don't know, maybe he doesn't see it, maybe he's too fucking stubborn to do the obvious thing."

"Hey, maybe this'll work," Shave says, tossing me a rolled-up towel while we work off nervous energy before an offensive meeting. We're alone in the hallway. "All I know is, I didn't sign up for this shit. Where the fuck's the goddamn blocking? How the fuck are we out there runnin' seven-step drops when I'm gettin' my ear dang near torn off? Nine stitches. I mean, *inside* the helmet."

"I'm worried about coach," says Danny Shugarts, our right defensive end who's off to a slow start. We're standing around in the parking lot late one night. "There's a rumor his son took a turn for the worse. I heard from one of the offensive coaches—I don't want to say who—that coach flew in a faith healer from the Philippines, and I don't hold no quarter to that voodoo stuff. If you want to know the truth, I really do think it makes Jesus mad."

Defensive tackle Meleki Faafeu looks like he's up over four hundred pounds, helplessly swallows cake alone in the big dining room. "Eat when I stressed," he says. "Eat when I sad. Eat when I lose."

"Underwood and Brohammer got into it," Townsel tells me. "Y'all ever seen a fight on a plane? I mean, those boys was bombing each other's faces. Thought someone would kick out a window, we'd all go flyin' off into space."

Marcellus Blake comes naked out of the showers, a dripping black Adonis linebacker with curlicues of dark hair sprouting all over him, his manhood half-aroused and practically the size of my forearm. He towels himself sensually and speaks, not really to me, though I'm the only person over here: "Already fuckin' sweatin' again. Coach say we gotta last longer'n anybody else. It's a war of nutrition."

*

As the backup quarterback, Hinkler needs at least a few reps in our new four- and five-receiver sets, and waddles to the huddle reeking of entitlement. Hoverman quickly says, "Dallas Right, 39 F Stab King."

"Whaddaya mean?" Hinkler starts counting players. "What're you doing?"

"Running the offense, jackass. This is my rep. Get your ass out of here."

Hink backs away, eyes big. We can hear him muttering, "He can't throw a 3. You can't throw a 3 to save your life." By now the linemen are tittering.

"What the fuck is going on in there!" says Nugent. "Hinkler, where the fuck are you going, you scrotal lesion?"

"God damn you," Hurricane Hink says. "God damn you."

"Hey," from Richards, the giant left tackle. "No blasphemy."

"I'll blasphemy if I fuckin' want to. God damn him. That's what I fuckin' say." Hoverman grins thinly.

"Say it again," Richards growls. "Go ahead. Say it again."

"God damn Hover-fuckin'-man. God fuckin' damn him." So Richards punches out his arms like he's done ten thousand times—the move that made him a multimillionaire—and takes Hinkler by the shoulderpads, but Hink frees himself and ducks away whooping, runs toward the practice goalpost, Richards chugging after him, swinging his fat arms.

Watching them go, right guard Tommy Way says, "He'd never say that if he really believed he could tell God who to damn. People used to believe they could. Look at that boy, actin' crazier than a sprayed roach."

*

Gasper watches practice holding his crutches. He doesn't need the crutches anymore, but the team's disability insurance is apparently plum and not worth risking. He's got those same wraparound sunglasses on from the first time I met him, and his ID badge around his neck. He nods his head in tune with a song only he can hear.

We go out for soy burgers at a crunchy Dearborn dive, and he says, "Three things different in pro football than in college."

"One," I say through a dry mouthful.

"Obvious: money. Oh, I know, the best recruits probably get paid in school. But not that kind of coin. So your pros, obviously, have more disposable income than they know what to do with, leads to trouble."

"Two."

"Kids. They start dipping their wicks into everything that moves, they start spawning a new generation. Sometimes even with the same woman, sometimes even with the one they married. This means less free time, a dent in disposable income, less hanging around with other players looking for trouble. Or else more responsibilities to pretend don't exist. Sidebar on kids?"

"Granted."

"Smart kids aren't delightful. As gofer deluxe, I've driven around my fair share these past couple seasons. The ones who are privileged little punks and mini-thugs are annoying as shit, but at least they're good for some comedic value. But smart kids, precocious kids. Ugh. Think about it: they lead with their intellects, it's their way of impressing you, and earning love. There's nothing delightful about someone trying to win your love by being smart."

"Three."

"This is the key one. Cheerleader tits. I know it's sexist as hell, but it's true. I'm sure you had some swell ladies at

Upper East Anglia, or wherever it is you say you went to college. And they get fine-looking women to cheer at Texas and UCLA. But I swear to God, the reformed pole dancers and wannabe centerfolds on any given Sunday sideline could supply enough silicon to float Intel for a year. You watch 'em this weekend, nice and up close. Take a good look when they do the chorus line bit. They jump and kick, but their boobs never move."

"So. Coming back to work any time soon?"

"This from the asshole who treated my foot like a Rubik's Cube? And I know, I know, you don't know what a Rubik's Cube is, I get it, I'm old." Gasper finds a sesame seed on our tabletop and presses his finger down hard on it. "Anyway, that's not the question you want to ask."

"Well? Anything from Ronnie the K?"

"We talk. Oh, Ronnie and I have a long and complex relationship. We piss on each other's leg. But it's fine, Nick. The situation is, how you say, defused. In the meantime, how are you feeling about Sunday?"

"Like I can't believe it," I say.

"You got the desperation mojo, man. There's this thing Sumon told me. 'A dog in desperation will leap over a wall.'"

"Listen, there's…. I'm probably going to need more…*stuff*."

Gasper scratches his forehead. "I figured that might explain lunch. So how's it been going anyway? Using the latter-day tools of ignorance?"

It's gone rather spectacularly well. HGH has seemingly made my energy level higher, my wits sharper. I still get sore—my legs are feeling it right now—but the extra workouts since I've been using have put nine more pounds of muscle on my frame, so I'm up to 176. The morality of taking a banned substance is background noise. Gasper was wrong about me. I tell him, "Fine. No problems."

"Well. Get me the cash and I'll arrange another delivery."

"Thanks. Hey, who're you betting on this weekend?"

"Oh, come on," Gasper says. "How could I pick against my pal?" He pauses for a comedic beat. "I'll probably just sit this one out entirely."

When I get in my car alone feeling my tired feet and calves bickering as though they'd like some kind of trial separation, I see my phone has a missed call. But it was Townsel who rang, not Henny.

*

"Yawl get off the line quicker," says Lester Jefferson, in a running backs meeting. "Come on, gahs. Look right here. Watch the man's balance. Yawl's smarter than this. And here. Toombs, he's on yawl's inside shoulder man. You read the blitz right, but how yawl gonna break yawl's route inside? He's *on* yawl's inside shoulder."

*

"You fucking terrible!" says Bow Wow in a receivers meeting. "How do I rewind this fucking thing? DeNoon! You fucking terrible! Tell me what you thinking here. It's a 6. Square in. Square *in*! Dig the fucking route, boy! You throw off your quarterback's timing when you pitter-patter you fucking little footsies like that! Why the fuck your quarterback trust you, you run a route like that? Somebody help me fucking rewind this fucking thing."

*

"All right," says Nugent in a full-offense meeting. "Maui Right Rub-Dart F Juke Gone. Hoverman, that's a piss-poor rub. Set a pick. Set a pick and let me worry about if it gets called. This one's Split Right 414 Swing V Queen, who's hot here? Tight end's hot. Wallace or Schenk. But I want the outlet out of the backfield cutting hard. Four yards. Four yards and cut real hard. This one, we're in Quads Right here, this one's gonna work Sunday. Ace 628 F Flat. We didn't run it this morning, but I also like Trey Right 680 Corner Cut King. Shave, make the read. It'll work."

*

Saturday night at the team hotel I drift off and dream that Zeke Hoverman and I are at a funeral in our football uniforms. It's unclear who's died. Hoverman holds his helmet at his side, and his dreadlocks—which he's shorn in real life—have returned in their leonine glory. We're outside and the air is cool (even in a dream this is a relief) and the sky gray. Two dozen people are dressed in black, heads down, eyes closed, and I notice everyone has bare feet. The open grave is deep and tufted with grass at its edges. Someone is down in there, in the dark, and I assume they must be digging. But then I hear a woman's moan, all pleasure. I look around the mourners but nobody else seems to hear. Hoverman touches my arm and says something while smiling, but I can't make him out.

In the way of dreams, the scene changes and I'm at a poker game. But the playing cards are ultra-small: the size of Scrabble tiles. When I throw away two cards and draw two others, I keep accidentally grabbing too many, so there are always eight or nine cards in my hand. I try to play honestly and keep only the ones I was supposed to receive, but everyone at the table gets mad and accuses me of cheating.

I awake at 4:30 a.m. and realize it's the day of my first regular-season professional football game.

*

You can hear the crowd from our locker room. It's a howling unlike anything the preseason can offer.

I'm dressed and already have my helmet and sticky gloves on. In my second go-round, I've been told to relinquish #84 and shed any vestiges of being a wide receiver. This time I'm #25.

The players are milling, having performed a walkthrough this morning, having worked up a lather in warm-ups just minutes ago. It's nearly time. We're standing close at the center of the room, pads jostling, random utterances rising from the crowd: animal grunts and howls. Coach Fond's priest gives a benediction which I frankly don't hear, though I'm dragged down to one knee by somebody, and I think this:

Football is beloved because there's a scoreboard, because the rules are arcane but perfectly known to millions. Is there any wonder the slowest of slow-motion instant replay has evolved through football broadcasts, where we *must* know whether this shoe definitively touches the sideline marker or if the ball jiggles brownly in the wanton receiver's mitts as he hits the turf? It is perfection because *everything will be known.* Anyone who says the sport is simply a venal substitute for warfare and that it satisfies the modern human's suppressed bloodlust needs, they've either advanced to a higher stage of dealing with life's unfathomability and should be followed like yogis, or are uncharitable to a fault. The beauty of statistics and formations and (yes, by heavens) instant replay is they let us touch bottom. And of course there is no bottom to life, which is wonderful but awful, and so we pretend: for a few hours, we allow ourselves to be charmed by a common spell. The first time one of my college games was televised— by some regional sports network with a two-camera setup and a tiny production truck—I DVR'd the broadcast and saw *myself* in instant replay, saw my body frozen in mid-lunge as the talking heads discussed whether the ball in my hands had broken the end zone's plane. It was sublimity itself.

"Boys," says Coach Fond, as we continue to kneel. "You-all can't do it for me. I know some of you-all would like to, and I appreciate that, but it doesn't work that way. You play out there thinking of me, you go' fail. No, go out there and do it for you-all's selves. Precision. Think about the heavens opening above, because they go' open and blood go' rain down. I know you-all have it in you. I know there's a reason we were put here. Blow a hole through them and make them bleed. Hate and precision and focus."

We run screaming into our dome.

CHAPTER 15

I'm out here, actually *in the huddle*, actually *part of the game plan*, trying not to look up at the stadium's latticework comprised of several tons of steel, trying not to read the advertisements everywhere, trying not to lose sensation in my extremities. For days I've told myself how to approach this: with no interpretation, no validation. Be in your body. Rise up close to your skin. I haven't blinked for ten minutes.

Like most offensive coordinators, Nugent scripts his first several plays and walks us through them beforehand, so I'm expecting our first call to be a simple counter run for Hoverman. Instead, Shave listens to the microphone in his helmet, smiles at us in the huddle and calls Doubles Sprint Rev Right Pass, a trick play. This puts Hoverman alone behind Shave in the backfield, Vance split left, DeNoon split right, Wallace on the left end and me snugly up against Pendleton on the right end, not split or slotted or anything, just smack dab directly *on* the line of scrimmage, staring up at #94, their left defensive end who easily outweighs me by a C-note.

"Check! Check!" Pendleton shouts, meaning he already forgot the snap count.

I say, "Blue! Blue!" meaning we're going on three.

Is this happening?

Om mani padme hung.

Shave takes the snap and pivots right, as though Hoverman will hit the 2 or the 4 hole, except Hoverman is busy sprinting the other way, directly around the left tackle. Along with the rest of the offensive line, I fire left and block down, allowing #94 to basically envelop me as he tries to stand up in the hole, anticipating the runner who'll never come. Behind me, I know Shave has spun completely around and is running what looks like a bootleg to the left, following Hoverman around the left edge. Shave is a big man and slow of foot, and when we've run this in practice and then watched film of it, someone commented he looks like he's running with gravy in his boots.

To my right, I can see a flash of DeNoon running his square-in, bringing their corner and free safety with him. To the defense, our movement looks like play-action—maybe *botched* play-action—and DeNoon looks like the intended receiver sprinting for the opposite sideline. I've been grabbed and mashed by #94, and allow myself to be tossed away.

Meanwhile, Wendell Vance (I know but can't see) is running a reverse. As Shave lumbers left, Vance sprints backwards, behind the quarterback, and accepts a pitch-back. All eleven defensive players shout "Reverse!" and stop their pursuit, change direction, and close in on Vance who almost certainly has the ball tucked under his arm and is running hell-bent-for-leather to get around the right offensive end.

Except it's not a running play. They've lost track of me, and I'm running a deep out on the right sideline. I turn with my left hand up and see big Vance give one final fake like he's really trying to outrun everybody and turn upfield, then he slows up and raises the ball in his big right hand and heaves a spiral at me. Me.

Me.

I'm 18 yards downfield and all alone. Vance has flung it perfectly, and I'm uncovered. All tension leaves me, there is the ball, there are my hands, no other facts need apply.

I catch and tuck, find myself a foot from the sidelines

and turn upfield. There's *nobody*. The closest white uniform is ten yards away, charging at me but taking a bad angle. I run with my scalp blazing, with fear mainlining its yellow venom directly into my spine. I go hard, straight along the side hashmarks, now I start to hear thousands of people screaming and I can see the blue end zone, the tangelo pylon, big defenders using diagonal lines to try and close in on me and also friendly faces directly to my right: teammates, coaches and staffers running after me with arms outstretched, rooting for my progress. I score with an exultant leap over the goal line. I look up at the end-zone grandstands and those voluble thousands have gone mad, are jumping on one another, shaking each other, pulling at each other's commemorative jerseys, howling, happy. My teammates close in on me and blot the ceiling, slapping my helmet hard many times, and then Tommy Way lifts me like a child, so my shoulderpads are above all others.

*

Unfortunately, Darquavis Greylock is a truck.

He runs it seven times in eight plays, helping Minnesota keep the ball for six-plus minutes and tie the score, then performing his Inferno Dance. Watching him go, Hoverman says to me, "If I had to tackle that dude, I couldn't make myself get up in the morning." Clancy Swift comes off the field with a haunted, blazing look in his eyes.

Our next possession picks up steam when we run a back-of-the-envelope formation Nugent installed last night: Hoverman, DeNoon and Vance in trips left, me in the slot and Toombs alone behind Shave. I motion into the backfield, Shave fakes it to Toombs and I get lost in the scrimmage melee, then break out by myself, away from their #90 who has short zone coverage but whose arms and legs look like jelly beans glued onto a potato. I catch a short pass and carry it 35 yards. But we bog down and settle for a field goal. I haven't sat out a single offensive snap.

"Come on, D!" Shave shouts, and the defensive coordinator Kolakowski gives him an ugly look.

Greylock gets shoved into our sideline after a nice run and nobody helps him up. We can hear him laughing at us in a sort of grunting fashion.

"He's not human," says Bolduan, the kicker. "He's a robot."

"They don't make robots that fast," says his long snapper, Calcaterra.

"He's a robot from the future."

On the next play Husseyn Norwell intercepts a flare pass and takes it deep into their territory, but Sugar Tits gets called for roughing the passer and it all comes back.

"He's reading the wrong book!" Hinkler says beside me. "Damn! Little less Bible, little more rulebook!"

"Shut up, Hink," says Hoverman.

Shave comes over after a consultation with Coach Fond and shows me a few digital images of their defensive formations, then leans over to show Hoverman. He says, "Look at this. We got this. We totally got this. The Mike is my little plaything. He just follows my eyes. I mean, you can't see it, but in this one I'm totally looking the way he's running."

"Then don't look at me," I tell him. "That guy is huge."

During a TV timeout I decide to watch the cheerleaders. In honor of Halloween, they're either dressed as sexy witches or spooky prostitutes.

"We're not supposed to fraternize," Bolduan says. "They wouldn't talk to me anyway, because I'm just the kicker."

"Don't sell yourself short," I say, watching them shimmy in sprayed-on hot pants.

"I *am* short," says Bolduan.

I walk over to the two giant receivers, Vance and DeNoon, who are chatting coolly, helmets off, arms crossed.

"Here he come now," says Vance. "You giving me half

that bonus check, right Mouse? Me and Nooner drawing all that attention away from you."

"I would. Unfortunately I didn't get a bonus check."

"You'll have to owe me. Oh, get that two-four! Jump that out! There you go! There you go, kid!" The crowd also approves of a play I wasn't watching. Vance is the kind of charismatic guy who swallows personalities, who makes you want to have his opinions and talk like he does. His voice is high, especially when he gets excited, and woe betide the soul who disagrees with him on a football-related matter. He considers himself a leading authority, takes pleasure in trying to guess Minnesota's plays before the ball is snapped. "Draw!" he shouts, in that cool and domineering way. "Watch this, Mouse. Halfback draw." But they throw a screen to Greylock, and I search Vance's expression for some hint of humility. His smirk offers none.

"27 will bite on the double-move," DeNoon says, drinking water brought to him in tiny paper cups. "I'll get him in the second half."

"Two-seven bite on any damn thing I *want* him to bite on," says Vance.

I think what a picture we must make on TV.

*

It's 21-13 bad guys at the half and everyone sits around the locker stalls wearing thousand-yard stares, listening to position coaches buck them up. Geathers is illustrating a blocking technique to Norwell, Schenk and Julian Edwards, who was called for a block-in-the-back in the second quarter. Across the room Kolakowski exhorts his charges: "He's just a man! Chop him down! Chop his ass down!" Nugent and Coach Fond stand together near a blue trash barrel consulting in whispers, staring at their shoes.

A trainer brings a syringe over to Toombs, who has his jersey off and lifts his undershirt, takes the shot directly in the left side of his ribcage. His face is stone, his Mohawk glistening.

"Not bad," Hoverman tells me.

I nod, and watch him pull down his sock to care for a turf burn that's turned his shin to gristle. He pats the blood with a towel and swallows several pills. "Don't get squeamish," he says. The flat-screen above our lockers isn't tuned to the halftime shows, instead simply displays an infinite graphic loop of our upcoming home dates.

"Good shit," says Shave, hobbling past, protecting his hip which took a big shot. "Just keep that shit up, you two. We're moving it." In the insecure way of quarterbacks, he wants to be praised in return.

"You, too," I tell him. "Some great pre-snap reads."

"Aw, I do what I can."

Nugent gathers up the offense and lists five or six plays he likes heading into the third quarter. He says, "The defense needs us to pick 'em up. So here's the thing: our adjustment is no-huddle, five-wide, pedal down. Pitch-and-catch, know your reads. Jimmy, great job out there, keep it up." Those who've stripped off part of their uniform start hitching back up. A trainer comes past with another syringe, making eye contact with every player by way of asking if anyone needs it. The energy level is low until Swift throws his helmet across the room, breaking a folding chair in half.

"Fuck!" he says. "Auuuuuugh!"

So we all scream unintelligibly. Men butt one another without headgear on. Coach Fond has nothing else for us, simply rolls up a piece of looseleaf paper and walks out ahead into the tunnel, back out onto the field.

Before I leave the locker room, Nugent grabs my arm and says, "I want you to know how extraordinary it is, what you're doing. Off the street, right into this. I'm very proud of you, Morrison."

Hearing this, Vance flutters his eyes and makes a kissy face, in a way that makes it impossible to hate him.

*

A security guard high-fives me as I walk back to our side—an overweight, middle-aged black guy with thick glasses—and of course this seems entirely plausible yet also crazy: how could I be so close to the center of this storm? My knee-jerk is to feel both unworthy of this guard's attention because who the heck am I, and also stupidly annoyed more people aren't recognizing me personally because what the heck more do I have to do? Well, do I know what life is like with a chip-free shoulder? Love—in one of its forms—is cascading from the rafters.

Minnesota fumbles the second-half kickoff. We're on their 17; the frenzy is so hot Shave does the archetypal "quiet-down" arm wave to these adoring thousands. Hoverman gets two on a slam, DeNoon catches a bubble screen and takes it three more. Shave draws them offsides, but we're still inches short. Quick as can be, with no huddle, Shave goes play-action and takes a shot at DeNoon in the end zone but it's too high. On the play I take my first real hit of the afternoon in blitz pickup, trying to get in #94's way. He blasts me backwards so I land against Shave's knee, and the quarterback crumples on top of me. Everything sounds muffled and hollow. But we're both okay. Nugent decides to forego the field goal and I come off in favor of a heavy package. Hoverman gets the first down.

"There it is, Zeke!" I say.

Beside me, Nugent puts his hand over his headset microphone and says, "31 Trap Cub. Get in for Hoverman." This is a single-back running play. "Now! Before I change my mind."

So here I am: swelling, bursting. The middle linebacker watches me line up at tailback and starts gyrating, pushing his strong safety back because he figures it can't be a run. The defense pinches outside pre-snap, ready to blitz Shave hard and force a mistake. First and goal, Shave takes the snap, whirls, and the seas part as I accept the ball in my gut. I jab-step the Mike and he crumples leftward disgustedly. I skip into the end zone: the first in-game carry of my professional life.

*

"Play fast! Play fast! Hey. Let the game come to you! Do everything right!"

"Hey! He's blocking before the play!"

"I'm hungry! I'm hungry today! Look at me! I don't give a damn! I'm hungry today!"

"We gotta rotate! We gotta rotate!"

"Last time when we was in Minnesota, these boys got real disrespectful! But they in our motherfuckin' house now! They in our house now! And we gonna release these big dogs, send 'em after they ass, and send 'em back to Minnesota where they belong!"

"He's a runner! He's a runner! He's not protected! He's a runner!"

"Far West Right Slot 16 Stop on one."

"It don't matter where the battle is fought at! It don't matter! You know why? We physical! They finesse!"

"Hey! When we put you the widest, you know he's comin' hard inside! You gotta win one-on-one!"

"That was a big-time answer right there!"

"Play like pit bulls!"

"Blue 18. Weak. Weak. Weak. Weak."

"This is our championship! They got fat while we starved. It's our turn!"

"Get on top! Get on top!"

"Uhn! Uhn! 'Booty sittin' higher than a flight of stairs. Some can make it clap. Some really can't though. Them Alabama girls said it's all in the ankles.'"

"We gotta get in the end zone, man. We gotta get in the

zone."

"I Left Zoom Z Left 13 Double Kick on one."

"Don't cut back. Trust your speed."

"Big Booty Judy!"

"We ain't playin' today. They gettin' they ass whupped today."

"Don't let one bad play turn into a bad day! Get 'em fucking going. We just gotta make a fucking play! And by making a play, I mean doing your job."

"Gotta feel it baby, gotta feel it! Gotta get six! Gotta get six!"

"You can't even touch quarterbacks anymore. Two years ago that would've been a K.O. shot."

"Hustle your ass off!"

*

I take a backhanded handoff from Shave—something new to simulate play-action—and get maybe two yards before the world caves in on me. I'm at the bottom of the pile, a legendary place of biting and poking and clawing, but it's not so bad.

Maybe I'm always falling in love. Then again, the desired thing, the lusted-for thing, can it ever truly be an object of love until you're granted admission? Perhaps what I've known about myself during my various exiles (without knowing it) was my capacity for *this feeling*, this rapture in here with a ton of human flesh piling and then unpiling from me. Express myself, yes, via physical work and pain or whatever métier you choose, but clamp down the exposure, and sabotage myself by expecting the worst, because if I'd known it could feel like this—it could *sound* like this—I'd have torn my chest open for Henny and for football every day of my life. What would happen if you lived life that way? Ready for love, but ready to bleed? Blades of artificial grass are gummy against my lips and eyebrows, polygons of light shift above me though I can't move my head to look up at them, the sweat-soaked football is still clamped under my right arm despite tugs from all around and reads "Wilson" and, in smaller letters, "The Duke."

Someone spits on my arm.

*

Greylock scores again, and does his dance. Then Vance gets in the end zone for us, and mocks the dance, ensuring he'll be all over the highlight reels.

As will I. As will I.

Our defense holds them to a field goal: Sugar Tits makes the key play on a third down, crushing their quarterback and knocking himself out in the process, so smelling salts are applied and he tries to walk to the wrong sideline. We're down 31-27 with just under three minutes to play, no timeouts left.

Hoverman's on the bench. I play the slot. It becomes a game of wind sprints: line up, run your route, hurry back to the line, get set, run another route, hurry back. I'm running underneath and sideline stuff and don't get a ball my way; it's worse for Vance and DeNoon, booking it straight downfield then hustling back to do it again. At the two-minute warning, with water bottles shoved into their facemasks by attendants, they seem cooked.

We're on their 41. Hoverman is back in, gets a draw that goes nowhere, and nets us thousands of boos. Two more pass plays, underneath grabs by the tight ends, more booing, it's hard for me to even see what's going on. I look up and the clock is running. Shave takes a snap and whirls around, hammers the ball directly at my head. I lift my arms and the ball sticks to my hands, I run upfield and generally toward the sidelines, I nearly fumble when a safety slaps my arms, but I get out of bounds for a short gain. What down is it? My lungs feel molten, I can hear individual shrieks in the crowd. We can't get lined up properly and draw an illegal formation penalty, which at least gives us a chance to huddle.

"Double move," says DeNoon to Shave. "Don't care what shit Nugent's calling. Out-and-up." DeNoon is one serious cat. He looks at his quarterback with the angriest squint he can muster.

"Motion into the backfield," Shave tells me. "They'll be coming. Give me time. All of you. Give me time."

It shouldn't work. Minnesota is playing zone, hanging back. Even if a cornerback bites on DeNoon's fake, there'll be a safety on his half playing centerfield. But Shave has that laser arm. You never know.

I motion. The snap comes. White jerseys swarm our line under; my assignment is block whoever gets through, but it's a jailbreak. I choose #94, ostensibly because he's taking a circular route and is therefore hardest for Shave to evade, but probably also because this is what stubborn people do. He mauled me earlier, and I need to get him back. I watch his belt and lean toward him, feel his left arm sweep under my right, feel him literally begin to lift me off the ground with a swim move. I can see Way and Pendleton, I can see their *eyes*, which isn't a good thing: it means the right side of our line has broken down, too, and they've spun around in retreat. My momentum carries me into #94's hip and I think: I'm getting a pretty good piece of this guy. But I don't really know. The noise is unbelievable, like a jet engine. Is the play over? Has Shave been sacked? Is the ball in the air? #94 is leaving me behind, I can feel him getting around me, and I want to grab his jersey. The urge is difficult to resist. I stick out my right hip, spin to impede him with my butt, press against his in-motion weight like a little brother holding shut a bedroom door against the onslaught of an elder. I begin to fall, chunks of rubber from the field are spraying up around me as though triggered by gunfire, #94 is completely free of me and I thud helplessly to the ground, my fists wrapped around my facemask in despair.

*

But Shave has enough time. He gets the throw away before getting crunched, DeNoon has a crack of daylight between corner and safety, and the ball is on him so fast it's hard to believe. It is beauty. Touchdown. We win.

*

"Let's bring it up! Let's bring it up!" Coach Fond says in his mellow baritone. A staffer whistles for the locker room to hush. "Just for a second!" says Fond. "Don't it feel great? Don't it feel great? Don't it feel great?"

We cheer our momentary love for one another, manifested in our love for this man. It's bedlam in here: players are taking off their pads, some have already jumped in and out of the showers, Shave has the game ball squeezed tight in both arms, DeNoon is listening to someone on his cell.

"I knew you-all had it in you!" says Fond. "I gotta say, I knew it. Of course we can. That's what you-all gotta put deep into your heart. That's the feeling, and it's a feeling close to God. Of course we can. Best dadgum win I can remember, what you-all just gave to me. 'This is why we don't get discouraged, given that we received this ministry in the same way that we received God's mercy. We don't focus on the things that can be seen but on the things that can't be seen.' You focused hard. And I thank you. I thank you. And we'll see you-all on Wednesday!"

My heart is full. I'm choked by emotion. Reporters stream into the locker room, and players don't care: they get naked, do interviews with their privates hanging out, sort of a weird brotherly surge of secure masculinity (or, one could argue, barely suppressed sexual ambiguity). I'm still in my jersey and pads, though. I can't sit down. Love. Just…love.

*

"How tall are you, Nick?"

I'm in the press room. Apparently, the reporters must be fed.

"What does it say in the media guide?" I ask, knowing I'm not in the media guide.

They ask me what it feels like to burst on the scene like this. I give them clichés. They'll play up the underdog angle, write cracks about my size. There are an awful lot of cameras. How many times have I yelled at the TV watching some athlete getting interviewed, because of the uncreative, dunderheaded, disingenuous answers he gave? But now the lights are blinding, and I don't particularly want to share what's just happened to me with strangers. This is a realization: the jockspeak doesn't unfurl because they're stupid—well, not mostly—but because there's little to be gained by meting out bits of feeling to those programmed not to feel it too. And there's something to be said for the old stand-by: "I can't really put it into words." That's exactly what it feels like. There is no translator savvy enough.

"I think we did," I say. "We just banded together and, you know, just *focused*."

When I've taken the questions our p.r. guy wants me to take, when I walk to the locker room that's mostly quiet except for a few guys getting treatment in back, when I pack up my bag and smile at the ceiling, I walk outside to discover a blizzard has struck during the game. A foot-and-a-half of snow covers the players' parking lot.

CHAPTER 16

You can never look at a place on television the same way once you've been in it. Watching film later in the week, seeing our heroics, the big dome with the green-grass floor doesn't look smaller so much as it does dingier, and thoroughly located in Euclidian space. Evidently I carry around a GPS in my head, which constantly places the movie-reel memories of that day in context: when I first came out of the locker room, it was stage-left; yes, when I laid this block, the scoreboard was winking directly above me; my back was to that end zone when this highlighted pass was deflected.

It's a debunking, I suppose: the brain's regular work. It's like repeating the same song over and over in my head. I suck marrow from that past ecstatic moment and also decode it into common terms.

It's impossible for me to think about that day, and view this life as illusion.

*

A few weeks later, I'm at lunch sitting with Hoverman, Vance, DeNoon and Toombs. We're the starting skill core, though we haven't planned our meal that way. But maybe we congregate instinctively. Did I follow Hoverman to this table? Was he following someone else?

"Y'all watch *Celebrity Hip Hop* last night?" says Vance.

"Aw, man," says DeNoon. "That show again."

"All right. I know *you* don't watch it, punk. You already *told* me that. Now let me ask these other shitheads."

"Never seen it," Hoverman says. "But I don't watch anything but film during the season."

"Hooverman got a vacuum cleaner up his ass. Mouse? Toombs? No? Damn, boys, how you not gonna keep your finger on the pulse? Life ain't just all about football."

"It ain't?" says Toombs. "Last non-football thing I watched on TV was somethin' Barney. Maybe Spongebob. I don't even know where the dang remote *is*."

"You missing good shit," says Vance. "Who's the girl in that movie with Tom Cruise last year? Shit blowing up, Tom Cruise is a spy? They got her learning how to rap. She fine, she fine."

I say, "I think I saw that movie. Was that the one where he had to get into that room and they hung him from a wire?"

"Shit, Mouse, that one came out in the '90s, man. Y'all too busy doing the Pythagorean Theorem to notice what the common man doing?"

"You kidding me?" I say. "Compared to you guys who know what the defense is about to do just by where they line up or how they're leaning or whatever, I'm short-bus, man. It's all I can do to keep up."

"Yeah, you all right, Mouse. You stick with ol' Wendell. He show you the ropes."

Hoverman says, "Like how to refer to yourself in the third person."

"First lesson," says Vance, "is pay attention, little Mouse. You dudes never know what's goin' on up here," he taps his forehead. "I get all kinds of ideas for shows from watching *Celebrity Hip Hop*. Make just one idea like that happen, and *pop*! Money come rushin' in."

"Shit," DeNoon says, mouth half filled with bread.

"Next idea be your first, Hollywood."

Vance likes the unexpected, strikes poses you don't necessarily believe he believes. At the end of our game in St. Louis last week, one of their young linebackers came up to Clancy Swift while everyone was shaking hands and asked him to sign his cleats. Swift did it, TV cameras caught it, and now everybody's asking us whether it was some kind of breach, like the competition of the game is subverted because everyone's too buddy-buddy. You'd expect Vance to take the veteran's line, how back when *he* was a rookie, the young players knew their place, and you didn't fraternize with the enemy. Instead, he tells reporters, "Don't see nothing wrong with it. Kid grew up wearing a Clancy jersey? Shoot, get it signed, boy. It's after the game. We already whipped they ass." But when someone left a stack of motivational hardcover books in the locker room—easy p.r. to show how well-rounded today's athlete is—Vance went off on a tirade with media stragglers hanging around: "The fuck I wanna read a fucking *book* for, man? I heard some bitch on TV, she loves reading this one book because it make her feel like she really *in* Africa. Bitch, if I start readin' this book, what do you mean I'm gonna feel like I'm in Africa? *I'm standin' right here,* and it's fuckin' cold!"

Sitting here now, eating far healthier than the rest of us (including an incredible volume of wheatgrass juice) but still striking you as the street-wisest dude ever, Vance switches to his exaggerated suburban patois and says, "I encourage you fellows to think outside the box of your football-playing lives." He grabs DeNoon by the shoulder. "I met the guy who wrote the last Wesley Snipes movie and we workin' on a little something. Why not? I can act like anything you want, and everybody knows who get the most pussy around here."

"Ah, Wesley Snipes," Toombs says to his food. "Poor brother."

"Big house got him," says DeNoon, shaking his head.

"Oh!" says Vance. "Y'all don't know shit about shit, but

Wesley Fuckin' Snipes y'all heard about!"

*

We win three more in a row. Suddenly we're 5-4 and Detroit is talking playoffs.

But in our most recent victory, I felt something pop in my left calf. It didn't force me out of the game, but it's been with me every minute since. The trainers hook up electrodes to stimulate the muscle, give ice baths and massages, and every time someone asks me how it feels, I say, "Much better."

It's a lie. Nugent told me not to come out on the practice field for precautionary reasons and I made a display of reluctantly agreeing, but the truth is I can't run.

*

It doesn't help that, as Vance said, the weather has gotten obscenely cold. Every outdoor surface has a foot of frosting on it. Getting muscles loose would be difficult without the calf. As it is, when I walk Aggie in the morning I feel crippled. I live in fear of losing my balance on the parking lot ice and out on Enterprise Drive where the tire dealerships and self-storage facilities hug I-94. The dog takes it easy on me, recognizing a gimp when he sees one.

Saturday we fly to Dallas. We convene in a conference room, walk through the game plan in our travel clothes and slippery dress shoes, with some of the guys flinging around footballs so they bounce off partition walls and hotel workers poke in their heads to check on us. They feed us from a buffet but by eight I'm hungry and phone Vance. He says he's busy. I connect to Tommy Way's room, and he says the offensive line is about to go out for steaks, and I'm welcome.

So it's me and seven behemoths at a back table in a chophouse, laying waste to a cattle drive's worth of meat. I admit: it smells good. But I stick with salad and sample every vegetable they have. I take a long string of abuse from the 350-pounders for my sissyhood, so much that our waitress—a bee-hived woman my age with long cerise fingernails—keeps piling it on: "Can I get y'all more lamb chops or New York strip? And can I get y'all anything else for your pet rabbit down there?" The linemen love her, laugh as though they've got t-bones stuck in their diaphragms.

A small boy struts from up front and says, "Are you from Detroit?" We pass around a piece of paper and give him everyone's autograph. "Thank you. But I hope we kick y'alls butt tomorrow!" and this gives everyone great hilarity, too.

In fact, everything is funny. Nobody drinks more than a couple beers, but we all become purple-complected at a mildly racy joke and a funny story about an old teammate who accidentally sunk his boat in the Gulf of Mexico. Bettany, the starting center, has a quarter pound of barbecue sauce stuck in his beard and Way reaches a fat hand as if to drag a piece of cornbread across Bettany's cheek, which makes us all squint and slap the table in hysteria, rattling silverware.

All of a sudden, this is where I am. I know these guys personally, after seeing them on TV for years. It happens this fast.

It's possible to imagine that these are the quaint Saturday night rituals pro football players have repeated for fifty years. Out and about in some strange city, yes, but constructing a cocoon, blotting out the actual geographic specifics. Keeping to ourselves, spinning yarns, chewing meat, guffawing. We could be anyplace, and also any time; I can imagine us finishing this meal and climbing onto a train for a barnstorming tour. Every team has factions, I suppose, and maybe everyone doesn't like someone. But right now the sepia-toned feeling of brotherhood blots out everything, and is wonderful. I look around at these chubby faces and feel gratitude. I listen to them, though the content of conversation doesn't matter: all is nervous anticipation for tomorrow.

When the check comes I read it first and nearly faint, but the upstanding members of the offensive line spot my share. On our way out, I feel someone tap my coat sleeve. It takes me a moment to process his happy face. It's Ronnie the K.

"We meet again," he says. "Please forgive me for interrupting your night, Nick. I wanted to congratulate you. It seems you've taught The Man some new tricks."

"I've…really got to get going. Those guys are my ride…."

"Oh, c'mon. I'll pay your cab fare. I'd like to introduce you to my friend Sophia." He spreads those small hands and indicates the woman across from him. She wears a red halter dress and an indulgent grin, and alongside her cinnamon skin and dramatic décolletage the rest of this steakhouse loses luster. I shake her hand. "In answer to your first question," says Ronnie, "I get to as many games as I possibly can, and this was a good weekend for me to fly on down. In answer to your second question, no, I haven't seen our mutual friend Patrick for a month. Would you like to sit?"

"Thanks, no. We have curfew. What's my third question going to be?"

He folds his fingers together. "Let's see. It's got something to do with bullets."

"I was there. I heard shots, I saw the holes." I watch Sophia for a reaction. She sips from a martini glass and twirls a coil of her hair.

"Nick, I just…. Well, I don't know what to tell you, my brother. It wasn't me. It wasn't anyone who works for me. We got off on a very bad foot, but I'm a fan of yours. Darlin'," he turns to Sophia, "this young man might be the bravest dude you'll ever meet. He's out there every Sunday, getting pounded on by the baddest men in the world. At his size. Stand up, darlin'. Stand up, let me measure you two." She smiles to gauge whether Ronnie's kidding, and sees he isn't. She shrugs and gets out of her chair, steps out of her bright red heels, takes my elbow and spins me a little. At her touch, some bitterness seeps from me. I feel her rump and shoulders press against mine.

"Let's see," Ronnie says. "Oh, it's close, very close. But Nick wins by an inch. Imagine that. This man plays professional football. It simply boggles the mind. It speaks to dedication and talent, my friend. You got something inside you most people can't imagine. I can't imagine it. Can you?"

Sophia sits back down and says, "No."

"Has Gasper paid you?" I say.

"As a matter of fact, he has not. But do I look worried? He's good for it, Nick. There are much finer things to concern ourselves with."

"He's good for it."

"I have other ventures. I'm diversified. There are bigger fish to fry. I'm a bit embarrassed to ask, but can Sophia have your autograph?" Sophia chuckles and looks me squarely in the eye for the first time. She's mostly free of makeup, has a lovely heart-shaped face and a long neck, and she bares teeth in a schoolgirlish way that indicates life is play. She most certainly doesn't want my autograph.

But I sign. I sign the back of a business card, then Ronnie gives me a fresh one. It reads: "Ronald Kirkland, President, The Kirkland Agency."

"When they come to you with a contract extension," says Ronnie the K in his dark brandy voice, "don't sign anything until you talk to me first."

Out of loyalty to Gasper, I make a display of folding his card in half. But I do put it in my pocket. I tell him, "Funny: I don't see any bodyguards around this place."

"Bodyguards. Man, you got the wrong idea about me."

*

Back at the hotel, I get on the elevator and a huge guy I

don't recognize says, "What floor?"

"Um, twelfth."

"Sorry. Private party." Behind his shades, he doesn't seem that sorry.

"But my room is on the twelfth."

"No it ain't," he says. "Don't lie. Get off the damn elevator."

I do. At the front desk, I hand them my keycard and with much chagrin report I've forgotten my room number. They say 1254. Yes, they're sure.

"They told me it's a private party on that floor," I say, but nobody's listening. The lobby, bustling just a few hours ago with wine drinkers, appetizer-noshers and complimentary video-game players, is vacant. Now my life acquires a modern, neutron-bomb feeling. I push the elevator button again.

"Kid," says the bald, bearded black man. "You got a big fuckin' sac. And two arms that ain't broke. Wanna keep it that way?"

"I'm in 1254," I whine. "I'm rooming with Tom Calcaterra. Go ask them at the desk."

He raises his eyebrows. "You from Detroit?"

"Yes. Let me on."

"And you stayin' on twelve. Not on eleven with the staff and whatnot."

"I'm a player!"

"Boy, we get up there and they don't know who you are, you gettin' yo' ass killed."

*

It's a party, all right. Every door is propped open, and players are roaming the hallway, moving from room to room with women under each arm. Walking through the corridor takes me through a gauntlet of R&B tunes, so the people are mostly inaudible, except when one of the female guests shrieks with laughter. I reach 1254 and its door is open, too: Calcaterra is nowhere I can see but Toombs is sitting on my bed with a topless blonde in his lap, alternately kissing her mouth and her nipples. He tells me, via eye contact, to get out.

There's chanting down the hallway's other end, where Swift and Blake are holding a push-up contest with naked women sitting on their backs. Several players are shouting encouragement and waving money. Inside the floor's final suite I see Wendell Vance standing in profile, looking out at us here in the hall; I walk in to say hello and get an inadvertently full view: he's got a small brown woman doubled over in front of him and he's clothed but his zipper is open and he's smoothly pounding the woman from behind, each stroke in time with the music and the woman's head is turned sideways on the mattress, her eyes are closed, her mouth is etched in a frozen 'o' as her whole body shakes receiving this gigantic man, rapt with pleasure or pain. Vance sees me walk in and doesn't react strongly: his smile grows a little wider, he closes and opens his eyes to show me what a good time he's having, throws his head back and loosens his shoulders to dance and pump along with the current song's rhythm. I step out.

This scene is repeated in many rooms, though I find several of the guys in a suite playing poker, with no women around. Calcaterra is here, along with Hoverman, Hinkler, Shugarts and a few others, puffing cigars and throwing down cards. The music is no quieter, but Calcaterra sees me and clears a spot beside him, beckons me. I rub together the fingers on one hand, knowing their stakes are certainly higher than I can afford. But I watch the game for a while and between songs I say, "Isn't it bed-check soon?"

Hoverman says, "They greased Geathers and Jefferson to look the other way."

In his cowboy hat and dark glasses, Sugar Tits yowls and rakes in a big pot.

"And where do the women come from?" I shout.

"Vance has been planning for weeks!" says Calcaterra. "Getting girls on Facebook, telling 'em to show up here tonight! Hey, I saw one walking around wearing your jersey!"

I say, "Really?" and everyone at the poker table laughs, and falsettos back to me: "*Really?*"

I sit on a couch and watch them play. I drink a beer, turn down a cigar. The TV shows a college game I don't care about, though it's funny how easily I can spot the pro-ready players now. And wouldn't all those big kids on the screen give anything to be here? There goes DeNoon sauntering completely naked past our door, waving to us all as he passes, and here's Husseyn Norwell with a six-foot-tall black woman wearing bra and panties looking for an empty suite, poking in their heads and grinning at us sheepishly, continuing on their way.

"I think Norwell's with a dude!" says Shugarts, and everyone laughs.

The poker continues endlessly, around and around. The college game ends and late local news starts, which someone immediately shuts off. Circulated heat courses up through vents—it's Texas, but it's freezing outside—mixing with the jock humidity in here and leaving steam patterns on the window glass: smudges, fingerprints, and what looks suspiciously like two footprints, toes pointed at the ceiling. I hear the poker players shouting happily: "Hey! Hey!"

Ronnie the K enters the suite. Shugarts gets up to give him a hug. Hinkler and Hoverman bump potatoes with him. Ronnie trails a tall blonde behind him; Sophia is gone. They clear a seat for him at the game, but Ronnie trips in my direction, clapping and laughing, hunched over as though pained. He says, "I didn't want to ruin the surprise!"

"I don't get it, Ronnie! If you're this big shot, why torture Gasper face to face!"

He keeps smiling, and leans in. "Gasper?"

"Yeah!"

"What can I say, man? That dude is a trip!"

"I'll pay whatever he owes you!"

"Fine! Done! Now you'll have to excuse me! I have to take all these boys' money and get 'em drunk, so you all get killed tomorrow!" He winks. The lovely blonde stands behind him, as Shugarts deals him in.

My calf throbs and I don't recognize any of the songs that are playing. But I have to admit: I want to. Honestly, right now I'm just a little tired of setting myself apart.

I decide to take a walk, to see if there's really a woman here wearing #25.

And there is. She's tall, pale and brunette, and when she sees me she grabs my wrist, brings me into a room that's been ransacked but is free of teammates.

"I cannot believe! Nick! How is your mother Pamela and your father Charles? What is like at the Middleton College? What is like to have David Blum for the agent? I am Aletta. I am born in Budapest. Is in Hungary." She fumbles through her purse. "You score three touchdowns this season." She says it *totch-dons* and has very blue eyes. "You will sign shirt?" We're standing face-to-face in the middle of this room.

"Wait. I've played in four games. How do you even have my jersey down here so fast? How am I your favorite all of a sudden?" She wears too much pancake, covering up bad skin. She extends a Sharpie my way, presents her chest so I can sign. I do, nimbly, over her left breast.

Her color becomes high, and she shows her straight teeth. "You are very handsome, Nick, and I see you play. You play very well!"

"Thank you."

"You are very beautiful to meet."

"I don't think I've ever really had a fan before," I say. "It's not like I get recognized."

"Number *one* fan," says Aletta in what I recognize is a practiced tone. I see luggage wheels poking out of a closet, a suit jacket covered in plastic, coins on the desk. I wonder which teammates this room belongs to. Then I look down and see my hands are on Aletta's hips.

I hear myself say, "You don't even know me," but my hands don't move.

"But I know you, Nick! I see you! I know you very well!" I can see she has a pierced tongue. Henny got her tongue pierced when she moved from Massachusetts back to Manhattan, claiming ignorance when I teased her about the supposed sexual advantages. But the piercing bled regularly, and Henny let it fill in.

"Hungary," I say. "I've never even been out of this country. What's it like in Hungary?" We're standing even closer now.

"Is not exciting. Is most not exciting place ever-ever. The men are, *pff*, worms. Nick, these other players," she gestures out the door, to the hallway, "so much bigger. One day they will hurt you?"

"Maybe," I say. "But I'm a small piece of leather, well put-together."

She pulls the jersey over her head, revealing spectacular, surgically enhanced breasts. Hero worship is gone from her blue eyes now, if it was ever there. She's my height, she pulls my face down to her nipple. My nose clanks against a sabretooth incisor she wears on a thong around her neck. I see the door is still open, and reach for it. It's hard to say whether I'm lost or found.

*

The next morning, in the visiting locker room, I present myself to the trainers and ask for an injection. They shoot my calf with amber liquid and sit me in a corner. I watch the second hand of an old-fashioned clock, like one from an elementary school. Teammates are banging around just outside the door. My calf burns hot, then I become distracted for half-a-second, take stock again, and the sensation is gone.

I feel nothing. I touch the skin and it's like I'm not there. It's like pressing on a glazed ham.

CHAPTER 17

Thursday they run a feature on me in the *Detroit Free Press*. I cooperated self-effacingly, and the reporter—a buddy-buddy young guy I didn't trust—made a big part of his story the fact that I didn't want to be singled out, that I was resistant to his charms. The public likes an underdog, and so he built me up as an everyman. He latched onto the "Mouse" thing and ran with it: lots of clever metaphors about cheese and cats and traps. The article's really kind of a chunk of garbage. But I buy ten copies of the paper, mail one to my parents, then realize I don't have anywhere else to send the other nine. But there are a couple interesting quotes.

From Brian Nugent: "He does everything perfect. He's the answer to the question: what if a regular-sized guy did everything perfect? Could he be a pro?" This levitates me right off my hotel couch; it's the purest form of soma that could ever be absorbed by my regular-sized body.

But from Zeke Hoverman: "You're not supposed to root for a guy who's basically your competition, but I have a hard time not rooting for him. He doesn't do anything all that well, I mean, he's not really fast, he's small, he can't jump, all that stuff. But give him this: he knows the playbook and he goes out there and he plugs away. Obviously nobody knows how long it'll last."

Overall it's a puff piece dedicated to the magnitude of

me, but I fixate on Hoverman's backhanded compliments. Not fast? Can't jump? I don't want to. I know I shouldn't. But I burn.

I still can't practice because of the calf, but I dress quickly and get out of the locker room, into the bubble. Calcaterra and the punter, Scoggins, work on their fourth-down routine, and I field kicks and visualize turning upfield, making moves, escaping all. This is the calm before they start piping in crowd noise, so I can hear foot inhumanly whopping ball. Then here come more guys, including Vance and DeNoon.

"Mouse!" Vance says. "You gonna tell us what happened with that fine piece down in Dallas? Brother closed the door. You believe that? Close the door on his boys?"

"Mm-hm," says DeNoon.

"She your biggest fan, man. She took pictures of you and put 'em online."

"I know it," I say, watching another punt arrive like a tracer.

"Don't worry, though," Vance says to DeNoon, "nothing that show his rooster. Nothing get you kicked outta the Ivy Club, Mouse. But everybody wanna know, man. You bust that onion?"

I see Hoverman walk past, stretching out his back and hips as he goes, paying us no attention. I don't say anything, but I look at Vance and wrinkle my forehead, shrug my shoulderpads.

"He did! He did! Damn! Da-Yamn!" Vance and DeNoon exchange a low-five, then Vance comes over and hits my helmet, and offers *me* a series of low-fives, which I accept. "Didn't think you had it in you," he says. "You act like you above it all, baby, above the *fray*." I hear another punt-thud but I'm smiling at Vance and someone shouts "Ball!" and I raise my arms defensively but Vance sticks out his left hand the ball comes down and lodges there, effortlessly. He spirals it away underhanded and shakes a finger at me.

Later in practice, I'm on an exercise bike watching the offense work. Hoverman comes by drinking some neon orange concoction from a water bottle, and I say, "Not fast, too small, can't jump."

Hoverman says, "What?"

"Nice to know you're rooting for me anyway, though," I try to keep my voice neutral, "while I keep plugging away."

"I hurt your feelings, Morrison?" He pushes sweat from his eyes and smiles. We speak loudly to be heard over the fake crowd noise. "I intrude upon your little fantasy? Come on man, it's just the business you chose. Man asks me a question, I have to give him my honest opinion. What did I even say, anyway?"

"That I don't belong." I've stopped pedaling.

"Bullshit."

"Yup. You pissed on your territory."

"Well," he says, "it's *my* territory. I'm a free agent next year, man. Running backs don't last past thirty. Have to make your bank while you can."

"And who cares about the team."

"Shit, dude, I'm out there busting my ass. You're riding a bike. I got a quad so bad it looks like I got hit with a baseball bat, a broken thumb, probably a concussion though I didn't tell anybody about it. You think I don't lay it on the line for the team? Besides, what the fuck did I really say? You're an okay athlete, but you know where you're supposed to be and you don't make mistakes. Which part do you have a hair across your ass about?"

I put a finger over one nostril, and blow snot out the other.

He says, "Didn't we have a big heart-to-heart in training camp, you told me all this shit about how don't listen to what anybody else says? I mean, you really want me to fuck you in the media, Mouse, I'll fuck you in the media."

I want to punch him. I start cycling again, and the calf

barks.

"Everybody's so goddamn sensitive," Hoverman says, walking away.

*

A sharper-witted journalist could actually boil down my season so far to a montage of post-game handshakes with other undersized running backs. They seek me out, these third-downers: Tremain Booker of Tampa Bay, Kensington Rhee of Philadelphia, Arthur Chimelis of Dallas; each is taller and heavier than I, but each has no doubt been told a thousand times his lack of size would render his dream impossible. Yes, there I was after the easy win over Tampa, tromping to the locker room and feeling Booker tap my pads to give me a hug, and he said into my helmet earhole: "Keep doing what you're doing." Here was Rhee with one of those ColdGear hoods still covering his entire face except a three-inch slit around his eyes (looking like nothing so much as a Muslim woman in a burqa), putting his hands on either side of my helmet, pressing his face against my mask presumably so I'd understand the sincerity of his comments, and saying, "You an inspiration. You an inspiration, man." By the afternoon of that frigid Dallas win, I understood the brotherhood to which I belong and looked for Chimelis myself: with staffers, reporters and other players swarming around us, we chitchatted about his family, my dog, the new cleats he's lately been using…nothing to mark us as mini-players.

*

We lose in Green Bay. I'm a game-day inactive because of the calf. I'm angry, so angry, that it still hurts like this. Why the hell am I taking these shots if they aren't helping me heal faster? At four o'clock on Monday morning, having returned with the team on a chartered puddle jumper and reclaimed Aggie from the kennel, I make a pyramid of my many photo IDs and shopping cards, and watch replays of the Sunday night shows where talking heads and ex-jocks explain what our psychology must have been, the obvious degree to which we weren't ready to play. They are very assertive, very final.

I flex the calf. What good am I to them? They could cut me tomorrow. I can't miss any more time. I can't. It's not a very Buddhist line of inquiry, I know. But mine just now is a divided self, and I can't imagine players like Vance or Shugarts or Swift allow themselves such solipsism. When in doubt, *go!*, and do whatever you need to make the going irrepressible. I fill a syringe and give myself a second shot of the day, and nearly allow myself to take a third before visions of an overdose leave me sweating and shaking.

And then I dream.

In one, I must produce dozens of urine samples all at once, and am flogged for my dehydration. A team of lizard doctors straps me to a gurney and jabs me with a hundred needles to take blood, until my arms wither like deflated balloons. In another, my bones and organs grow at such an extreme rate, they begin softly popping out of me as I walk around, and I must press them back under my flesh so nobody will notice. I wake shouting, then meditate back to sleep.

CHAPTER 18

I still take the painkiller before we line up against Washington. Nugent asks how I feel. I tell him I'm ready for anything, ready to play the entire game. I try and hold his eyes as long as I can.

On the game's first offensive snap, Shave hands it to me on a simple draw and I take it twelve yards, emerge from the pile clapping hard and signaling first down. Later in that same drive, I catch a wheel route over their outside linebacker and nearly score. Hoverman plunges it home, and we all come off the field like brothers deafened by the crowd. On Washington's first series, they complete a nice screen then hit a couple decent runs, but then Faafeu hits their halfback with the power of a dump truck and the ball squirts away, Marcellus Blake covers it, and the offense is back out there. Nugent insolently takes a shot on first down, a go-route to DeNoon who has to fight off a corner and a safety just to knock the ball away. This play calls for Hoverman and me to line up in I-formation and charge forward as though it's a run, but then split apart and pass protect, and I get a good shot in on their defensive end as he's engaged with Pendleton. He falls and it rings his bell a bit, and I feel like Superman. The game telecast goes to commercial and we stand around watching this behemoth defensive end sitting up, holding his facemask, shaking his head and blinking his eyes. Trainers help him stand, and he looks around and points at me.

"Tempo!" shouts Nugent. "Tempo!"

Wallace catches one over the middle, Vance makes a sideline grab, Hoverman moves the chains with a plunging run that has Nugent clapping with his laminated play sheet. Shave says, "24 Slam" and gives me a look, which means I'm the halfback directly behind Shave, and Hoverman's the fullback, split to the right. All there is is go, and I do: a hole opens and I see Hoverman blast the Mike linebacker and I see what's about to happen with the safeties the instant before it does: these two men are puzzle pieces, the strong safety was cheating toward the line on the offensive right side but overcommitted, so he hurries back toward the middle, and I can see the free safety coming down toward me, also hell bent, and there's going to be a window for half-an-instant, and if I can accelerate and hit that spot, I'm gone.

I ask the calf.

The calf is noncommittal.

And I'm caught—I mean, *blasted*—from my right. It's the same defensive end I hit just a few plays ago. He sends me pinwheeling into the stadium air. I land on my back with my feet pointed up, but carry so much momentum I roll onto my shoulders and then the back of my head. The crowd says, "Ohh!" I hold onto the ball.

A moment, here, on what it's like to be hit, to be *really* hit, in professional football. I can't imagine there's anything else like it in any other sport. It's equal parts malice and shock, with a smattering of delight. You hate the traps they've laid for you, you hate them before they ever touch you, you hate with the heat of one perpetually afflicted. Everything in you is devoted to foiling their plans for your body, and there's an arrogance that comes with this, that you consider yourself capable of this. There's arrogance, also, in having been extraordinarily good at *not* being hit for one's entire life. I mean, everyone playing in this league—certainly everyone who touches the ball in this league—has been dominant from an early age, uncatchable, unhittable. No, I wasn't bigger than the children, teenagers or collegians against whom I played, but I was so much better it wasn't fair. When they tackled me, it was usually by an ankle; when they rattled me, it was rare enough to be forgettable. So when someone at this level really gets you, there are gradations of surprise. Physically, everything in you is compressed: bones come together more closely than they should, organs slop against their neighbors. Your body feels condensed and dispersed by the hit, ice-cold and ablaze. Your mind spends a few instants unaware of the brick wall you've just slammed into; it says, "Legs keep pumping, where was that linebacker, get outside, cut upfield," even as you're in midair, horizontal, helpless. Often, that's all you get: then a blackness, or confusing images if your eyes are open: a spiraling ceiling, a hashmark that sticks on your retina. And the delight? Well, you are the conquered, and there is grudging respect for the conqueror. This is what you are told football is supposed to be. Here is brutality. And self-love for being able to endure it. Camaraderie, no matter what the team, for other men who endure. So the gilded pain— thinly gilded—of a surprise spinal adjustment.

I get up. I flip the ball back to the middle referee (I see three). I shout "Whoooooo!" and reach up and slap the defensive end on his helmet, and make sure a smile of grudging admiration is on my face.

We win 45-10. I score on a little shake route in the second half, long after the result is in question, and fling the ball into the stands.

*

I dream of Henny at an outdoor pool, naked in a chaise lounge, waving hello at me then embracing Wendell Vance, who casually removes his swim trunks, parts her legs and slides himself home as an adoring public cheers him on.

I get up early and drive Aggie to the nearby baseball fields and we ramble around in the snow. The wind is so extreme that for a moment I'm in a cyclone of loose ice particles. But the twister batters me, yet still I stand. The wind moves its toy away; the blown snow disappears into the outfield, across the street. What's left behind on the ground is two-feet deep and glazed with urban soot, plus blown into strata, so here by the benches these snow banks look like sand dunes.

The key is stop thinking. Don't think about what it's doing to me. Don't think about what is and isn't cheating. Don't think about the fact that on my own, I wasn't good enough for this. It's a compromise. So what? Hell, isn't this the exact thing Henny was talking about? *Not* holding myself up as some pinnacle of righteousness? Being willing to get messy with the rest of humanity? Who would I rather be? I can be the schlub who couldn't go in Green Bay, or I can be the guy who toughed it out against Washington.

"What's it like getting everything you ever wanted?" says Gasper. We're in a bar on Michigan Avenue, in the Necklace District. He's brought along his new girlfriend, Laurie, who works for the state in some clerical capacity and has two kids. "My God," he says. "Don't look so aggrieved when I say that. Doesn't he look aggrieved?"

"Aggrieved," says Laurie sweetly. "Yes." She's a round-faced, happy-looking woman about whose romantic perversions Gasper has told me much. She hugged me virtuously at the evening's outset and carries herself with the muscled grace of someone who's borne children then run marathons. Still, it's hard for me not to imagine her standing on her kitchen counter like a high diver, heels perched over the edge, stooped over and requiring Gasper to give her a pre-coital pickle-brine enema.

"I'm not aggrieved. It's great. I'm having a great time." Gasper pulls a face. I say, "So what's everything *you* ever wanted?"

"Me. Don't go by me. I want everything. The whole world and everything in it, for me to pick up and scrub against my brain. I want it *all*, baby," and he grabs Laurie from behind, and she gives a yelp.

"There used to be a better place, further down the avenue," she tells us. "It closed down. And what was the club in Dearborn with the Statue of Liberty in the back? And there was that one in Canton, before it was Tryst it was Sneaky's and it had this giant mural. Those are gone."

"Boohoo!" Gasper says. "It's a tragedy. Let's sit around and count off how many failed businesses in Detroit we can remember. Think we can get to a thousand?"

"Well. It's a sign of the times."

"A sign of the times," says Gasper, "is that gentleman right there, staring at our famous friend. It's all right. Yes, you. Don't be scared. Come on over."

"Mouse?" It's a heavy guy in a turtleneck sweater, carrying half-a-beer. "Whooooo! Mouse Morrison! Hey Tommy, look!"

Several football fans crowd around us and introduce themselves, shake my hand. An Asian woman stares at me from across the bar, trying to locate my face in her memory. I'm a little giddy. Laurie is a good sport, but Gasper looks peeved, which is unlike him: he's not the jealous type. Perhaps he doesn't like seeing me magnanimous, a pose I'll admit I rarely have cause to strike. Well, for a few minutes it's a buzzing little coterie which I know Gasper is for, so I think maybe his great requirement is *he* should always be at the center.

"I take it back," he says after the fans have departed. "You're not aggrieved. You're weltering, my friend. You're a pig in slop."

"Don't be such a turd," says Laurie. "Nick, it must be so cool. You work for years and years, you're the underdog. And it finally pays off."

I make a shy display of grinning away this praise, but it's

true that something in my life's current feels like it's shifted, as though my perceptual abilities have changed: the few faces walking past are particularly handsome and old-fashioned, streetlights visible through this window paint classics on wet asphalt, the soft sounds of bar chatter are from any of a hundred previous years. I'm like a snake that's sloughed off its old skin, and barely understands the sensitivity of its new one. "I saw Ronnie the K," I tell Gasper. "He was in Dallas."

"Who's that?" Laurie asks.

"Guess what," Gasper says, "I think I'm coming back to work next week. The gravy train was never forever, I guess." Covertly, he makes monster eyes at me, *shut up shut up.*

Laurie needles him. "Fine. Ignore me, but tell me this: when you look back at your four months of getting paid to do nothing, what do you see? Did you make yourself useful? Did you get lots of projects off the ground?"

"I got *you* off the ground, little missy." Gasper steps backward, and now that I see him in better light, he appears to have a black eye. "I gorged on much Freud. I smoked much weed. The great American novel, alas, will have to wait."

Laurie massages her own temples. "My God. The bullshit."

Later, in the name of cigarettes, Gasper and I walk outside, where the snow falls thick and he looks down on me, breathing smoke, a little ticked off. We stand in the purple glower of a neon sign, nodding at the bouncer and the traffic. There's a 20-story Neo-Renaissance hotel across the street— though most of its windows are dark—and three orange-striped construction barrels just down the sidewalk, signifying nothing.

He says, "I haven't yet shared all aspects of my life with her, right?"

"Is Ronnie the K an agent? Like, a player agent?"

"No. I mean…no. You have to be officially certified to do that kind of thing."

"He's just a bookie, right?"

"I wouldn't say bookie. I mean, yes, bookie. But kind of a Bookie to the Stars. He takes action from people who can't be seen placing it."

"He sells discretion," I say.

"I hooked him up with guys on the team. My *pals* on the team, not a single one of whom ever called to see if I was all right." Gasper actually does light a cigarette. "That's a pretty good-sized comedown, when the world takes a few minutes out of its busy day to let you know exactly where your place is in the pantheon."

I say, "What happened to your eye? Somebody hit you?"

"It's just a stye," Gasper says. "Pale people get them."

"I've seen styes. Nobody's eye ever looked like that."

"It looks worse with that purple light on me."

"Have you settled up with Ronnie? I'm assuming you'd have told me if there were any more episodes of people trying to snuff you out." I decide just now not to tell Gasper about my offer to pay his debt. I stare at his reddening hands and we both acquire snowflake eyebrows.

He bites his cheek, winces at me through his patchy red beard. "And I'm assuming you're still shooting recombinant hormones into your gut."

I receive this like a punch. The concrete wall behind me presses my shoulders. "Why do you mention that?"

"I don't know. Maybe I'm a little tired of the implication that I'm the immoral one who needs looking after." We're out here without coats, and Gasper shivers a little. "Listen. Sumon talked to a guy. He doesn't think Ronnie the K had anything to do with those shots, either, and nothing's happened since. Maybe I'm getting out of high-stakes mischief. Anyway, don't worry about me."

"If anything," I say, "I think of you as…. I mean I think of you as *highly* moral."

His grin demonstrates pain. "Morality. I don't know. I'll tell you one thing. When someone tells you they expect a higher morality out of you it feels…dismissive."

It's very cold out here, but we stay. Nobody speaks for a while. We watch various hipsters show their IDs at the door. Finally, I say: "It was Laurie's kids, wasn't it?"

"What?"

"Your eye. One of Laurie's kids landed a clean shot."

He laughs. "The little girl packs a mean right cross."

We grin and rock on our heels. I say, "So Ronnie takes bets from guys who are actually on the team right now?"

"He always did before." The guy in the turtleneck sweater is leaving the bar and he shouts my sobriquet, happily sticking out his tongue, hoisting up his arms and giving me the double-horns sign. I wave back. "Look at you light up," Gasper says. "A pig just waiting for his slop. A pig waiting for the slop to drop."

CHAPTER 19

Ahead of our trip to Buffalo, I get a text from Natalie Cook. She wants to meet before the game, and she's all I can think about during Wednesday's practice. Natalie and I dated when I lived in upstate New York a couple years ago; she was a doctoral student doing some kind of ethics or political theory dissertation: a serious woman I met in a coffeehouse, wearing my aviator's jacket and blue muffler, knowing I looked more compelling than the hairy art-school boys and pasty academics around me. She considered me a break from her usual type (studious, intellectual, flabby), and I liked her, too. She was tall—taller than I—and blonde, but with a weird, inhaling, horsy laugh and too-close-together eyes, and she read voraciously and didn't care about football, but hated most of her fellow students and was wound too tight, set off too easily. Or was she? Now in the clover of my progress, I look back and wonder if Natalie might not be just the ticket. Well, I feel my inner balloon lifting higher. The calf feels pretty good. Standing in layer after layer of long underwear at practice, trying to keep the falling and blowing snow out of my helmet, I remember the warmth of her big featherbed.

Our left corner Kevin Hamill practices catching passes with only his left hand, and asked why he says into the wind, "Coach told me to be more amphibious."

*

Pot Roast says they want me upstairs, and my bowels loosen. Not again.

Coach Fond's private secretary meets me getting off the elevator. She gives me a wrinkled brow, which reads: Aren't *you* a little tree gnome? We walk down the half-lit hallway and now it's clear to me: they've found out about the injections.

Fond's office is an airy homage to power: its walls are white and unadorned, there's a desk at one end, a small couch by a window at the other, and only a long expanse of blue carpeting in between. Fond and Brian Nugent are dressed in jackets and ties, sitting on the couch, arranging papers on a coffee table. Nugent gets up to shake my hand. I'm not used to seeing him visor-less. Fond acknowledges me with his eyes, but doesn't smile. He says, "D'you pray, Morrison?"

"I guess sometimes," I say, unable to swallow. "Kind of."

He nods slightly and unhappily, looking back to his papers. One sheet droops at the corner and tremors in his hand. "Thought maybe you-all had an explanation for what you-all have done for us lately."

Nugent chuckles, is how I know Fond has told a joke.

"Never in my life," says the coach, "has so much...." He's still distracted by the papers. "What was I go' say there, Brian?"

Nugent folds his arms. "You've never seen so many column inches devoted to so few person inches." He grins with one side of his face.

I say, "Am I in trouble, Coach?" hearing my own telltale heart go wild.

Fond purses his lips, feels for something in his coat pocket, looks up at me. His complexion is brown, his hair completely black and sweaty-looking; neither color seems natural. The longer he goes without speaking, the more I hate him. I can't help it. If everything meaningful in my life takes place by degrees, alone, training, then a moment like this is without equivocation: it contains validation or it doesn't.

A door clicks behind us, all the way back near the desk. It's Chick Hechtkopf, the team's general manager. He shuffles into the room comically, like an actor coming onstage to sit beside a late-night interviewer. I've never met him in person. He has a giant gray head, and he, too, is unnaturally biscuit-brown. "Here he is! Here he is!" He shakes my hand. "Do we have the kid's agent on the phone, Starling?"

"Sir," I say. "No disrespect, but I'm freaking directly out. Can somebody tell me what's going on?"

"You didn't tell him?" says Hechtkopf. "You didn't tell him? Son, we want to make you a rich man! Why don't I just…. Listen, I have a meeting. I've got to meet some reporters. But Coach Fond will tell you. We're making you a two-year contract offer. It's a pleasure. Goodbye!"

I look at Fond, who looks haggard. He shows me a few teeth but doesn't say anything. He's distracted by these papers. It's left to Nugent: "You've been terrific. I can't tell you, Nicholas. We're not letting you get away. It's a great story, you're a part of the Detroit family now. Personally, I don't care what size you are. You're a football player." There's emotion in his voice, and I love him completely for it. Fond, the figurehead, sits like a golem whose stare has been carved coincidentally to point in my general direction. Nugent is the man who feels, as do I. He says, "We have a chance at the division title. We're 7-5. So there are a lot of strange-but-true stories going around, son. It's winning time."

*

They offer me a half-million-dollar signing bonus, and two years' salary amounting to $1.4 million more. When Dave Blum tells me, his voice trembles. It's not huge by pro football standards, but it's the biggest football deal he's ever done. I hang up my cell, standing just outside the cafeteria. I touch my stomach—the few inches which are my preferred injection site—and hear players' voices through the wall. I walk to the locker room, sick with exhilaration, frowning hard. Some equipment kid in winter gear nods at me, but I only register the nod after he's walked out into the blizzard.

This is what I think: What if I become satisfied, and lose my edge? (So there's also a faint sickness at failing to be overwhelmed by happiness.) Above all else, the most important thing is not to be changed.

Boy, Dilgo Khyentse would laugh and laugh at me.

*

We have meetings about the Buffalo game plan, and Vance interrupts everything to say: "Here it is. It's all right there in front of us, boys. We gonna take it?"

"Hell, yeah," says DeNoon.

"You gonna take it?" Vance says, much louder.

"Yeah!" everyone shouts.

"Y'all get up on my back," from Vance. "Get. Up. On. My. Back. I'm telling you right now: I'll take you there!"

"Take us there!" a few people in the meeting room shout, like a congregation.

"I'll take you there!" says Vance.

"I'll take you there!" many of us answer.

"I know a place, ain't nobody cryin', ain't nobody worried, ain't no smilin' faces lyin' to the races!"

"I'll take you there!" says DeNoon, and now we're all singing this old Motown song, with Vance going, "Help me now!" and "Help me y'all!" and the rest of us clapping and singing, "I'll take you there!" and Lester Jefferson doing the bass line by slapping his hands against a desk, Bow Wow doing his grizzled half-smile thing and clapping along, Shave and Bettany grinning sheepishly and lifting their hands like choir members, Vance now up in front of the whole room clapping his hands above his head to get us all in time, a few grunts and hallelujahs coming from the back row, suddenly my heart is up in my mouth with love for everyone in here. Soon nobody knows the rest of the verses but everyone's still chanting, "I'll take you there!" and looking wet-eyed at one another, Tommy Way is flat-out crying while also smiling, the brotherhood is thick and spontaneous. Eventually the song collapses and we all cheer wildly, Vance is still up there, leading us to clap faster and say, "Hey! Hey! Hey!" and the noise is wild and uncontrolled, and it's certainly not about football anymore, because no man in here is thinking about a game or himself. Vance bows and pumps his fist and we celebrate the gold-liquid feeling in our chests.

CHAPTER 20

The FAA must have relaxed its standards of what constitute safe conditions. Our charter leaves for Buffalo in a whiteout. Above the quilted cloud cover, of course, paradise awaits us. The sun, old stranger, presses warmly on my window-side cheek.

*

From one dying Rust Belt town to another, and it's even colder here. This afternoon, Natalie texts me the name of a restaurant. There's no way to avoid doing this like the prodigal son; I'll have to play it ironic, to deflate the possibility that I've returned a self-important jerk. Anyway, I'll be who I'll be, and the rest will be up to her. But I can't help picturing us locked together, her legs around my back.

She walks in pregnant. I'm sitting in a new Greek restaurant that smells of souvlaki and fresh paint, and here's Natalie, big as a whale. She also has new bangs and a rainbow scarf around her neck. She doesn't see me, waddles to the hostess, then they both look my way. Her chin cleft is still there: sensual if a little masculine, and her eyes are still very close together. She waves as if at a departing steamboat and wobbles this way.

"Oh, relax," she says, reading my expression. "You're

not the father, for fuck's sake. I haven't seen you in like two years."

Aside from the disconcerting Prince Valiant hairdo, Natalie hasn't changed. She flounces into her chair and instantly is whinnying that ridiculous, room-shocking laugh of hers as I tell the Aletta story, eager to show her that I, too, have moved on to new partners. She eats bread slathered in olive oil, nodding violently. She drinks from a ginger ale bottle and still does this weird thing, ending a sip with her mouth open, deathly afraid of backwash. She has two great big hitcher's thumbs.

"I'm eight months in," she says. "It's hell on the writing, I've basically stopped."

"Remind me your dissertation topic again?"

So she tells me about Hannah Arendt, *The Life of the Mind,* and the process by which a person uses will: that one's will is absolutely separate from one's thought processes or intellect. To be honest, she goes on with such rapid fire— blurting either to impress me or prove to herself she still has command of the material, or both—that I lose the thread, which eventually she recognizes:

"Oh, Nick. I'm sorry. I can see what I do to you. But you were always such a good sport when I talked like this."

"Was I?"

"Most people go around telling different folks the same stories over and over again, to the point of drudgery. They just sit waiting with the mental file cabinet, ready for the right moment to slip in this or that *bon mot.* But there was always a receptive quality about you I liked. You didn't mind where the conversation would go."

"Well, thanks."

"Don't thank me yet. You also very much gave the impression that while you had the patience of a saint, you didn't actually give a shit. Or at least that you were above it all, and no amount of cajoling was going to make you invested. Hence I'm not surprised you can't remember my topic, even though you basically listened to me talk about it every day for the better part of a year. But I know. You get focused. You're a very focused person, and I'm so happy it's working out for you."

She has no rings on her fingers, I see, and feeling stung by her assessment I'm tempted to ask about the father. But she's watching my eyes closely, and heads me off at the pass: "He's in the Marines. Really, he's just a guy, and we spent last winter hanging around. He moved back to San Diego. He offered to help me take care of it. But I decided no."

Natalie orders and eats an incredible amount of food. She has tzatziki sauce and baklava crumbs on her face. I remember her in one of my practice jerseys and nothing else, hips and legs powerful but elegant; she begged for me to get in the shower with her, then gasped and sighed in the steam. Her breasts were tiny for her big frame (she had to crouch a little for me to take her from behind) but hers was a graceful, athletic body, notwithstanding so many hours in the library and so little exercise. Ah, but despite the mess she's making, she's beautiful when she laughs: mouth open, eyes scrunched, teeth even and white. We talk for more than an hour, she touches my hand many times. I guess she's really the only girlfriend I've ever had, except for Henny.

"I can see you've changed," she says. "You seem surer of yourself. Then again, you never seemed to care much what other people thought, I guess."

"Really? It feels like that's all I ever care about."

"No, I can see it in you. And you have harder lines around your eyes, and your jaw looks very handsome, more pronounced." I wonder if this is the HGH. "I'm glad you came to town, Nick. I'm really glad to see you. Don't worry, I'm not subtly hitting you up for money or something. I have no ulterior motives. I just heard your team was coming here, and I thought it would be nice see you again. They tell you to listen to the hormones when you're in my condition."

"I'm glad, too," I say, deflated by the knowledge of our

incompatibility.

"Do you remember when we met, Nick? We made eye contact at the coffee place, and I recognized you from other times you were reading in there, but you'd never said a word to me. I had to pursue you, which isn't usually the way it goes with me. But after all, I guess it fits. You were sitting there, probably memorizing plays. Waiting for someone to say something."

*

Julian Edwards hurts his knee covering the opening kickoff, and Geathers says I'm next man up as gunner when we punt. Nugent chews gum and makes a face hearing this, but then consults with Coach Fond and nods. The calf feels good. I still took the pre-game shot, but everything feels all right. It makes me exultant.

The special teams guys—Brohammer, Schenk, Ahmad Custance, Conrad King—are crazy. They work themselves into a frenzy while we have the ball, privately rooting for us to get to fourth down. In the second quarter Shave gets blasted face-first into the snow and we have to punt; I stay on the field and the rest of those maniacs gather around me.

Brohammer calls the protection: "Max cloud! Max cloud!"

"Kill kill kill kill kill kill kill kill," says King.

"Fuuuuuuuuuck!" says Custance.

"Rip off heads! Shit down necks!" says Schenk.

"Yeahhhhhhhhh!" I hear myself say. "Yeahhhhhhhhh!"

"All right, Mouse!" says King. "All right, Mouse!"

"Yeahhhhhhhhhhhhhhhhhhhhhhhhhhhhhhh!" I shout.

Custance hits Schenk in the facemask with his open hand, and Schenk goes, "Do it again! Do it again!" We line up. Scoggins, the punter, is apart from the blockers and gunners, way behind, miming his drop-and-boot motion. He's out here playing in his wedding ring.

Calcaterra snaps and Buffalo doesn't come after the kick: they peel off to set up a return. I'm firing downfield with two bigger men impeding me, trying to shove me out of bounds, elbowing my head, punching my ribs. Through the snow, I can see their returner catch the punt and jab-step in the other direction, making our first man miss, and then come my way. The bodies get close. I feel someone with their fingers worked up under the back of my shoulderpads, yanking me. I stay wide, pinch the sidelines, contact is made all around me, bodies are slamming, mouths are grunting, someone slips in front of me and someone else stomps on his stomach, Ahmad Custance shouts, "Shit!" and I see him fall hard, then a Buffalo blocker comes screaming my way and hits me under my chin and I see my own feet in the air, I'm spinning, my breath disappears and I slam the artificial turf, and I look up and the returner has cut inside just in time for King and Brohammer to meet him right around midfield and they drill him: a three-way helmet collision that sounds like rifle fire and sends the returner flopping to the ground, sends the ball spurting away, in my direction, I struggle to my knees but several men clomp over me and crush each other to find the football, meanwhile trampling one of the officials whose black hat flies off as his head hammers the ground. I hear whistles. Then I hear men yowling, "Mine! Mine! Mine! Fuck! Goddammit! We got it! Get off me! We got it! Fuck you! Fuck! You!" Brohammer is up, screaming something at the referee. The downed official's eyes are open wide, but see nothing. King and the returner are both still down; on hands and knees, King vomits a bit, while the returner's leg twitches awfully.

*

We celebrate a tight win. The mood is euphoric in the locker room: Vance rags DeNoon about a throw Shave made late in the game: "Perfect toss! Perfect toss! Yo, Shave, what do they call that back-shoulder fade?"

Shave shouts across the room, "The Old-Man Fade."

"Right! The Old-Man Fade. 'I can't get open anymore. Just put it right here.'"

The music is loud and about six tons of professional athletes shake and groove, adorn themselves in earrings and gold chains, or else stay naked: freshly showered, towels discarded, clomping to the beat in shower shoes. By instinct, reporters huddle around the periphery busily checking their digital voice recorders, consigned, as ever, to society's second string. I finish buttoning my shirt, and beside me Orlando Bolduan says, "Did you see that fucking Buffalo mascot? That blue fucking hairy-ass bison mascot? He made like he was pissing on me right as we were coming off! Lifted his leg on me and everything!"

I tell him: "That's not right."

"No shit it's not right! I'm wound up! Most people don't get fucking pissed on by a eight-foot-tall ugly blue bison!"

"At least not since the frontier days," I say.

Deep in the night on the airplane home, I'm seated in front of Vance, who says, "You dudes ever play for that Otts motherfucker? He Buffalo's coach now, but I played for him in J-ville. Asshole don't allow jewelry, hats, beards, long hair, t-shirts. He don't let you wear white socks. He don't let you cross your legs in meetings."

"My college coach," says Hoverman, across the aisle, "wouldn't let you celebrate when you scored. I mean, nothing. Hand the ball to the ref. So I had the video guy tape me doing an end-zone dance. I break this long run right before halftime, I hand the ball to the ref. But up on the video screen they show me losing my shit, doing the Cabbage Patch and the Worm. Coach couldn't say jack."

Toombs says, "Best celebration ever, that dude who frisked that other dude after he scored. I laughed my ass off."

"That number 72 Buffalo got," Vance says. "Rang my bell so hard today, my unborn kids feelin' it."

"Oh, you got born kids," says Toombs. "You just ain't heard about 'em yet."

"I remember Buffalo had me take their pre-draft evaluation test at the combine," Hoverman says. "It was like 600 questions. One of them was, 'Did you ever put a cat in the microwave?' Seriously."

"Number 72 a fat fuck. How he move that fast? My fucking back, man."

"He got a size 23 ring finger," Toombs says. "My boy Dunlap on their team says they got rings together winning a bowl game in college. Fucker's finger is a size 23."

Hoverman shakes his head. "'If you found $10,000 in an unmarked envelope, would bring it to the police?' 'When you were a boy, did you ever pull the legs off a spider?'"

"Size 23 finger," says Toombs. "Imagine you with some skank and you give her the Shocker, and you got a size 23 finger?"

Vance says, "Every year, Otts tell his players, 'I gotta choose between you dyin' and you fumblin'? It ain't close.'"

"'Were your father or mother ever addicted to drugs?'"

The plane rocks crazily in a pocket of turbulence. "Oh, shit," says Vance. "Number 72 just hit us again."

I feel someone tap my knee. It's one of the quality-control kids who says Brian Nugent wants to see me in the front of the plane.

His is the only illuminated overhead light up here. Coach Fond often has his son with him, but rumor has it the boy was too sick to make the trip. Nugent has a row to himself and is hunched over his computer; he asks me to sit. He's wearing his ubiquitous visor, and that prim little rosebud mouth is pulled to one side. But he says nothing. I've been up here for a private visit a couple times, as have most of Nugent's bishops and rooks, but he isn't usually coy.

"What's up, coach?"

"Seriously?" he says. "You're a fucking idiot, Nick." He unzips a small pouch and places something atop a notebook.

Three clear, small, empty bottles.

A band of silver-sparked adrenaline sluices from my feet to my face. My instinctive reaction is to wish for Nugent to drop dead of a heart attack so I can steal this evidence. I'm a jackal, and I hate myself. I feel shame and self-righteousness. How little we know ourselves until we're cut open. I'm remorseful for what I've done, but just as remorseful that I've been caught.

"Tell me it's not yours," says Nugent.

"It's mine."

"You're goddamn right it's yours. If I can have an intern dig through your hotel garbage for five minutes and find this shit, how do you think you'll keep it out of the newspapers and off the Internet?"

I hear him speaking, barely, over my heartbeat.

"Nicholas, if some reporter had found these, there's no question you'd miss the rest of the season. There'd be nothing I could do for you."

It isn't really registering. I think: are these the tools of focus, or relics that profess focus isn't enough?

"You're a point of great pride for this program. That block you laid on their strong safety today, I don't know how you do it. He's coming like a freight train, he outweighs you by seventy pounds, but you stuck your nose in there and bought Shave an extra second. I didn't think you'd get up. It hasn't always been easy to be your backer with some of the more traditional thinkers around here."

He wants me to react. I say, "Thank you."

"I mean, a reporter pays your hotel maid a few bucks and gets to walk around your room while you're not there, right? Or the maid just finds it herself, knows who you are, makes a phone call. As it is, you're lucky it was me. But I still have to bring this to Coach Fond."

I feel sick.

"We're a family, Nick. If I didn't tell Coach Fond and later he found out, he'd feel he couldn't trust me."

I rasp something, some words even I don't understand.

"I'll try and put in a good word for you," he says. He mouses on his laptop, dismissing me by looking away.

CHAPTER 21

After a white-knuckler of a landing back in Detroit, I tell my cab driver that the planet seems unhappy to have me back on the ground.

I open my hotel room and hear the air suck inward, a cracking noise as though I'm about to ravage an Egyptian tomb. This is my life. We are thrown into the world and take our time getting the hang of its spin, then we grow up, see the world, and adjust to an even brisker torque. And maybe these accelerations are always happening, and maybe one way to buffer the resulting queasiness is love and connection, but I know several teammates who would testify that clutching another person doesn't slow things down at all. Because the life we know (the one we *truly* know, at bottom, at 4 a.m., with the bedclothes pulled up around our chins) only *seems* to stop for love. These past ten weeks—as life has changed maybe forever—have introduced my fastest spin yet. But I'm still standing. And if I've used those injections to make me stronger, well, few men experience the world at these wild gyrations and it feels as though extreme measures are warranted.

All this is what I tell myself.

There are three weeks left in the season. In the wake of the Buffalo win we're 8-5. I spend two long days at the facility, avoiding everyone I can avoid, laying low, studying and lifting and treating the calf to so many whirlpool baths it probably thinks we live in a dishwasher. I don't see Coach Fond, and nobody mentions HGH to me. It almost becomes possible to believe the conversation with Nugent didn't happen. I haven't stopped using.

Tonight I come home, but Aggie doesn't greet me.

I have a few moments of dislocation, thinking I must've accidentally left him at the kennel.

But no. I find him.

He's on the bathroom floor.

He's alive. He's alive and panting on his side, and he doesn't move when I say his name. I touch him and he doesn't react. I offer him a treat, and he doesn't lift his head.

I phone an emergency animal hospital and carry Aggie out to the car. I drive while patting the poor boy's head, scratching his muzzle, placing my finger in his ear, something he's always loved. I've taken him for granted. To say the least. He sprawls on my lap, tongue out. I squeeze him against me, essentially doing my same old thing: begging him not to go, begging him not to leave *me*.

I present him at the hospital, and they rush him into the back for tests. It takes an hour, and I picture him in some cage, waiting for attention, and it's too much for me: I scrape the floor with my hard plastic chair and cover my eyes. This is real. This is *real*.

A short woman in a white coat steps into the room and reads my name aloud. "Agamemnon has bloat," she says. "His stomach is twisted, and gas can't get out. His esophagus is also closed off, so he can't throw up. We think he's in shock from hypotension, and this is obviously very serious. We'll need to do surgery right away."

I pinch my nose as I listen. I turn away and stare at a pile of old magazines and a water cooler, thinking how tragic I must look. I sign the paper and rub my eyes. This is real.

*

I'm here for hours. It's a hopeless, bactericidal place occupied by good people, doctors and staff who save lives. What do *I* do? I mean, what do *I* do? The floor is tiled teal, olive and gray, a horrid mix declaring its institutional aloofness. But the walls feature happy signage: "Moving Tip 12: Don't Pack Your Dog And Cat In The Same Box" and "Beware Of The Dog & The Cat Is Not Trustworthy Either" and "Nice Dog; Crazy Owner." Aggie, my ward. The doctor says his chances are fifty-fifty.

Many times I've told myself I'll play with him more once the season ends.

Whenever someone opens the hospital door, a blast of the outside enters.

I jog my knee to stay awake, and the calf feels great. Time moves so slowly.

*

He pulls through the surgery. The doctor wears Aggie's blood on his scrubs and tells me the dog's not out of the woods yet, but he's a trooper. I set my jaw and swallow.

I'll have to leave Aggie in the hospital for a few days. I walk outside. It's still dark out, but I discover it's 6:15 a.m. And it's snowing again.

For some reason, I sleep on the couch. Every time a car goes by, a box of lighted geometry trails across the living room.

*

I'm puttering around the next morning, looking at his food dish, his snacks, his leash. I phone the hospital but there's no news. I can't watch television, I can't read the game plan. I notice a spider web up in the living room corner, but can't see its author. I think about getting up to sweep it away, but don't move. It was too difficult to sleep without Aggie leaning against my legs.

I phone again and make a big self-effacing production, for which I hate myself: "I'm sorry, I know I just talked to you, I know I just called a little while ago, and I'm sure I'm being really ridiculous and annoying, but could check on him for me again?" I want to be told by this nurse that I'm not ridiculous and annoying, that she understands. But she's all business and tells me there's no change in Aggie's condition. I phone the team complex and eventually get Pot Roast on the line. I bravely tell him about the emergency, and hope he'll be sympathetic. But he merely takes the message and says Nugent will certainly expect me for the afternoon session.

I try to think whether this is the worst day of my life.

Hours go slowly. In a half-conscious state, I decide I should keep a vigil at the hospital, maybe ask if I can see Aggie resting. Then I think I should go next door and tell Townsel what's happened, but of course he's over at the facility. Then I realize I haven't taken my shot this morning.

I sleep and dream about Henny, just Henny, sitting in a chair, smiling, talking about nothing.

I wake up groggy, pissed off, aphasic. There's a second knock at my door; I realize the first one has woken me up. I'd like to be the kind of person who could just sit here, who doesn't care if a knocker has to depart from my door unsatisfied. But I hoist myself up and tiptoe to the hotel peephole. It's a guy in a limo driver's cap, preparing to knock again.

It rushes back to me: there's a Fan Appreciation event at the stadium, complete with a bigwig auto parts sponsor who specifically requested my presence. I promised the p.r. guys I'd show. When I skipped this morning's practice, they probably panicked and sent a limo to fetch me. I let the driver in; his face sinks. Sure enough, there are eight messages on my phone.

"Why don't I wait while you clean up," the guy says.

What can I do? I trudge past the kitchen, past Aggie's water dish, into the bathroom.

*

The drive downtown is smooth. It's barely snowing and there's little traffic. My feet are cold. There they are, side-by-side: Detroit's football and baseball stadia, the former domed and shoveled out, the latter clumped over with snow, so its light towers loom like vanilla lollipops. Beyond these monstrous creations, downtown sends its needles skyward, until it meets the lake. We park in the players' lot and I walk past streetlamps draped with team-logo banners.

I pass through the locker room and into the tunnel. The noise in the stadium is surprisingly loud, considering no one is in the seats: some trick of aural physics multiplying the voices of a thousand fans running harum scarum on the field. Nearly everyone wears some variant of the team's blue color; from this distance, it looks like the turf has been invaded by colorful bugs. Walking forward, I see several teammates, padless but in jerseys, mingling among the crowd, shaking hands, signing autographs. I don't have a jersey with me. I want to turn around and go home.

"Nick!" It's Sumon, who's here with his kids. He shakes my hand and we watch from the throng's perimeter. "I am glad you are here. Chankrisna and Sanda have told all their friends about Uncle Mouse." I want to say something about Aggie, but the words won't come. Sumon scratches his dark hair and says, "Imagine the love that will come if you make the playoffs!"

A p.r. guy named Devin spots me and scurries over. He has one of my jerseys with him, and fits it over my head. "Thanks for coming, Morrison," he says. "We've got an autograph table set up just over here." I'm evidently in high demand. There's a line of kids who peer over and through one another, looking for a glimpse of their patron saint. I sit down and shake the first little boy's hand.

"Mouse!" he says ecstatically.

"What's your name?" I ask him.

"Mouse mouse mouse mouse mouse!"

The boy's father says, "You can make it out to Ben."

"Mouse mouse mouse mouse mouse mouse mouse mouse mouse!"

I'm so worried about the dog, and I'm exhausted. Sitting here I realize it feels very stupid that I'll be going to Minnesota for a football game on Sunday. The effort such an endeavor requires, a veritable airlift, the immense coming-together of flesh and treasure. The empty seats in the bowl above us mock the very idea, hint at a seriousness for which my life has no room. And Coach Fond might be looking for me over in Allen Park this very moment, to punish me. A long time goes by as I sign little slips of paper and occasionally gaze in wonder at the impermanence all around us. It masquerades so effectively as permanence, doesn't it?

Over there are Danny Shugarts and Ed Scott, entertaining several dozen children with a two-against-the-world football game and tumbling to the FieldTurf whenever touched. Toombs has his own brood with him, one of whom sobs inconsolably to be held. Shave has an autograph table on the other sideline, and I can see him hugging a gnarled old lady. Hoverman stands alongside a redheaded local reporter who wears a shockingly short skirt, both of them motionless and smiling in front of a mobile cameraman whose floodlight is on, all of them waiting to be cued by a studio anchor. I feel pride. And it curdles into shame, but recovers and settles in as interconnectedness, fragility, solace. Shugarts takes a nearby breather and folds his arms: a man's man, kind and tough and without guile. And of *course* Ronnie the K is here—now apparently the Zelig of football in Detroit—strolling to Shugarts in a three-piece suit, gregariously pumping his fist, and I swear also slipping him a wad of folded money. Ronnie takes a few steps in my direction, leans way forward with one arm extended until he has my attention, and gives a little wrist-wave. Then he's off, smiling.

Later Sumon comes by again. "We have not seen you at the bar. Please come back. I will take a picture of you maybe, to hang. And how is your charming blonde friend, Nick? How is Henrietta?"

*

Before I get dressed that afternoon, I peak into the equipment manager's room. Gasper is back. He's mustering dirty laundry and cleaning out the Aqualift. "This is the life!" he says.

"Can I help you carry anything?"

"Yes. My ego, please. It's somewhere down there around my ankles. Y'know, when the luster and romance of being around a team goes away, it really just comes down to inflating footballs."

"You're overqualified, is what you're saying."

"No. I'm about perfectly qualified. I just don't *like* it anymore."

When I stride out onto the practice-bubble field, I see a dozen guys gathered in the far end zone. I walk past several smirking trainers and serious-faced Hoverman, going through his extra-stretching ritual. Everyone else is doubled over laughing in their practice gear. Several of them are in the process of taping Butch Hinkler to the goalpost.

"You think this can hold me!" he shouts, his hands trapped behind his back. "I'll tear this motherfucker outta the ground!"

"Naw, naw," says Vance, putting the finishing touches on Hinkler's ankles. "This ain't enough. My boy here needs to learn some whaddayacallit. Humility. Hink, you got a stuffy nose?"

"I got a stuffed jock strap!" Hinkler says. "I got a white anaconda! Your mom liked it just fine last night!"

"Asshole," says Vance, "can you breathe through your nose? Yeah? Then somebody tape this motherfucker's mouth." A cheer goes up from this small crowd, and they slap a rectangle of athletic tape up under his helmet, cheek-to-cheek over Hink's face. "Make no mistake," Vance says in his easy manner, "after a season talking the way he do? This clown deserve this shit."

The left tackle Richards is here with his giant arms folded, like he's mulling over the universe's mysteries. He steps forward, nodding his head, and everyone else hushes. Richards taps the side of his face with one finger, looks down at his own clean white practice jersey. He snaps, as though an idea has just come to him. He says, "Gatorade."

So someone fetches a cooler of Gatorade and they pour it over Hinkler's helmet (which is itself taped to the post). Vance says, "And be sure you feed the anaconda," so someone yanks out Hink's uniform waistband and purple liquid goes splooshing into his pants, down his legs, Hinkler recoils and groans, thrashes but is held fast.

"All right," says Tommy Way. "How about this?" He's got an armful of referee beanbags pressed up against his big belly and starts pitching them at Hink, trying to get them caught in his facemask.

"Mm!" says Hinkler. "Mmm mmmmm, mm mmm mmmm!"

"Let me take a shot."

"Hand one here, Tommy."

And as everyone practices horseshoe tosses against Hink's face, Brohammer sneaks up behind him with a can of Cold Spray and lets loose on his backside, freezing the skin through those soaked uniform pants.

"Mmm! Mmmm! Mmm! MMMMM!"

I turn to Tommy and say, "He's madder than a mule chewing on bumblebees," and the big guard shrugs at me and nods.

*

The show must go on. Everyone jives and taunts, and the scout defense (with Townsel opposite me playing left corner a few times) doesn't stand a chance. Shave is in rare form slapping backsides and chest-bumping on most every toss. "It's like they can't handle the heat," he says after a bazooka throw. "It's like I'm Mr. Heat Miser. All I do is crank open the pipes," he makes a muscle with his right biceps, "and they all melt away. Pro R 94 Z Batman, on one, on one. Oh! Look at that. He hits the curl, too? I mean, this guy. This guy!"

DeNoon deadpans: "Nobody told me Hink was starting this week."

"It's not all of Hink," says Toombs, "it's just his mouth."

Shave and I have this thing worked out, when I'm in the weak slot and he sees a single deep safety cheating toward the tight end. He touches his knee, and I'm supposed to run a skinny post. Only we've run it enough by now that everyone in the league knows what it means when he touches his knee, so now he takes me outside the huddle and says, "I'll just look at you. I'll just make big eyes at you, and that's how you'll know."

"Your eyes are always pretty big," I say.

"No, I mean I'll do this."

"Right, what I'm telling you is I can't tell the difference between that and your normal mouth-breathing expression."

"Fine," he says, "I'll never throw it to you again, rodent."

"Have I mentioned how good-looking you are, Jim? I mean, what a looker."

"So just do it, all right? I'll go like this."

"Give it to me again. Just so I can get a mental picture."

"Like this."

"You look constipated, Jimmy. You sure you're not constipated?"

CHAPTER 22

Darquavis Greylock strides over to me several hours before our rematch in Minnesota and says, "Merry Christmas, man. God bless." Several players from both teams are out here stretching in sweats. Greylock is six-foot-two, 220 pounds, towers over me and nearly breaks my wrist with his handshake.

"Ow," I say. "Yeah, I hope you have a good one."

He laughs. "I'll be in meetings all day, same as you, I imagine. Probably not what the Bible had in mind. You guys are looking pretty good; must be fun to think about maybe playing in January." I admit it is. "Congratulations on the new contract. What were you doing this time last year?"

"Let's see. I have to think about that one. Sulking and whimpering in my ex-girlfriend's apartment, I guess."

"Ha. Hey, but don't do that, man. Enough people in this world want to run you down, without doing it yourself. Finishing up my fourth year, and at least I've learned that. How old are you, Mouse?"

"I'll be 28 in January."

"That's great, dude. I'm 25. They finally figured out what they had in you, right? Well, hey man, good luck today. Gonna have to try and stop you guys. I don't know if you're a Christian, but read that Bible. A lot worse ways to handle your down time after practice and watching film and stuff."

"Thanks, Darquavis. Thank you. I do still have a lot to learn about doing this and also having a life."

"A life?" he says smiling, walking away. "Hm. 'Having a life.' What's that?"

*

Helplessly, I give myself an extra injection, standing in a filthy bathroom stall. I clack around on my cleats, roll up my jersey, and stab a new spot on my belly, so as to avoid cysts.

*

There's a noticeable hatred in this game. I feel it envelop me, feel it give everything a sharp, reddish tinge. The first break I get from hyperventilating with hate comes near the end of the first quarter, when one of their linebackers goes down and doesn't get up. He isn't moving. Immediately the sentiment is: "Good!" But as he stays motionless for longer and longer, as trainers call for a back-board and immobilize his neck then unscrew his facemask, I'm chastened. Some players from each side pray, as do many fans. The rest of us mill around, looking elsewhere. Because this is a hint of mortality and we are, of course, immortals.

*

We're losing at halftime. I sit beside Calcaterra and he says, "There's a red giant star in Orion, and I just saw a thing that said it's about to explode. And when it does, it'll be so bright that from Earth it'll look like we have two suns and there will be no nighttime for a while."

"Really?" I say. "When is this supposed to happen?"

"It could happen today," he says. "Or any time in the next million years." I look at his fingers. The nails are strange: not particularly damaged by our profession, yet somehow perfectly circular, with no corners on their distal edges. They look like flesh-colored thumbtacks. I shudder at them, then tell myself: What am I shuddering for? Why is this so awful? Who am I to declare what normal is? I feel love for strange Tom Calcaterra and his scientific curiosity.

I say, "Buy stock in sunscreen companies."

Coach Fond says nothing. He hasn't spoken to me in more than a week. His body looks emaciated, his teeth too big for his mouth. He confers with Nugent and Shugarts for a few minutes, but the content of their conversation remains unknown.

Before it's time, I go out into the short-ceilinged hallway that leads from the visitor's locker room to the field. I want to clear my head. I got on the airplane, I got on the bus, I slept, I dressed, I ate a few times. Maybe it's impossible to want these experiences—finally making a team, finally getting respect, finally being inside these walls—without clutching the things that are no good for me. Ego. Approval. Fear. I thought I could work hard for the pleasure of doing it, but now I'm not sure.

Despite my best efforts, I still regard impermanence as pain.

∗

Our first possession of the second half, Shave says, "Here we go. Houston Left, 91 F Corner Queen." After a nice gain to DeNoon, he says, "Dallas Right, 86 F M Gone, on two, on two. Mouse, you play outside. Vance, run the cross." It works: Vance catches it 11 yards downfield and turns up, I come back to the play and deck his man with a fulminating block then stand over the fallen defensive back, daring him to get up and pursue. Vance takes it deep into Minnesota territory.

"Thunder 47 F Cut Slide," says Shave. We get to the line, and I'm set to run a corner route out of the slot. Their fans have cranked the volume to ear-bleed levels. Shave does his pre-snap stuff—fidgeting and pointing, shouting dummy audibles though he knows we can't hear him—and then I see him turn to me and make something like an "eyes-open" gesture, the one I'm supposed to recognize as replacing our traditional knee touch. Maybe. But he doesn't linger, he hunches behind Bettany, hands ready. Is he telling me to run the skinny post? Do they have a single safety high? I can't exactly tell. The corners are up, ready to bump Vance and DeNoon. Toombs has an outside linebacker on him in the other slot. No, wait, this looks like two-deep. What does Shave see?

I decide to have faith in my powers of perception; there's something vaguely Buddhist there, maybe, isn't there? (What would Dilgo Khyentse say?) I decide to run the post. At the snap, the inside 'backer facing me blitzes, and I jet toward the end zone, bending rightward and seeing Shave's arm go up. Oh, no, is he throwing the corner? I'm about to turn and look behind me, then a dot appears over several helmets, this out-of-place splotch hanging like a brown balloon above the defensive linemen's heads. But no, it's not hanging. My God, it's on me. It's the football. It's *on* me. I can't conceive of a football moving like this, and if it isn't aimed at my throat, I don't grab it. But it is, and I do: touchdown. My first in six weeks. The big room gets quiet.

*

My teammates surround me in the end zone and I slam the ball into the turf.

But Jim Shave is down.

He's rolling around on his back, clutching his left shoulder. He tries to get up, but our doctors press him to the green floor. On my way to our sideline, I stop to see: Shave's eyes are squeezed shut, his teeth are bared. He says, "Ahhh! Christ! Ahhh! Fuck! Ahhh! Christ!"

The trainers suspect he has a broken collarbone. He's probably done for the year.

*

And so our season rests with Hurricane Hink.

A series of short Greylock runs sets up a Minnesota field goal, and we're down 10. Six minutes left in the third quarter.

Nugent doesn't explain anything to me, but when he gathers the offense around him for Hinkler's first drive, the last thing he says is: "Split Left 43 Gut." This means we'll have a more traditional formation—a halfback (Hoverman), fullback (Toombs), two receivers (Vance and DeNoon) and tight end (Wallace)—on the field, but not me. I guess this is because Hinkler isn't comfortable in the spread. I clap my hands, and stay put, my heart hanging somewhere around my navel.

Hoverman runs it for three. Toombs catches a short pass for eight. Hinkler almost throws a pick, but gets lucky on a bad drop by the defender. Hoverman goes for three, then six, then two. Wallace makes a nice grab to put us in field goal territory then fumbles, but it goes out of bounds. Hink takes a shot at Vance in the end zone, but it's way overthrown. Bolduan runs out and nails a field goal to get us within seven. The offense walks off the field and I barely recognize them.

"Great job," I say to Hinkler. "Way to move 'em."

He grins at me, but looks nauseated and overwhelmed.

On Minnesota's next play, Husseyn Norwell makes an acrobatic interception right on our sidelines, definitely getting one foot down and apparently dragging a toe with the other, and the officials call it a good catch. We bounce around like crazy on the sidelines, and Minnesota challenges the call. So there's a long delay during a TV commercial and the subsequent analysis of instant replay, during which Norwell happens to be standing near where I'm out of bounds, and he says, "You hurt? Why ain't you play last series?"

I shrug.

Norwell says to their No. 81: "If you was coach, wouldn't you have Mouse playing out there?" and the Minnesota player says, "Oh, yeah. He dangerous." Further review overturns the call, and Norwell curses loudly.

*

I watch the fourth quarter unfold. I stand near Nugent, ready if he asks for me. I'm angry not to be out there, angry Shave got hurt, angry Hinkler isn't more flexible. Fond and Nugent are trying to coax their backup quarterback through the game, trying to hang close and maybe steal it at the end. If we win, we're one more victory shy of a playoff spot. If we lose, the task becomes almost insurmountable.

Townsel is here, in street clothes, clapping. I remember what it was like for me a couple seasons back, inactive on game days, devastated to be so close. Townsel wears it better than I did. His eyes are clear, and his cheers sound heartfelt. I watch these Minneapolis fans holding their heads, crossing their fingers, issuing prayers. I watch the cheerleaders preen. I watch Hoverman and wish someone would break his arm.

Someone clicks a knuckle on my pads.

"Punt return!"

And ridiculously, I take it to the house and tie the score.

*

Minnesota kicks a go-ahead field goal with three minutes to play. Now Nugent has no choice: he can't protect Hinkler any longer. We'll have to go hurry-up. That means I'm on the field.

Sure enough, Hink takes too long, seems tentative about formations and pre-snap reads. Vance stretches as he's falling, barely converting a fourth down, and he gets up screaming, "Come on! Come on! Come on!" We're sluggish. *I'm* sluggish.

I find myself watching the scoreboard, watching the game clock tick backwards. Tommy Way throws up in the huddle and nobody says anything. The play clock nearly reaches zero and we have to burn a timeout right before the two-minute warning. Hink slinks to the sideline.

"Don't this beat all?" DeNoon says to me, in his mock-casual way.

"I guess it does," I say.

"Hey, it gets easier," he says, sipping water. "Don't get your thong all bunched-up under there."

"It gets easier?"

"Fuck." He holds up one gloved hand parallel to the turf, showing me how rock steady it is. "Come on, man. It's just football. You worried they'll knock your head off, you won't have any fun."

"I guess I am a worrier," I say.

"Mouse, you a tightly wound dude, but what, you already scored twice today? What you got to be tightly wound about? You ain't got nothing left to prove. You're good. Make another play. Make the next play." I admit it sounds easy.

Hoverman walks by and says, "Come on boys, we'll sleep when we're dead."

*

Hinkler throws a screen my way, but it's over my head. He dumps one off to Toombs (and you can hear a few of our fans in the building shouting: "Toooooooooooombs!"). He misses Vance open going to the post, leading him too far. We huddle up and everyone feels bad for the kid: it's his first significant action, and he's messing it up terribly. DeNoon and Vance clap and shout to rally the guys, a propping-up that's unbecoming, considering how quiet Hink is. All we need is a field goal, but we're stalled at their 49. It's third-and-long, with 21 seconds to play.

Hinkler listens in his helmet and says, "Thunder 79 F...."

Wait, what?" He stands up out of the huddle and looks over at Nugent, as though the coach can hear his question. "Thunder 79 F what?" We have no timeouts left. "Thunder 37 something. Just go out! Let's go, let's go! Just get open!"

We hurry to the line. I have no idea what I'm supposed to do.

Hink gets the snap with a fraction of a second left on the play clock. From the left slot, I run straight down the field, a defensive back glued to my hip. I turn around, knowing I'm covered, and am witness to one of the craziest plays ever.

Hinkler rolls to his left, stepping forward to avoid a defensive end's charge. He pats the football, lifts his arm to throw, then jerks it down, having faked out an onrushing linebacker. He drifts back to his right, pointing, still hoping to find someone open past the first down marker. Now he runs harder, toward the right edge, selling the run so maybe one of our defenders will leave us, and we'll get open. Or maybe he'll charge out of bounds so we can take one last crack on fourth down, but how much time is left? Is he past the line of scrimmage yet? I allow my arms to get tangled with my defender's, a precursor to a possible downfield block. I turn and look again, and Hink has gone around the edge, is steamrolling toward the marker. He's got it! He'll get the first down! I let my man go, for fear of a holding call. Hinkler is very near the sidelines, and a safety is lining him up for a big hit. Then comes the crazy part: Hink plants his right foot in the turf, stiff-arms the safety who falls past him, and continues upfield. There's a huge roar. Hinkler—who's no faster than Shave—is lumbering straight down their sideline, picking up more yards, getting us into field goal range. They're catching him from behind, reaching for him…and he cuts *inside*, into the center of the field. We have no timeouts! I look at the clock. It says 10 seconds. This is huge mistake; we won't have time to kick our way into overtime. There's Hink, chugging with his mouth open and his tongue hanging out, kicking up his feet to avoid a defensive tackle, taking a glancing blow from a linebacker but continuing on. I run his way and get a good block on a different linebacker, falling on top of him. Hinkler is past me. One of his shoes flies off, lands near my head. He cuts again, back the way he came, stumbling with one cleat. Vance is in the end zone, sprinting to the middle of the field and Hink points left, Vance comes screaming forward and absolutely crushes a cornerback in position to make the tackle. Hinkler has a hitch in his giddyup as he capers forward, the ball dangerously loose under his right arm. The clock reads zero. One final defensive back grabs him around the waist, a tackle from which there will be no escape, and Hink topples backwards, using his momentum to pirouette on his stocking foot, falling, stretching back over his head with the ball, and somehow, some way, he collapses into the end zone, and the officials raise their arms: touchdown. We win.

Maybe it turns out this was Butch Hinkler's story all along.

CHAPTER 23

I bring Aggie home Tuesday afternoon. He won't eat and will barely look at me. He has a morphine patch adhered to a shaved rectangle on his trunk, and a massive sutured slit from stem to stern along his underside. I ask him to get up and go outside for a pee. He won't, and looks at me with imploring brown eyes.

I carry him into bed, and hand-feed him a few brown granules of special food from the vet. He rests against me, his head on my chest. He grunts with each exhalation. Aggie had a gastropexy, and now his stomach wall is actually attached to his right side. This noble soul. I stare for a very long time at his morphine patch, and simultaneously touch that particular inch on my stomach.

A couple days later I catch him drinking water. Then he limps out into the snowy parking lot on his own for the first time, and he halfway lifts his leg to pee, as opposed to his prior aggrieved squat. I clap for him and smile. There's no better feeling than to know he's on the mend: it's the breezy wonder of getting away scot-free.

But when we hobble back to the hotel, Aggie stops in front of Townsel's door and looks at me.

"Wrong room, boy," I say. "C'mon, Aggie. C'mon just over here, you can make it."

But he pants and stays put, slowly waving his tail.

"You wanna go see your buddy? You wanna see if Townsel's in there? Good dog!" I knock, and indeed Townsel is home. He's shirtless and has a playbook in his hands.

He says, "Aggie! Aggie dog! You're walkin' around, boy! I can't believe it! Good as new! Look at this li'l prince!" He stoops and gently hugs the dog, scratches his white-black mane. Aggie kisses him on the cheek.

"He's doing great," I say. "He's tougher than Sugar Tits on a goal-line stand. He wanted to come say hi."

"Dang right he did! Come on in!" So we pace on into Townsel's room which is mine's reverse-twin. I peel off my down jacket, remove my ski hat, discard my gloves. Aggie thumps to the floor and sighs, glorying in Townsel's ministrations. "Look at this little man! Who is this guy! Look at that face! Look at those eyes! Gonna take him down to Texas! Gonna put him on the state flag of Texas!" Townsel is gritting his teeth so hard.

We spend half an hour here, and it's nice; our proximity notwithstanding, Townsel and I haven't hung out regularly. He's anchored himself more thoroughly in his suite than I have in mine: he's got family photos propped on tables and his kitchen counter, a silver crucifix nailed into the door, his own comforter draped over the living room couch, and a life-size stick-on rendition of Clancy Swift hanging on a wall, a gag gift from an unknown benefactor which Townsel wound up taking half-seriously as an inspiration. He and I talk about the upcoming New England game. I'm careful to speak with him as equals, which we of course are. We're teammates. But I couldn't stand for him to think I was big-timing him in light of my success.

"All right," I say. "Whaddaya think, Aggie? Ready to get going? Come on, dude. Let's do this thing. Let's do this thing like a chicken wing on a string at Burger King." But Aggie keeps his chin on the carpet, blinking up at me. "C'mon. Let's go." He doesn't move. "All right. Let's do it."

"Okay, Aggs," Townsel says. He puts his hands on the

dog's shoulders to force him up, but Aggie groans and rolls onto his side. He squints at me, then scrubs a forepaw against his face in an adorable, puppyish way. Townsel looks at me, too.

"You feeling like you wanna sleep here for a little while?" I say, still sing-songy. "You wanna stay here for a little while?"

Aggie's tongue lolls out, and he pants his assent. His face, so expressive, reads like a mixture of gratitude and fear. Townsel says it's fine, he'll bring him back over in a little while. So I kneel down and give my dog a kiss on his furry forehead, scratch the inside of his ear, and leave him. I've got a DVD of every defensive snap New England has played this season back in my room, and I'm obliged to study.

*

I'm walking in the facility parking lot late Friday night after meetings. Someone is already out here, standing against my car. I think it must be Gasper, but then I see broad, leather-jacketed shoulders and a knitted Rastafarian hat. He turns as I approach. It's Zeke Hoverman.

"Hey," he says in a tired version of his voice.

"What's up?"

"You know. Thought maybe you'd want to go get a beer or something."

"Mm. I don't think so, Zeke."

He grins. "Man. That article was a month ago, dude. The fuck you carrying a grudge for?" He thuds my rear tire with the heel of his dress shoe. "My agent says Hechtkopf offered me a new contract. Six years, 37 million. Fifteen guaranteed."

"It's not the article," I say, not knowing if this is true. "I'm beat. You signing it?"

"I don't know. I haven't told my wife yet. She'll say grab the cash. This summer, if things didn't get better quick, I was looking at a shitty extension, maybe near the minimum. She'll say don't look a gift horse. But there's something to be said for testing the market."

"Elevator up," I say.

He inhales deeply. "We could win the whole goddamn thing. I can't believe I'm standing here saying this shit, but we could make the dance and do damage. Then imagine the offers. How the fuck did we go from winless to this? How'd it happen?"

I drop my gym bag onto the pavement's flattened snow. "New starting quarterback. New coordinator."

"That's probably it. Though sometimes I get the feeling it all happened because of one little mouse."

"That's pretty flattering. But you don't sound happy when you say it."

"I did think one thing," says Hoverman. "Put my stats and your stats together in one player? That's almost 2,000 yards from scrimmage, maybe fifteen touchdowns. *That's* a player who'd have broken the bank." He folds his arms; his voice is quiet. "Hell, more than money. Those are the kind of numbers eventually get you to Canton."

"Yeah," I say. "If only I hadn't been born."

"Nobody to blame but myself. I let it happen. Maybe I didn't believe enough. It took you to show me, hell, maybe it took you to push me." He nods and offers me a handshake. I take it, feeling odd. His hand is freezing and his breath comes in heather-colored puffs. "Probably it's my own fault."

"Can you imagine if we really did win it," I say. "Hink under center for a crazy playoff run. They'd never stop talking about it."

"Yeah, now you got me jazzed up a little," Hoverman says evenly. "I can really see it. I don't know if I could really see it before this season. And you're coming back here next year."

"Looks like it."

He nods. "You see, though. That's what I'm afraid of. They're starting to call you and me Butch and Sundance, man.

Go figure: the great white hope gets half the billing. When I'm the one who does the heavy lifting."

"…"

"Which, I mean, like I say, you helped me. But at the same time, it's hard not to start figuring it out on the back of an envelope. How much bank did you and your lover-boy Nugent wind up costing me? They're offering fifteen million guaranteed? It should be thirty."

I pick up my bag and unlock my car. "I guess I'll get going."

"Hey, I know a couple things," he says. "I got me a little dirt to shake up the situation. I got some infor*ma*tion." I flounce down into the driver's seat, and he steps away. "Come on, man. You've had the same thought. You've wondered what life would be like around here without ol' Zeke around."

I slam my door shut, start the engine, my face feeling hot.

He's got his arms folded and is still saying something down into my car, but I can't hear him. I pull out into the parking lot and feel the car lurch into a long skid. I barely avoid a wreck, and screech out of there.

When I get home, Aggie isn't there; Townsel hears me come in and says the dog was howling, so he came in and rescued him, took him for a short walk, and once again Aggie wanted to retire in Townsel's room. It's late and I thank him. I go to bed alone.

And I think: Hoverman knows about the HGH? And thinks the coaching staff doesn't? He's in for a rude awakening. I'm one step ahead of him.

Then I understand what he meant. He'll go public. He'll tell the world, or he'll tell the commissioner's office. Oh, no. But he wouldn't. He wouldn't. He's not that guy. He was just blowing off steam. He's done too much for the team, tried too hard. I've seen him bleeding, I've seen him screaming on the verge of tears. Even if he won't acknowledge it, he wants to win even more than he wants a bigger contract or more credit. It was just talk.

This is the vortex that swirls around me. I keep looking at the clock expecting it to be nearly morning, and it's always fifteen minutes later than the last time I looked. It's a punishing night, locked in this ten-by-ten box with my thoughts.

*

The next morning my phone rings. It's Tom Calcaterra.

"Emergency," he says.

"What is the nature of your emergency?"

"Seriously. I'm not kidding. It's emergent."

"All right," I say. "What is it?"

"I don't think it would be wise to say anything more over the phone."

"But you *called* me." My stomach flops. "What are you talking about?"

"Really, I don't actually know. But they asked me to call a few people. They want everyone in here now. Come to the complex. If you've got anyone there with you, bring them. I think there's going to be a meeting. Top priority. The highest priority imaginable. I mean anyone on the team. You know, if you've got someone not on the team there with you, you definitely shouldn't bring them."

"I'm eating cereal here, Tom."

"Two hours from now. I'm led to believe it's an order."

*

We're in the full-group meeting room. It's seven in the morning on a Saturday; nearly everyone is here: in sweats, wearing shower shoes, eating breakfasts out of Tupperware or to-go Styrofoam, fidgeting with phones. And Coach Fond is seated in the front row, which is unnerving. We all watch the back of his motionless head, like children recognizing a parent's mortality. Danny Shugarts and Clancy Swift have a hushed but animated conversation up in the back; I can't hear what they're saying. Hoverman sits with Wendell Vance; Vance has on an expensive striped dress shirt with the tails untucked, and he scratches his scalp furiously. Calcaterra doesn't know anything, other than when Fond asked him to make a few calls, he looked ashen.

Chick Hechtkopf, the general manager, enters the room by himself and looks up at us. He throws back his shoulders and says, "I'm not at liberty to say very much, because this is a pending legal matter," he says. "Last night, Brian Nugent was charged with possession of narcotics and drug paraphernalia, and is awaiting bail."

All oxygen leaves the room. I see Coach Fond sink microscopically in his chair.

"He was apprehended by police in a hotel up in Livonia. He was allegedly smoking crack cocaine with his girlfriend. I imagine that's what you'll hear from reporters later this morning, and that's all we'll say about it for now."

Vance goes on scratching his shaved skull. Calcaterra's leg is hopping wildly.

"Needless to say, this puts us all in a difficult position, but as of this morning Mr. Nugent is on a leave of absence pending further investigation into his legal status. It should go without saying that you have absolutely no comment for anyone who asks. Tomorrow, you'll take the field, and Edward Kitchen will be your offensive coordinator. I know he'll do a wonderful job, and that we'll all make a seamless and smooth transition. It's one more win for us, and we're in the playoffs, men. I know you can do it. Thank you for coming in early."

I look at Vance and Hoverman. Their faces are stone. Hinkler looks stricken. I feel someone touch my shoulder: it's Townsel. The offensive linemen stand up and shuffle out. Someone coughs. Coach Fond is still here, arms on the desk before him, his sweaty dark hair pressed about in disorganized licks. What's he waiting for? Does he want the room behind him empty before he'll move?

"It's all right," I hear Hinkler say, softly. "Nothing changes. The plays are still the same."

A bubble in my stomach pops.

"Mouse," says Townsel. "Nick. Let's go."

He's standing over me. I'm the only person still sitting. Everyone else is gone or going. I back look down and Coach Fond's seat is vacant. I say, "Edward Kitchen?"

Townsel nods. "Bow Wow."

*

I love sports. I love playing football, I love watching it. I love pretty much every sporting event on TV, though this fall I haven't had much time to watch. As a kid, my sensibilities were shaped viewing a basketball dynasty in Chicago, a baseball renaissance in the Bronx, and a young mixed-race golfer stunning the Masters. I was a jock in high school, so to some my sports-obsessiveness was explained away by my peer group, and I admit it's not always the easiest group to belong to: they can be loud and obnoxious, vulgar, condescending. But I think there are a lot of sports fans in the world who understand that *being* a sports fan is fundamentally ridiculous, but that it's also okay. Many more things in the world are more important than who wins the title this year. But caring who wins doesn't make you a troglodyte. Meaning is where you make it, and there *can be* meaning in the narratives sports weaves, there almost always is authenticity somewhere buried in there, and having contact with it can be exhilarating and humbling and wonderful. It's all pretend, yes, of course. But it can be fulfilling. And I've always wanted to play football in that same spirit, to be a person who cares about his team but also maybe recognizes it's all a little bit silly. This is what I've wanted. But it feels like something has gone wrong.

It's like I've woken up nearly three months later and forgotten every lesson about attachment, about conventional and ultimate truth. Look what I've striven for! Now I have money, complicated friendships, the avatar of relative fame and, technically speaking, a drug habit. To make matters more confusing, I know this: while contemplation on ridding myself of attachment brought me out of my funk last year, it also freed me up to more completely pursue this life of conventional achievement and striving.

And now it seems I've been rescued. Did Nugent ever even tell Fond about the HGH? I feel guilty about my relief. He was the one who believed in me.

*

Bow Wow gathers the offense Saturday night, before we go home. In effort to rise to the occasion, he's replaced his usual profane shouting with a whispery diction, and he punctuates every word with thumb and forefinger tight together, as though he's oil painting.

"You strong. You strong-minded men. Here's what you have not done this season: you have not let what nobody said get you down. You strong enough to block out everything. Tomorrow? No different. I been there every week right there with you. We already been doing it together. You prepared, you know what to do, you think about the game and none of this other bullshit. Everything just the same."

*

Except once we get out there against New England, Bow Wow's play calling reverts to the Mesozoic Era. It's I-formation, single-tight-end, three yards and a cloud of dust. I don't play a single offensive snap in the first half. Richards gets hurt and has to be carted off, moving Pendleton to left tackle and putting wide-eyed rookie Ruvell Underwood in the game; Underwood allows sacks on back-to-back plays, leading Hinkler to toss the ball disgustedly to the sidelines and incur an unsportsmanlike conduct call. Bow Wow wants to pop his cork, but thinks better of it. Instead, in his withering, hate-filled voice, he says, "That's all right! Motherfuck! That's okay! Shitbags and cocksuckers! Get 'em next time, Butch!" I return a single punt in the first stanza, and get hit so hard I nearly bite off my tongue through my mouthpiece.

Walking past me at halftime, Hoverman says, "Well isn't your uniform clean?" It's occurred to me it's not impossible Hoverman was talking about information he had on Nugent, not me.

We are lifeless and grim. Kolakowski has the defense down the other end of the room, and he's lighting them up. We're here puttering and coughing by ourselves. Bow Wow is sitting on a chair over in the corner, stooped over with his elbows on his knees and his old hands up around his face, staring at us. In three syllables, Wendell Vance sums it all up: "mm-mm-mm" in declining register. I don't know where Fond is. On the way back out, I walk alongside Bow Wow and say, "Maybe we should spread 'em out. Just to mix it up a little."

Bow Wow looks as though I've woken him from a dream, and answers, "I think I got the tunnel vision."

*

We lose big, and now our hopes ride on the season's final week.

The nights after a game are brutal. It's more than just sensory overload and it's more than solitude after a performance, though these are cruel. It's also the relative density of time: resting here in bed, time comes in clumsy chunks, compared to the fine slices made by energy and paranoia just a few hours earlier. The body is glad for rest, but the mind won't quit; I'm here, but I'm also back there, swarmed under by color and noise, filled up with purpose.

Sometimes I wake up in the wee hours of a Monday morning and think of sticking my thumb in a blender.

CHAPTER 24

The drumbeat begins for our final week, the only week that matters. Way back in the season's second game, the team lost in Chicago by three touchdowns. The winner of the rematch goes to the playoffs.

Monday I get to the facility and have two fingernails drained, where my left hand was crushed between helmets yesterday. The trainers hook the calf up to a stim and I sit for a while, looking at a laptop. The *Free Press* website has the gruesome details about Nugent's arrest—he was incoherent when the cops got him, his girlfriend is 17—including his leaked mug shot. My phone is ringing off the hook, unknown numbers, probably reporters trying to get me to comment. Eventually I turn it off. Gasper staggers by toting something heavy and gives me a longsuffering grin. Later he asks about Aggie's health.

I go into the weight room and hear my teammates grunt and gasp. My legs are worn out from the long season, so I focus there, quads and hamstrings, rep after rep, getting encouragement from a strength-and-conditioning assistant named Kyle. After an hour, it's an ice bath, a hot shower, lunch, and some of Vance's wheat grass which superstition has me believing will fight off the cold many of the offensive guys have contracted. Then it's film time.

It's not pretty. Lester Jefferson has his laser pointer out, and Mr. Good Guy is gone. He says, "Yawl a bunch a retards, ain'tcha? Yawl just a bunch a not-listenin' bunch a retards. You pass-protectin' like it's the first day a camp. Zeke, you look so stupid missin' this blitz, I'm embarrassed for you, I truly am." Bow Wow comes in and stands in back, overseeing. He doesn't say anything. Then the full offense meets and goes through Sunday's tape again, play by play. Hinkler has a notebook out and he's filling it with his mistakes.

Then we run. Bow Wow puts the offense out in the cold and snow and runs us the entire way down a practice field five times, ten times, until everyone is bent over, kneeling, prostrate. Bow Wow doesn't say anything.

Before we leave for the day, Coach Fond speaks to us. "You-all have to be ready." He's reserved and grim, and one side of his mouth begins to twitch and dip, something like a stroke patient's. "We go' get ready to play, and we go' win. You-all are a different team now, men, from where you were when we started. And now I want to read a passage from Ezekiel:

> This is what the Sovereign LORD says: Repent! Turn from your idols and renounce all your detestable practices! When anyone separates themselves from me and sets up idols in their hearts and puts a wicked stumbling block before their faces, I the LORD will answer them myself. I will set my face against them and make them an example and a byword. I will remove them from my people. Then you will know that I am the LORD.

"You got a choice. You can let the pressure get to you, men, or you can stay true. You-all build up idols and stumbling blocks in your hearts, I know you do. What you go' buy. Who you go' buy it for. Get rid of all that. Stay focused on what matters. We go' forget all the nonsense that tempts you-all every day, and focus on what really matters. This here. You-all. You-all, and what you do the next time we play a game, is the only thing that really matters."

When I get home, Aggie is in Townsel's room.

*

Tuesday is off, and most weeks that means we stay away from the facility. But Clancy Swift announces a "voluntary" workout and everyone shows up. There are no coaches; just us, the brotherhood. Hink is quiet and Vance pulls no pranks.

Relentlessness is the coin of this realm. To be on the team, you're either an elite athlete even by professional standards, or you're relentless. You pound on, the same way the days pound on. The general public, at a grocery store, in a movie theater, in traffic: they're like phantoms to me now. Their incidental conversations are babble. They hint at lives that seem like secrets. I know I'm the one in the exclusive club, but they're the ones who seem in on something. When I can see them. Sometimes they're a blur. If ever by happenstance I run across a teammate away from the facility, I recognize that he feels it too. We are confused instruments at rest. And so finally I'm convinced that much of the world really is illusory. But what's in this building, in these rooms and on these fields, and what's waiting for us Sunday: that's a reality I can't get around. It's coming. It's coming so fast.

Just for a change, I walk up some stairs I've never taken, walk down a hallway and around a bend, and find a tiny old lounge with a couple vending machines and a broken foosball table. Townsel is sitting in a plastic chair, staring into a small bag of potato chips.

"That's kind of crazy," I say. "What is this place?"

Townsel smiles beneficently. "Unofficial practice squad office. This is where me and Gregory and Barlow go sometimes. You know what it's like on the squad."

"Hard living."

"Nice to get away."

I sit with him. "I heard a rumor Custance has a concussion. Have they said anything to you about it?"

"Yeah."

"So they might activate you for Sunday?"

"Dunno yet. Don't want to get my hopes up."

"You've done everything they wanted," I say. "You've worked. You've turned yourself inside out. You'll make the team next year for sure. Feel like you've learned a lot?"

"A real lot. Watching you Morrison. You're our patron saint, man. Serious, every time one of us gets down. 'Look what can happen. Look what Mouse did.' Make us work harder, make us hit the playbook."

"I'm a lucky guy," I say.

"Nobody say it's luck."

"No, I mean sometimes you get bogged down in the middle of it, you can still feel sorry for yourself."

"Hopefully we make the playoffs," says Townsel. "What you got going on in the offseason?"

"You know, I haven't given it one second of thought. I don't know. Thinking about it now, the idea scares the hell out of me."

"Maybe we could train together. Everybody say you're a beast, man. I'm not the only squad-dog who'd do it, if you let us." He eats a chip. "Why's it scare you?"

"I have no idea. I guess because if I get to do it all over again, maybe I won't do it as well."

"See," he says, "I think that's the beauty of it. Maybe you'll do it *better*. Can I ask you a question? Don't mean to take advantage. But I mean, I been hitting people my whole life, since third grade. But I'm a Christian man, y'know? And I never played with murder in my heart. I always had the size, I always had the speed. But they told me I wasn't a killer. It's why I never got to a big school, why I didn't get drafted, because they said I wasn't furious enough. That's what they wrote down, 'Not furious enough.' You a smart dude, Morrison. Am I ever gonna play in this league if I don't get murder in my heart?"

I look at the treats hanging in curlicues inside the vending machines. I say, "Never compromise what you believe," and it tastes like ashes.

*

Wednesday morning we're in the meeting room, breaking down Chicago's film. They're a 4-3 defense, heavy on two-deep coverage but with a lot of exotic blitzes mixed in, and their middle linebacker tends to drop and cover the seam. The dude can really run, but he's 260 pounds, so I believe I can out-quick him. We watch a half-hour of zone blitzes, one after the other, watching their free safety time the snap and come hard with the Will linebacker. Our coaches assume Chicago will target Underwood, the rookie sub at our right tackle slot. Chicago also loves to stunt their left end with a three-technique tackle, which in theory could mean I'd wind up having to get in the way of a 310-pound behemoth. But all this presupposes I'm on the field.

We lift weights for a half-hour, then it's out in the bubble for practice in pads and shorts. Hoverman and Calcaterra have a bet whether or not Bow Wow will have us hitting. He doesn't. It's full-speed, but two-hand-touch below the waist, the same way Nugent did it. We even practice some of Nugent's funkier formations which gives me a chance to run around a little bit. Things are looser. Jokes are told, smiles are cracked. We stampede into the cafeteria for lunch, then into the meeting rooms again to watch film of the practice we just performed. Afterward, I get more treatment on the calf.

Hinkler is in the cold tub next to mine. Breaking ten minutes of silence, as though bursting up out of a trance, he says, "This is gonna be the most important day of our lives."

I think about this for a while, as the freezing water does its worst. I remember in college I could only do thirty seconds at a time; now I'm up to fifteen minutes. "*This* will be?" I say. "*This* will be the most important day of our lives?"

"Shut up, Mouse. Why does everybody around here automatically disagree with everything I say?"

I look down at my legs. They're red on the way to purple, but I just grit my teeth. "I didn't say I disagree."

Bow Wow gathers us up Wednesday evening and says, "Don't be the guy. Don't be the guy who peak early. You not focused enough. We practice this play, what, five times." He's skimming through today's footage. "Look at you selves. Watch you selves. Every time, something different. One time Hink don't take a deep enough drop. One time DeNoon pitter-patter his little footsies. Schenk, this time you just fall over. Look at that. Somebody shot him. Somebody shot Schenk and he fall over. You ain't clean. You ain't clean enough."

Coach Fond makes an appearance. His face seems shrink-wrapped, his eyes barely open. Bow Wow turns the room lights on, but Fond says no, he doesn't need to talk to us. He sits off to the side and listens, and in the blue reflected light of million-dollar video equipment we stare at his profile: cheeks wasted, chin less proud, only the great Roman nose a reminder of his famous televised face. It occurs to me perhaps he's quite ill.

CHAPTER 25

Thursday we get the beginnings of our game plan, Bow Wow's first. He's scripted a dozen plays, and I'm involved in several of them. He's not such a stubborn jerk after all! Zoom Split Left 414 Swing V Queen. That's clearly for me if there's a single safety back. Dallas Right Switch Right 88 Dig Queen. Press Right Horse 826 H Chase Jack. Split Right 628 Backs Flat. I like that one. Easy money.

"All right," Bow Wow says. "Boy wonder, Hink the genius. See this? They in dime here. It ain't always just Cover-2 with these assholes. You see the strong safety's coming. What we checkin' to?"

Hinkler says, "It's Cover-0, so I want a double-move. Hoverman slides in protection to get the safety."

"How he do, Mr. Shave?"

Jim Shave is in the meeting, wearing a sling after collarbone surgery. "I'm flexing out the Y, so if their end does drop into coverage…." The film progresses, and indeed we watch Chicago's defensive end backpedal at the snap. "Now he's in trouble. He's got deep-half help over the top with the dime, but that's a throw you can make. You'll take a hit, but make that throw."

Hinkler nods and writes in his notebook.

The edge is coming back. By Thursday night we're testy. Brohammer and Ronald Waltz get into a fistfight in the showers. Waltz is hopping around protecting his broken leg, Brohammer's nose is bleeding. We break it up eventually.

*

I drive home and Henny is sitting on my couch. She sweet-talked the guy at the front desk.

"I wanted to let you know I'm engaged," she says.

"You're what?"

"I know, it's too fast. He's a producer. I'm getting a part in a movie next month, and we went out to celebrate and he popped the question, and I heard myself saying yes. If you want to know the truth, Nick, I'm scared to death."

I put my keys on the kitchen counter, remove my heavy coat and wet boots. I see Henny's overnight bag in the bedroom.

"You'd like him," she says. "He's a little more deadpan, a little more *boom*. But seriously, you'd like him."

I recognize she has a new affectation: she slightly lisps her 's' sounds now. California for ten weeks has changed her speech for the sake of sweetness, to presume intimacy where there is none. Looking at her—face still bronze, hair still light, that body squeezed into a mock-casual ensemble—brings pain into my chest. I hear myself say, "You could've told me this over the phone."

"Do you have a girlfriend now? I know it doesn't really matter, but I'm just curious." I don't answer. "I don't like to think about you kissing somebody else."

On the one hand, I bitterly wonder whether it's her impending nuptials or my football success that's driven her here. But I also see her brown legs and shoulders, I see her patting the couch inviting me to sit with her. I would love to tell Henny to hit the bricks. Why isn't life like that?

"I've been watching you," she says. "I watch every game. I tell everyone about you, what you went through to get here." Her smile drifts away. "It seems like maybe all you needed was me to get the fuck out of your life."

I stand next to the window.

"I know I ended it forever between us," says Henny. "So I have no right to ask for anything. But it really scares me, Nick. Was I really the thing standing in your way?"

I'd like to tell her yes. But I say, "Of course not."

"No?"

"Come on. We both know I'm the biggest problem I ever had. Everyone's responsible for their own life."

"Okay. I feel like there's a judgment of me in there somewhere."

"Not at all. You never did anything to me that I didn't let you do."

She blinks, and rubs her palms against her knees. "Wow. That was pretty mean."

"You'd like me now," I say. "You trained me well. Now I do whatever it takes." But hearing myself makes my indignation buckle. Softer, I say, "It's true, though. I'm turning into a selfish ass."

She says, "Oh, bullshit. You think too much. You're not an ass, and sure you're selfish, but you know what? Everybody's selfish. Everybody wants things that make them feel good. For some people, those things involve other people suffering, but that's not you. You're the best person I know, Nick."

My God. What if that's true?

We talk a long time. She tells me about L.A., the begrimed apartment she rented and the house in the hills where she now resides with her fiancé. She takes acting lessons, has quit eating starch, drives to the beach every day. Well, she's the greatest self-inventor I've ever known, and one result of living this way is sometimes you wake up and you've crab-walked incredibly far down a narrow path just to see if you can. And the pillows may be fluffed and the morning light deliriously beautiful, but you realize if you don't turn back now you may never be able to. She laughs at something I say, covering her face as a hysterically sad person might, then she stands up and comes near, pushing me against the mini-blinds with her hips, hugging me so I feel her chest heave with giggles. Then she looks at me, very seriously, very close.

With her lips a few inches from mine, I say, "I'm cheating."

In her drowsy, sultry way, she says, "What's that supposed to mean?"

I feel sadness ripple through me. "I'm doing those shots. HGH. I already started doing them before you left."

"Oh." She's pressed against me, working her fingers under my shirt. Her face is hot on my cheek; I feel her eyelashes flick. She sighs into my neck and finally says, "Well, so what? Other jocks do it, too, and they're bigger than you are."

A spasm flashes through me, a recollection of what it's like to be inside her. It makes no difference. It makes no difference if we do or we don't. Nothing makes a difference. I say, falteringly, "It wouldn't be fair to the other guy."

She kisses my neck, puts a hand against the inside of my thigh and begins to rub.

I don't care about the other guy. I'm supposed to care. He and I are one, all that. But here's what I think, as Henny's ministrations grow ever less resistible. I think: maybe I've changed for the worse, but surely I've changed. If not, my God, what's this all been for?

I squeeze her very tight against me, so her breath whooshes away and her arms go limp. I kiss her forehead. I say, "Where does he think you are, anyway?" and step away into the kitchen to look for something to eat.

Stung, Henny regroups for a moment then says, "He makes me come so hard. Nobody has ever made me come like that." She sits on the windowsill, blowing her hair out of her face.

I remove some protein-heavy imitation chicken pieces

from the refrigerator and mix them with enough mayonnaise for two sandwiches. We eat far across the room from one another, and she makes faces about the meat substitute. Between bites, she looks around and says, "Where's your dog?"

*

Friday is weigh-in. It's the most fun we have as a full group all week, everyone stepping up and trying to make their weight. That's not an issue for me, but it's a point of stress for the bigger guys, who get fined four hundred dollars a day for every pound they're over. The trainers call out a name and a weight, and the player drops his towel and steps on the scale in his jock, sucking in his gut, taking heaps of verbal abuse. Then the number is called and either the crowd boos (when the weight is made) or erupts into cheers (when it isn't). Vance is the world's raunchiest m.c. during these sessions, breaking everyone up with his putdowns and one-liners.

"Guy meets this hooker in a bar," he says. "She goes, 'I'll do anything you want, anything in the damn world you can think of for 300 bucks, long as you can say it in three words.' Dude hands over the money and he says real slow, 'Paint…my…house.'"

That gets Hinkler going: "Two hookers are standing on a corner. One says to the other, 'Hey, have you ever been picked up by the fuzz?' And the other one says, 'No, but I've been swung around by the tits.'"

And Toombs says, "This patient asks her doctor, 'Doctor, won't you kiss me?' And the doc says, 'You hot as shit, but it's against my ethics.' The girl goes, 'Please, just one kiss?' And the doc says, 'Sorry. No way. I mean, I really shouldn't even be fucking you.'"

Next we practice out of pads, then come the massages, brutal rubdowns designed to break up bad muscle adhesions and get us stretched in tough-to-reach places. They tell us Aretha Franklin will sing the anthem Sunday, and James Earl Jones will be our honorary captain. There are also rumors of a Saturday night pep talk from a mystery celebrity. Eventually reporters file into the locker room and ask us questions about the game. We look at the microphones and give them tapioca.

*

I knock on Townsel's door to see if Aggie wants to go for a walk. Townsel acts bright and shiny at the notion; he's embarrassed by the dog's preference for him. Aggie relents. He seems a little stronger. We maneuver through snow banks, get in the car, and drive over to the baseball fields in bright sunlight. There's no wind or clouds. We explore all manner of pee and unscooped poop, and as is his wont Aggie is fascinated but ultimately disgusted by other dogs' waste. By the time we've prospected the entire park, I've decided today's weather is actually rather grand. I clear a spot on one of the benches and schlumpf down in the snow. Townsel joins me, then Aggie sits beside him, careful with his sutures. From here I can see a receding hillside of vacant factories and blown-out mini-malls, the wreckage of an American city.

It's almost certain now that Townsel will play in his first pro game this week, on special teams, because of Ahmad Custance's injury. I say, "Imagine if somebody told us this summer we'd both be in the Week 17 lineup, a game for all the marbles."

He shakes his head. "Unbelievable, man."

"I don't even want to say anything, that's how great I know you'll do. I don't want to act like it's even in question."

"Wish my grandma was gonna be here." He gives a funny smile. "Hey. I'm sorry about Aggie, man."

"It's okay. He knows what's good for him."

"Now he knows you're next door. He gonna flip out if you don't live next door, be on the first bus to find you wherever you are."

"No, that's all right."

I look over at the dog, whose tongue hangs out like polished pink coral. He does know. I want to possess the same qualities as the man who rescued him way back in June. I still want what felt like higher motives.

*

I'm up at 7 a.m. Saturday and I pick a suit for tomorrow morning, fill a duffel with some random clothes, get in the car by eight. We have meetings until ten, then the walk-through: coaches scurry around us as we perform our routes and blocks as slowly as possible; they explain techniques, describe systems and variables, read off play-sheets, bark at us. Per usual Coach Fond isn't here, is likely up in the office that overlooks the bubble field. He's been a ghost for a month, and it's worse since Nugent left.

Everything is normal, everything is routine, despite the nervous energy of knowing what tomorrow means. Some of us are back in the weight room stretching. DeNoon says, "Nine points, fellas. Nine-point 'dogs at home. That's disrespect. They're sayin' you got no chance!"

"Just something for us to chew on," Hamill says. "Just something to make the hate stronger."

"The fuck those Vegas shitheads know about shit?" says Parnell, the left guard, whose tremendous midsection is bent over an industrial-strength yoga ball. His voice strains as his various abdominals tense. "I'm gonna take nine points of human flesh out they ass tomorrow."

"We're one win away from the playoffs!" cries DeNoon. "We're at home! Don't care who the goddamn quarterback is! It's disrespect! What team one win away from the playoffs should ever be a nine-point home 'dog?"

"Ain't nobody gonna believe in us but us!"

"They ain't in the locker room! They don't know what's

in y'alls chest!"

"It's only gonna make us stronger! We band together, we play with one heartbeat, we'll shock the world!"

"It's all right here! It's all inside these four walls!"

Jefferson has the running backs in for a special film session where we promise not to be as horrible as last week, then I drive over to the team hotel, eat an early dinner, go upstairs. Calcaterra comes in and we watch college football on TV. This is when you can start to feel the ball rolling downhill, the momentum of the week culminating in Sunday afternoon. It's nauseating, but it's better than I ever could've expected. Tommy Way and Marcus Schenk come by and sit in chairs to watch the game. Later Meleki Faafeu joins us and grunts down onto the floor in a barefoot yogi pose. Da'Norris Maynor knocks and comes in, and tells us our special guest celebrity is downstairs setting up in the ballroom as we speak. We turn off the game to gossip about who it might be. "I couldn't even get a good look," Maynor says. Then here comes Husseyn Norwell, and he says, "Man. I was just down there. I think it's Kid Rock." And we all like Kid Rock and we talk about it for a while and agree he'd be pretty cool. But there are still hours to kill before then. I think about meditating. Then I get a text from Gasper who says come on over for a visit, he needs to ask me something.

So I drive up to his house in Redford. It's dark early, and my headlights swoop across the lawn; I can see Gasper's helmeted gargoyle statue still writhing in pain, but buried nearly waist-deep in snow and soaked a darker color. I give the side door a shave-and-a-haircut knock.

"I have to ask," he tells me. "A little birdy told me the bitch is back." He's sitting on the floor, legs akimbo, and he's slurring a bit.

"I assume the birdy is Henny herself. I haven't told anyone."

"You kicked her to the curb. I was stunned."

I step around him, past the bedroom, and go look at the

front closet. The three holes are still there, unrepaired, though he's patched the exterior wall with sanded-but-mismatched fillets of putty. "I had you in mind when I did it," I say. "I thought you'd approve."

"I'm not saying I don't approve. I'm just saying the unmitigated willpower…. Anyway, she's bunkered in that snazzy casino-hotel downtown. Maybe using the roulette wheel to decide her next move. Red she goes back to California."

I step back to the living room. "Having your own little party here tonight?"

"No-ho! Just a typical evening at Chez Twigged. After a hard week of work, and all that. I almost said, 'work of week.' What are you gonna do about Henny?"

"She's marrying somebody else."

Gasper sparks his bowl, takes an eye-flutteringly long drag. In a strangled voice he says, "I'm sure that's working out great."

"It's not a matter of me forgiving her or whatever. It's a matter of staying away from pure self-destruction."

"Speaking of which."

"Yes?"

He gets up. He's wearing torn sweatpants and an overly tight Cake t-shirt that displays both his spoon chest and his nascent pot belly. "Are you sure I can't get you super high? No?" He walks into the kitchen, cracks open the fridge. "So you're, like, last on my list."

"I have to get back to the hotel sometime this decade, so if you're ultra-invested in stringing me along all night…."

"I'm supposed to deliver you an offer." He returns with a can of whipped cream. "Which on account of some prior conversations of ours I may or may not have spent the afternoon psyching myself up for, in light of your probably entirely justified and understandable objections and/or taking offense." He swallows a quick squirt of whipped cream. "And by psyching myself up, of course, I mean…toking myself down. Anyway, how would *you*, young man, how would *you* like to earn an easy quarter million dollars?"

I feel my face, already flushed after coming in from the cold, go claret. "What are you talking about?"

He gives me a look—a complicated eye-widening, brow-wrinkling, frown-deepening expression—that somehow in the language of facial semiotics reads: *Ronnie the K.* "Apparently," he says, "there is just amazing, unbelievable cash coming in on underdog Detroit."

I'm cotton-mouthed. "You…don't have to do this, Gasper. I've saved some money. I've got a new contract and a signing bonus coming next year. I told Ronnie I'd cover you, however much it is."

He smiles as though something hurts. "Nick. It turns out I may not have been completely honest." He's sobered up quick. "In that I may have given the impression Ronnie is just a guy who takes my action. The thing I didn't fess up to…. Sometimes he also gives me a little work on the side. So, y'know. It isn't a matter of my *having* to do anything." He glowers. "Hey, I'm fucking shady, dude. I'm already your damn drug dealer."

I sit down. I sit directly on Gasper's laptop, but don't get up to move it. This couch's armrest is madly peppered with cigarette ash. I pluck and smooth the fabric, trying to clean it off. Well, I guess the idea isn't a dramatic leap of logic, given my injections. I am grudges and shortcuts.

"Ronnie and I have a complicated relationship," he says. "Did you think I made mortgage payments out of a gofer's tips? This is Ronnie giving me a chance to get back in good…. Oh, shit. I just realized. Don't breathe. What if they test you tomorrow or next week or whatever? Are we gonna have to squirt some of Sumon's pee up your dick-hole?"

I gently put a hand on my forehead.

"Anyway, two fumbles," says Gasper. "I'm really…sorry about this. But if you're interested, two fumbles equals a quarter mil."

CHAPTER 26

I wake Sunday morning with my fists clenching the hotel bedsheets. Calcaterra is already downstairs at breakfast.

The bus is quiet. Some would say businesslike. Some would say nervous. Dozens of fans line the walkway into the stadium, and we slap five with folks in this gauntlet, smiling and dazed. Vance is walking in front of me and tells everyone he sees, "Be loud today. Be loud today." In the locker room the rituals begin. I shed my jacket and tie, start taping up my shoulderpads with double-sided tape. I get treatment for the calf. I stretch in the training room and watch DeNoon get poked with dozens of acupuncture needles, very quickly, as he moves his arms and legs and torso. He wears giant headphones and mouths words to a song I can't hear.

Back at my locker I sit with my eyes closed, meditating. I visualize the coming fury. I see arms and legs. I try and occupy the body they'll want to destroy. I see turf and menace and onrushing men. In this preparation, timing is critical. There's a buildup of emotion that will peak too soon if I'm not careful. I put on my pads and jersey. I look in my locker: a couple pairs of cleats and gloves, a towel, shower shoes. No personal effects. Nothing to betray the occupant's capricious heart. I don my helmet, press it against my open locker, so my face is partway inside. I smell sweat and umbrage.

So you're, like, last on my list.

Meaning there are others?

We walk to the field for warm-ups. I see Chicago players in one end zone, big, clad in white, soulless. I run sprints beside Townsel and Norwell. They're quiet. I leap and touch the goal-post crossbar. Fans are streaming in. The ceiling in here feels low. I jump again, pushing the calf, a preemptive strike against future pain. I line up on the 10-yard line and run dig routes, fielding soft tosses from Hinkler. People in the end zones are taping up funny signs. The scoreboard has a countdown clock. I sprint along the sideline and look up over my shoulder, testing the receiving background. I hear someone going "Ahhhhhhhh!" and I realize it's me. I'm near midfield and their stud defensive end, Baxter, is standing on the center logo and he says, "I'm gonna kill you."

"Me?" I say.

"Little mouse. Nobody done squished yo' ass yet. I'm gonna kill you 'til you're dead."

I walk away from him.

"You a fuckin' pussy, Mouse. You a tiny little fuckin' pussy. I'm gonna ass-fuck you. I'm gonna rape your momma. You a fraud. I'm gonna come in your house at night and cut your dick off and feed it to my pit bull. Mouse! Mouse!"

I field a practice punt alongside Brohammer, and he says, "That dude just said he wants to cut your dick off."

"I know."

"That's creative," says Brohammer. "That's some creative smack."

We head back to the tunnel and I stop and sign a few autographs: more little kids holding out slips of paper, beaming parents right behind. I try not to act as though it's a bothersome routine. I look everyone in the eyes and I say, "Enjoy the game. Have a good time. Make sure you cheer for us." I want those people going home saying I was the nicest athlete they've ever met.

As we all kneel in the locker room, our priest says, "God

created this day, this Sunday. He created it for gain, not loss. He created it for success, not failure. He created it for positive actions, not negative thoughts. God has given you talents in His generosity, and they are tools to be used, not treasure to be stored. He wants you to look inside yourself. Nowhere else, only inside yourself, where you can reach in and find what you need, and find Him. His angels are there. They will guide and protect you. Good luck, today."

Then Coach Fond steps in and quietly, so quietly, he says, "They whupped our ass pretty good last time. But you-all are a better team now. You go' whup their ass today."

We aren't sure he's done. He looks down at us, then puts out his empty hands. Clancy Swift stands up and screams, "I'm gonna go out there and rip some motherfucker's head off! Are you with me?" We all shout. "Are you with me?"

*

When we go back into our dome, everything is dark and confused. The p.a. announcer's voice over-reverberates, so I can only make out snippets of what he's saying. The lights are half-dimmed. Cheerleaders form two welcoming lines through which we sprint wailing, but their faces are pointed away so all I see are pompoms, white boots and bared midriffs. There's smoke and dry ice and muddled music; someone smacks my helmet. I see more TV cameras than usual, and a throng of credentialed passers-by toting electronic gizmos. Maybe it's the crowd that makes everything so hard to follow: they've found a new decibel level. The lights are coming back up. I'm playing catch with Vance on the sidelines. There's no depth perception. A staffer says something to me; I shrug at him. He points down at some wires he doesn't want me to trip on. Now that I look at the ground, I see other-colored cords, the first-down chain, some kind of electrical trunk line, some spray-painted markings. These systems, and I have no sense of what they do. It's just kind of hard to tell what's going on.

A military band plays the national anthem. Bow Wow comes over and puts his hand over his headset microphone. "We gonna use you big today, Morrison! You gonna be out there all day! You do your thing! Just do your thing!"

They play a mid-tempo hiphop song that starts out with a catchy chorus of child singers, and the stadium excitement ratchets even a little higher; I look down the row and see the mouths of six or seven of my teammates working in synchrony:

> *Reality is catching up with me*
> *Taking my inner child, I'm fighting for it, custody*
> *With these responsibilities that they entrusted me*
> *As I look down at my diamond-encrusted piece*

"Come on, mothafucka!" Vance yells in my face. "Come on!"

"Oh yeah!" says Way. "Oh yeah!"

"Our house!" DeNoon tells me.

Toombs says, "Play hard, play fast! Play hard, play fast!"

"Our house! Our fuckin' house!"

"Oh yeah! Here we go!"

"Bring the fight to them!"

Hinkler calmly walks toward me, makes a little eye contact, acts as though he's strolling past, then yanks my facemask and brings it up to his face and goes, "Whooooooooooooooooooooooooooooo!"

We win the coin toss and take the ball. The kickoff goes out of bounds, and yellow flags fly. We have great field position, and Bow Wow gathers us up around him and says, "You moment! It's you moment!"

Hink calls Dallas Left, 91 F Corner Queen. We break the huddle and Vance says, "You okay, Mouse?"

I line up.

The crowd knows it's supposed to be quiet when we've

got the ball, but they can't help themselves. Hink shushes them with his arms. I hear one voice above all the others. It's Baxter, their defensive end. He's directly across from Pendleton, and snarling. "You don't want no part of this! I'm gonna kill you, boy!"

The ball snaps. I charge out of the backfield, give the middle linebacker a juke, and run to the right corner. I turn around and see Hink backpedaling and sidestepping, in trouble, and out of desperation he flips it to Hoverman in the right flat. There's nothing there: Hoverman makes the first tackler miss but is swarmed under. It's a big pile, with Chicago players unable to control their exhilaration and leaping atop the fallen. We've lost yardage on this first play. I race back to help my teammates up.

Tommy Way gets off the ground and shoves a defender. Pendleton is under there, too, rolling onto his side. DeNoon and I both extend a hand to him, and drag him to his feet. A couple Chicago guys struggle away from the pile.

I hear shouting. I look down and Hoverman is face-planted on the turf, clutching the ball with both arms. Other hands are reaching, grabbing, pulling. A linesman next to me is still blowing his whistle.

I lean over to see if Hoverman is moving.

I hear him say, "I still got it! Get the fuck off! Get the fuck off me!" It's Baxter who's got his entire 290-plus pounds atop him, and who's trying to rip away the football. Now he's also got Hoverman's arm and is yanking it behind his back. Hoverman yelps.

Pretty much everyone else is up, and Baxter is making like he's recovered the ball, and doesn't want to get off. With his free hand, he's signaling first down the other way. He's still got Hoverman pinned, and is subtly bending the running back's arm the wrong way. Hoverman's movements become frantic thrashes.

I lunge at Baxter and grab him by his shoulderpads, to try and choke him. I feel an official's arms start to pull me away. I reach up under the earhole of his helmet and claw him viciously, then grab the helmet and jerk it. I hear him say, "Hey! Hey!" in a booming baritone.

"Blue ball!" someone says above me. "Still blue ball!"

I don't let go. I feel Baxter release Hoverman, feel him trying to swing punches up at me, but I've got him leveraged against the ground. I knee him in the stomach and pull harder on his helmet. He's going "Hey!" and I'm working my fingers up under the back of his helmet and finally pull it free, so it wrenches forward completely off his head.

He shoves me off him. I see his wrapped forearms and fingers there on the ground, all the little pads placed strategically around his uniform. He lifts his head and looks me in the eye, angry and perplexed. We're both still on the ground, Hoverman is away from us and is apparently okay, and Baxter backhands me in the chest, a smothering blow that once and for all signals our teammates that this is about to be an actual fight, and they all converge, trying to get between us, pulling me away, holding him down. I fling Baxter's helmet by the facemask, so it clatters away far down the field.

The referee points at me and lobs his yellow flag skyward.

"Who's a fraud!" I hear myself shouting. "Who's a fraud! Who's a fraud!"

It's a 15-yard penalty on me. Our drive stalls and we punt.

Townsel comes over to me on the sidelines—yes, dressed in a uniform, not his street clothes—and I say, "What happened out there?"

"You went off your nut, dude. It happens. He had Hoverman down. You defended your teammate."

"I don't like Hoverman. And if he got hurt, I'd play more."

Townsel grins. "I guess people ain't logical."

*

Chicago has a strong aerial attack and a punk quarterback, Lydon Merling, who looks at our sidelines after every play, talking enormous amounts of trash though we can't really hear specifically what he's saying. Vance takes the bait, jawing back, pointing with his mouthpiece, grinning with utter unhappiness. "Home Depot ain't got enough tools to fix those fucking teeth! His teeth so crooked, he gotta suck the running back's dick sideways!" But Merling connects on a deep cross and runs past us pumping his arms and going, "Yeah! Yeah! Yeah!"

They run a draw that has the desired effect: our defensive backs are caught pedaling, Marcellus Blake turns his shoulders to run with the tight end, and their rusher is loose in the secondary for a gain of 24. Emboldened, they run straight at us, five-yard gain, four, six. Scott comes off the field cradling his shoulder and Kolakowski shakes his head at him. Merling drops back, his orange-and-black socks blurring, his shiny black cleats somehow looking a little fussy as he sidesteps the rush, sprints left, then he throws across his body, a cannon shot that Hamill has a bead on but can't get. It goes through his outstretched fingers and settles in a receiver's hands. He cock-walks into the end zone.

I see Coach Fond's chin dip and his eyes squeeze in semi-disgust. His arms are folded. Hinkler claps his hands lamely, like it's no big deal. Calcaterra taps my pads and points to the Jumbotron, where a little boy's face is slathered in liquid cheese, and he waves a tortilla chip at the camera. I look at Calcaterra—Dr. Doom himself—and snort. Faafeu waddles off the field and Swift is berating him: "You wanna play three-technique! You wanna get up the fucking field! Tell Kolakowski! Make a fucking demand! Otherwise, you're the fucking nose! Man the fuck up!"

We take the kick back to our 38. Hoverman stutter-steps and gains 11. Hinkler throws it incomplete to Wallace. I run a little trigger route and make a catch, self-tackling over the middle before they can really lay one on me. Schenk is in, and gets an easy look on a zero route but tries to run before he catches it. I read his eyes as we go back to the huddle. Does he look complicit? I chip a blitzing linebacker and we topple over, so I can watch Hoverman streak around the edge following Parnell and Richards, he makes a *great* move, slicing between tacklers, stiff-arming a safety, dancing and finally toppling out of bounds. Back in the huddle Vance goes, "Whoo! Zeke, you the man. You got slave feet, boy!" We're on their 22 and Bow Wow calls a sprint draw for me. Hinkler plows the ball into my stomach just fine and I squirt through the A-gap, I plant my left foot and in the distance see the back wall of the end zone, I accelerate but something happens to my hand, the rest of me gathers speed but my hand lags behind, I look down and a much bigger paw is on my own, and the fact that I can see both gloved, taped-up, empty hands is how I realize I've fumbled.

"Ball!" about ten people say at once. "Ball! Ball!"

Stupid football. For a moment it barrels in the same vector I do, I skid to a halt and reach backward, but it caroms off my wrist and spins away, controlled by the type of hidden forces we always convince ourselves are against us. A Chicago player falls on it, and then it comes clear it was big Baxter who stripped me. He bends down to put his face in front of mine, and lays into me with a stream of invective that would make a drill sergeant cringe.

*

Jesus, so now I'm thinking about Gasper and Ronnie the K, and now I'm thinking about *not* thinking about them. Frowning Lester Jefferson comes over and his arms make a rocking motion, *two hands*, but mercifully he doesn't say anything. Nobody does. I sit alone.

Merling takes an ill-advised shot downfield and

Brohammer tips it up in the air, it hangs tantalizingly, but Norwell can't make the pick. As the crowd groans, Hinkler says, "Oh, man, we got spatula hands!" and takes a sideways peek at me. Merling sprints out again, toward our sideline, then while stepping backward fires a laser across the field, good for a gain of 17. He's wearing a long-sleeve white shirt beneath his jersey and it looks vaguely preppy, like he got chilly walking down by the marina.

They run it. A counter that catches Shugarts running way upfield goes for eight. A simple trap goes for five. They're pushing around our defensive front. Scott is back in the game, but now McIntyre limps out. The first quarter ends. I think about the picture I currently make, sulky off by myself. Maybe some other time I'd have gotten up and looked busy. But pure frustration gets me out of my own head. I crush a plastic-coated paper cup, leave its corpse beside me on the bench.

I can see Coach Fond leaning a little sideways to get in on a conversation Kolakowski is having with Swift and Blake. Kolakowski is frantically pointing at a clipboard he's holding, shouting, but Fond doesn't take his eyes off the middle of the field where the officials are standing around talking, waiting for TV to return to the game. Fond says a few things without looking at Swift or Blake, still gazing out at the field.

Faafeu makes a great, stuffing tackle from his anchor spot before the center, and Chicago brings in a four-receiver package. It's third and five, and Merling can't find anyone open, feels pressure and spins away from Thomas and Maynor, doubles back, gets a block, tries to get upfield as Swift pummels him shy of the marker. They're around midfield and I get ready for a punt return, but they decide to go for it. The fans loose their lungs. But Merling sneaks it himself and gets the first down.

"*That's* the kind of game it's gonna be," says Bolduan. "Conventional wisdom out the motherfucking door."

I turn around and try to see Ronnie the K in the first few

rows of seats.

Five yards, four yards, six yards, two. Merling misses a throw, then hits two in a row. Their No. 88 rollicks to the sideline and inadvertently smashes a photographer. The guy has on a yellow vest and his lens is as long as my arm. He pratfalls backwards, snowboots in the air, as a policeman tries to catch him. You can hear everyone go, "Ohh!" His camera and baseball cap go flying. He gets up smiling, holding his face.

"Be ready for a sight-adjust," Hinkler tells me. Shave is just over there, still sling-armed, listening to calls on a headset. "That sight-adjust we talked about, if the end drops into coverage. Shake it off, Mouse. We all believe in you. I believe in you."

I want to say something smart-alecky in response.

Merling is in control, getting too much time, finding the open man, showing no bias toward any one receiver. He overthrows his tight end on a seam route but even then the play takes so long to develop, it's practically like a seven-on-seven drill. They get four on a trap, five on a sweep. Finally, as though impatience causes him to end the suspense, Merling calls a double-move and connects on a 30-yard score. We're down 14-0 early in the second quarter.

"Okay," I hear Toombs say to himself, "this is ridiculous." But a few moments later in the huddle, he says, "You still believe? You-all still got confidence? I know we're gonna win! I *know* it! Call a play, Butch! Call a play, and it's gonna work!" The o-linemen fire out of their blocks. Hoverman gets seven. Toombs makes a great block on their Will linebacker, helmet-on-helmet at full speed. He gets up clapping, snorting, wanting to do it all over again. Bow Wow pulls me for a heavy package and I watch Hoverman glide for a first down. Maybe we've found something. I'm off the field, standing next to Townsel (who looks out-of-place in his uniform, like a photocopy of his head has been stuck on this tall, strapping body), doing body-English with each rushing play. I'm thinking *call my number, please call my number*, but this isn't an injustice: it's common sense with maybe a whiff of the doghouse, too. Vance runs a beautiful 4-route at nine yards with their corner playing off, and he breaks a tackle to get into Chicago territory. Our fans have suffered with our early knockdown but they cast off wariness and let Vance hear it. Every stab deeper forward is met with mass belief. I try watching just Hoverman's feet, the rococo toe-taps and crow-hops of which his conscious mind is oblivious; I wonder if my feet are half as talented. But I can't focus with such exclusivity: I keep looking up to see where the ball is.

Wallace sets a classic little pick over the middle and DeNoon makes a one-handed grab and is loose in the open field. I look for a flag, but don't see one. DeNoon's legs spin cartoonishly forward as he tries to out-accelerate two DBs, then as he's going down he laterals to Vance who reaches for the ball while cutting back inside with coaches on our bench screaming, "No! No!" but Vance gets around the only man who can stop him and hotfoots into the end zone. Everyone around me exults. Defensive players pump their fists while wearing ruminative expressions, and look up at the stadium clock for deliverance.

Merling swaggers onto the field, magnetizing more than a hundred thousand eyeballs. His hips jut a little too far backward, like he's protecting some pelvic stiffness that goes away once he runs. He's smiling and chatting up the referee. He stands there, one leg straight, one knee bent, like a sultan's son pausing before the harem. Fond is hands-on-knees, staring darts at the quarterback. I imagine him uttering prayers of damnation. Vance yells, "Damn that asshole's ugly! Look like he run a 100-yard dash in a 90-yard gym!" Bow Wow gathers the offense and kneels in our circle, jabbering about something he can't quite spit out, clapping his stub-fingered hands, everyone leaning in to listen. "Start right now! You run it, you catch it…don't tell me! Forget all that! No explanations! No excuses! Just look at the man and cut his fuckin' head off!" I read the little corporate insignia on his headset.

Merling marches them yet again. He's already 12-of-15 for 147 yards. Their left guard can't get up. He writhes around on FieldTurf. Little men (my size!) stoop over him with one hand on his diaphragm, speaking into his facemask. He scooches onto his elbows and people applaud politely. Hinkler goes, "Come on, D! Come on, D! Come on, D! Come on, D!" through the entire next play, as King and Blake stand up the ball carrier and Scott crunches him down. Merling tosses a flare that's short of the marker, and their kicker is good from 42. Then the teams go back-and-forth with a punt apiece.

Our next possession we go play-action right away and Hinkler stands tall, pats the football, launches a munition shot down the middle of the field, Vance has a step and the ball is a perfect bomb…and it goes directly through Vance's hands. He stands there holding down the top of his head, as though it might mushroom off.

Hoverman gets three. Then we run a fake reverse, where I line up wide right and at the snap charge directly at Hinkler. He fakes a handoff to Hoverman then stands there super-casually with his back to the defense, looking me in, like a dad out for a catch with a really small child, this relaxed posture that says, *My little man will get here eventually*, holding the ball out as my arms and legs pump in attention-grabbing fashion, and my job is to spread my arms wide—one high, one low—as I approach the ball, and bend over as though slugged in the stomach, barely hiding the fact that the transfer has not, in fact, taken place. All of this is done as slight hyperbole, because we don't really want the defense to bite. We want them to sniff it out and stay in coverage. Hinkler looks deep right, then quickly back to short left, to me, because I've continued running, turning upfield into a wheel route, and nobody is with me. He lofts what amounts to a swing pass and I grab it and go, straight down Chicago's sideline, getting a long way before anyone even touches me and then lurching out of bounds. We're down to their 12.

But on the next play, Hink's pass to Wallace is a little high, and Wallace deflects it into the hands of a waiting safety, who seems utterly stunned by this development and stands in our end zone, holding the ball, seemingly staring at it, then finally giving a few token steps toward the field of play and capsizing on his own. Chicago gets two first downs and the first half ends.

*

"What you need to understand is you ain't in this alone! You ain't in this alone! It ain't just about you! Look at every other man out there! You gotta know every other man out there is relyin' on you! Look into their eyes! Look right now! Do it! Look at each other! It don't work if you don't realize that!" This is DeNoon, standing on a chair, addressing the entire team. He gets some perfunctory *yeahs* and *all rights*, but we're a deflated group. Jefferson gathers up the running backs but before he can say anything, Bow Wow steps over. Before *he* can say anything, here comes Coach Fond.

"We need points," Fond says. "You-all need to score points."

For a few minutes I sit at my locker. We're down ten. Who else could it be, who else was on Gasper's list? And what if I accidentally fumble again?

"Our best beats their best," says Toombs. "We ain't played our best. But our best beats their best. Destiny wears blue, baby. We worked too hard."

I close my eyes.

A different voice pipes up. "Withstand the first part of the game. That's what we said. Withstand it. Now you made it through. Now you're back in it now."

I think about the first half. I can barely remember it. I can barely remember my killer fumble. It only comes back to me in isolated little strobes.

"It's all in-cuts, guys! Stopping them is all about penetration and in-cuts!"

"Thirty minutes! Everything you dreamed about! Believe, men! Believe!"

"Let's go, let's go! Let it roll! Let's go! Let it outta your ass!"

"They can't double everybody! Somebody got a one-on-one on every play! You got a one-on-one, you gotta win! Win! Do not be afraid to be great! Win!"

"Hey. Hey, if you think there's pressure, you know what? There is!"

"Put a smile on yo' goddamn face and let's go play some football!"

I open my eyes. Hinkler punches his locker. Shave walks over and says, "Idiot. Punch it with your *left* hand."

*

Bolduan kicks off and Townsel makes a great tackle inside Chicago's 20. Merling is out there whooping and waving at us again, just acting like an idiot. But he zips a nice throw to his tight end, then sprints out and gains eight on his own. I hear Marcellus Blake go, "Break his spine, just break his fucking spine." They run consecutive draws and the second one is wiped out by a holding penalty. We've barely blitzed today but we're coming now, jailhouse, and Ed Scott pounds Merling from behind, snapping his head awfully, sending the ball ownerless out into dome air. Their right tackle flops backward, their tailback takes the opportunity to steamroll Hamill. I can see the ball bounce out of proportion with its impetus, two small rolls and a sudden 15-foot hop, it's in Danny Shugarts' hands but he can't keep his feet in bounds. They punt and we have it around midfield.

"It's time," Hoverman tells the huddle. "Come on."

Hinkler is in shotgun, and we run five straight plays that

way: Vance runs wind sprints to keep the safeties honest while the rest of us catch digs, stops and screens. Six yards, five, two, six. They can't get to Hink when we run these quick gun snaps. From the bottom of a pile I feel the ball's pebbled flesh, I dig my forefinger into its seam, a tackler presses all his weight on my legs as he gets up but I just rest here, another car crash down, several more to go. Next I follow a good block by Toombs and juke Baxter, so he trips over his own feet, and I can imagine the TV announcer giving him hell for leaving lingerie on the deck. Eventually someone else slams me down hard. They always do.

On Zoom Split Right 414 Shoot V-Queen, Hoverman gets loose in the flat, the pass is brilliantly timed as he squares his shoulders, I'm on the ground after a block, and I watch Hoverman disappear leaving vapor trails: he has this next gear about which I can only dream, and it doesn't matter that a DB has an angle on him because he jets straight for the end zone, untouched. We run screaming down the field like marauders and beat Hoverman about the helmet and shoulders. He falls down spiking the ball.

"We got us a game!" Bolduan shouts. "We got us an actual goddamn game!"

The defense rises up for a three-and-out and the dome is deafening. But we can't move it either, and punt it right back. McIntyre is limping again, and DeNoon says, "If he was a horse, he'd be half-a-can of glue." Merling throws it several plays in a row and the ball never touches the ground. Five minutes left in the third quarter. Now I can't sit down. I walk along the sidelines closer to our end zone, so I don't have to look through my giant teammates. From back here I can't really see the particulars of the snap. I watch Norwell shadow a big receiver, watch them in near perfect synchrony as the play goes elsewhere, this balletic nothing that only we three will ever know about. They cut and sprint and decelerate and saunter and stop. I turn around and look at the crowd. Precious few individual faces are visible; somehow I only compute the blurry group as a whole. One little girl standing by the front railing in the end zone is eating a hamburger, and I see her clearly and I desperately want to eat meat. I can practically smell it. There's a weird rustling right behind me, and I turn and see: it's a cheerleader, a shockingly pretty brunette woman in tiny black shorts and tall white boots, waggling pompoms. I step aside to let her dance, thinking for just a moment that this would be a poetic way to meet the love of my life. But her gaze is fixed to a bank of lights far above us, while she gives a little *what-are-you-doing-here* expression.

A crowd-rumble turns into a big noise, is how I realize we've recovered a fumble. I see Merling on the turf. I see Clancy Swift doing a gravedigger routine and Montrae Thomas holding the football and doing a pretend-finger-roll thing in celebration. I run out there and Hinkler is telling everyone, "This is it! This is it! This is it!"

"Everything we been through!" says Vance.

"Don't try to do too much!"

"Right here! Right now!"

"Whooooooooooooooooooooooooo!"

As I line up in the right slot, I hear Wallace say, "Man, I can't feel my feet."

Hop Quads Right Ace 687 F Drag. Hinkler shouts, "Go!" and I motion toward the ball, jogging behind our linemen until I'm all the way past the left tackle, Pendleton. At the snap I read the Mike linebacker cheating up, passing me off to a nickel man whose posture gives him away: he's one nervous twitch away from jumping a short route, a stab or drag. It's still dangerous for me to run the skinny post; DeNoon and Vance are also on deeper routes, meaning the deep middle will be congested with DBs. But this is basic stuff. I accelerate where the nickel expects me to power down and I'm past him. If Hink lofts it I'll get crushed, maybe sandwiched by two defenders. But he steps into the throw, powers it on a rope. I reach with my left hand, jostle myself slightly off stride, *bang*, the ball strikes me and I deaden it, the fans become deafening static, the ball complies and snugs under my armpit and I'm off, zipping up the middle as DBs trail after and converge. Everything is changed. I see fear in their faces. I'd have scored on a perfect throw, but I gain 52 yards before they get me.

"Don't give us life," says Vance. "Don't let us keep breathing."

Bow Wow calls three straight runs. You can't fault him; Hoverman's playing great. But he's ankle-tackled on the third, and the crowd moans and boos. Bolduan steps up and drills a 29-yarder. 17-17.

*

The fourth quarter begins. I feel lightheaded and think about asking one of the trainers for some oxygen, but I try breathing deeply through my nose instead. Merling doesn't seem quite as cocky now, and this lack of cockiness reads as nerves. Vance shouts, "My man so dumb he eat food stamps!" but there's no way the quarterback can hear him. I've never attended as important a game, let alone played in one. I finally understand why they constantly tell us to stop thinking. There's no thinking in here. It's too loud, too overstimulated. Every command must bypass the frontal lobe, which is a kindergartener oohing and ahhing and clapping and pointing. If your duties aren't stamped into your DNA, you're lost. I feel myself thin and spread, lost to time. It's wonderful and a little awful.

"Yo," Hoverman says, "nice catch."

I tilt my chin at him.

Merling keeps it on the ground. An off-tackle for five. A plunge for two. A draw for five more. Hamill comes limping off so Yates moves from nickel to left corner and Townsel jumps into the fray, covering Chicago's third receiver. I feel a surge of pride for him. No question Merling is paying attention, though, and he takes a shot at Townsel, but he throws it under fire and it's over everyone's head.

"There we go, Townsel!" I say.

We're bringing heat but Scott is offsides, and Merling chucks it into the ground to take the five yards. Kolakowski rages until Fond moves microscopically in his direction, his mouth moving slightly, and then the defensive coordinator quiets down and straightens his ball cap. Merling hands it to the fullback, a harmless second-and-short play intended as a sort of multimeasure rest, but the fullback absolutely plows over Thomas and then Brohammer, and looks dumbfounded to be rumbling on his own. He's slow, so we finally crumple his legs, but the field has tilted. They're on our 31. Merling takes a foolish end-zone shot: Townsel and Brohammer are both playing back, the receiver is triple-covered, Townsel leaps with his hands spread wide, somehow I can see his big eyes, the ball is directly to him but it glances off one finger and then his facemask and thumps the ground harmlessly. He jumps three times in agony. Defensive teammates slap his back.

Merling takes advantage. He puts a post-corner where only a few men in the world can. His wideout's legs go limp, splashing within the end zone's perimeter, as his arms grab a football dropped from heaven. Touchdown.

"Back and forth," says DeNoon. "They can't stop us, neither. Let's go."

8:12 on the clock. Plenty of time. Hinkler hits Vance on a dig. I drive diagonally across the field yielding all sorts of attention, and Wallace makes an underneath grab. DeNoon catches a wide receiver screen and carries it for eight. Hurricane Hink's throws are deadly accurate. In the huddle he's quiet and focused. He says, "89 Z Reverse" and I'm back in the right slot, a simple play-fake to Hoverman, I actually get the ball on a reverse this time and streak around the left edge but the Will linebacker is there and he crushes me with a shoulder-shot to my head, my feet keep going and then fulcrum ceilingward, an involuntary pirouette giving me what feels like a full minute of disconnection from Planet Earth which ends as I crash to the turf on my hip but holding, squeezing, *cleaving to* the football.

"How the fuck does he get up?" says the Will linebacker.

"He made outta feathers and lint!" Vance says.

It's third and short. In the huddle I look at everybody's feet. I find them fascinating in kind of a nonspecific and philosophical way, which is how I know I might be concussed. Coach Fond takes a timeout. What do you do here? There is do the expected, heavy package, bust it right at them and eke out the first down. There is do the expected unexpected, heavy package, throw it, see if you can bust a big one. Or keep me out here, spread out the defense, *then* run it, fewer defenders to block. Or just keep the throttle down and throw-throw-throw, multiple targets, pitch and catch. After long consultation with people at higher pay grades than mine, Bow Wow calls 21 Slam. I amble to the sideline. We're doing the expected.

It's all about Bettany and Parnell. Bettany must battle the nose to a standstill. Parnell must get an inside seal on either the end or the three-technique, depending on Chicago's alignment. Then Toombs can bust through the crease to clear out defenders coming from the second level, and Hoverman can fling himself forward for the first down.

It doesn't happen. Hoverman is stuffed. Fourth and a short two from our own 40. Five minutes and two timeouts left. I'm near Fond, who's hands-on-knees again. His mouth is a dot. Computations spin. Without changing his position or posture, he says, "Punt."

*

Scoggins pins the returner deep, but he wiggles free and busts it upfield, further, further, it's a disaster, he's at midfield and finally clotheslined out of bounds. King, Yates and

Townsel slink off the field shaking their heads.

"One time, D! One time!"

"Kill they ass!"

"Come on!" to the stands. "Get up! Get up! Make noise!"

"One time!"

"Plug it up! Plug the middle!"

"Aaaaaaaaaaaah! Come on! Aaaaaaaaaaaaaaaaaaaah!"

Their tailback pounds out a four-yarder, staying in bounds. The fullback is stuffed on second down.

"Here it is! Here it is! We got 'em!"

"Get up!"

"*Please!* One time!"

Merling…oh, no. Merling's back to pass. A hotdogging little organized rollout, we hate him, he pumps left, there's a fade open right, Merling sticks it in there, it's a catch. First down.

*

We burn a timeout. They plunge into the line. We use our last timeout, they plunge twice more. The clock stops at two minutes. The field goal team comes out. It's a 32-yarder. It's good. 27-17.

A swell of sorrow settles on our bench. "Come on!" Hinkler says, clapping. "Two-minute drill and an onside kick. It's happened before. Don't lose hope." Vance and DeNoon have dropped their helmets and don't say anything. "Come on!" from Hink. "This is what we do! Outs and crosses! March it down! One missed tackle and we're back in!"

Brohammer leads the kickoff return squad out.

"All right?" says Hinkler. "We can do this! You guys with me?"

Townsel is out there as a blocker. Chicago squibs the kick, and it goes right to him. It bounces off his pads but he quickly gathers it up. He looks behind him, as though to lateral, then takes a few tentative steps forward, holding the ball in his hands, away from his body. Tacklers reach him *en masse*, he's hit low and high, and the ball…the ball…it's out, it's loose, Chicago has it, they fall down, they yip and squeal, that's it, all done.

*

Monday morning I go to a bookstore. I find *The Heart Treasure of the Enlightened Ones*.

The first page says this:

> In ancient India, rishis were long-haired ascetics living in forest retreats, sustaining themselves with whatever alms might come their way, and remaining aloof from family life, trade, farming, and other ordinary worldly activities.
>
> These rishis varied greatly in their degree of accomplishment and realization. There were some who achieved miraculous powers. But even such accomplished rishis had not yet cut the root of the obscuring emotions, and so they remained vulnerable to pride and attached to praise and recognition. Lord Buddha, on the other hand, totally eliminated ego-clinging at its root from the very moment he conceived the thought of enlightenment. How was it that he was able to do this? It was because he sought enlightenment exclusively for the sake of others.

CHAPTER 27

I ring the doorbell. A uniformed man answers and asks me to follow him in. We march past blackening portraits, over inch-thick carpeting, into a study whose casement windows each have an elaborate wrought-iron 'F' at their centers, and which overlook the lesser lights of Grosse Pointe. A caged fire roars.

He keeps me waiting twenty minutes. I inspect a rock-ribbed row of hardcovers, which looks as though it hasn't been touched for decades. I think of Gatsby's uncut books. But as nobody is attending me, I take down one volume—*Prohibition in Ireland*—and the pages riffle freely. There don't appear to be any novels; I read titles such as *The Origin of Yamato Japan* and *Saint Gregory the Illuminator*. This library could supply Gasper with enough esoteric facts about the world to last him a century. Oh, the Great Gasper. I haven't spoken with him since his big score.

There's movement from an unexpected direction: a hidden set of double doors opens. And in steps Hawthorne Fahrenthold, scion of a billionaire logging clan and the man who metaphorically signs my paychecks. He's around forty, very tall, pouch-eyed and grim.

"Nick," he says. "It's a great pleasure to meet you."

"Thank you. Thanks for having me."

"I'm sorry my secretary's telephone call came in such a

cloak-and-dagger fashion. First of all I just want you to know what a great season. I'm sorry we fell short. But you were just marvelous for us. Really. We're an underdog city, and you're an underdog player." He has his arms folded behind his back.

"Well, just…. Thanks for the opportunity."

"Unfortunately, I wish I could have invited you up to the house for a happier occasion."

I try to swallow. In the room from whence Fahrenthold just came, I can hear a playoff game blaring from a television. All afternoon my mind has run through possibilities, what this request for an audience could mean. The andirons and letter openers hidden in this room offer violent escape.

"And," he says, jaw moving only minimally, "I feel ridiculous keeping this such a secret, but for the moment we're trying to keep it under wraps, for the good of the family. You see, Coach Fond's son has passed away."

I feel something crack in me.

"I know how much a coach means to his players. He's a foundation and a source of great strength. Well, now you men are going to support him. Daniel Shugarts was just here, and Starling also specifically asked me to fetch you. He's right there, in the other room. Please go in and see him."

I do. Fahrenthold stays behind. This is a media room, as modern-looking as the study is austere. The game flashes on a gigantic plasma TV which has a series of smaller screens set in the wall around it. I don't see Fond at first, and scan several laptops, a videoconferencing setup, an Xbox, an espresso bar. Then I see a pair of feet uncross in a recliner. Coach Fond says, "Some pretty dadgum poor game managing. Can't use a timeout right there. Just can't."

I'm not sure if he's speaking to me. I say, "I wasn't watching, sir."

"Just a lack of discipline," says Fond. "You-all didn't see it, but just a minute ago, Philly go' have 'em stopped, they were getting the ball back. But they were offsides. A cornerback. A dadgum cornerback is offsides." He leans over the recliner's arm to look behind him, at me.

"Coach, I'm just…so sorry."

His chiseled face flinches and assumes an angry expression, as though he's annoyed I won't talk football. It passes quickly, and he turns away again, sinking out of view in his chair.

"You-all were his favorite," says Fond. "I ever tell you that, Mouse? In just half-a-season, you-all became his favorite player. Why'n you come on over here and set awhile."

I walk to him. My back and armpits are soaked. I sit on the couch, try and make sense of the football statistics phosphorescing out at us.

"I s'pose maybe it's because you-all aren't much more than his size," he says, smiling unhappily.

"Yes sir."

"No, I don't really mean that, Mouse. I think maybe you-all were his favorite because you work so hard. He used to come set with me up at practice. He liked the boys that worked." Fond's eyes are dry, and as he speaks, he gestures with one hand. We could be conferring about an opponent's nickel defense. I know that he and Danny Shugarts were in here praying just a few minutes ago. "They take one thing away from you at a time," he says.

I swallow.

"He was a sick little man these past few weeks. Can't say he had any idea 'bout football or much of anything else by then. I'm sure he'd be second-guessing his old man just like everybody else. 'Shoulda gone for it on fourth down.'" He scratches a big, shoe-leather earlobe. His thumb plucks at a button on the arm of his chair. "Well, maybe I shoulda. I'm told you-all still living at a motel, Mouse."

"It's a hotel, sir."

He nods. "I'm go' tell you why I ask. I know you signed that new contract and I know a man sometimes doesn't know what to do with money. But if'm not mistaken, that contract goes for two more years. Maybe time to put down some roots."

I don't say anything.

"Y'see, Coach Nugent had a conversation with me before he left. He told me you-all were using that drug, the growth hormone."

"…"

"And a man who treats his body that way, and a man who doesn't have a home?" Fond has edged forward in his chair. He looks very old. "This game eats you up, son. It takes all our time. I didn't have a family until I was already an old man. Are you a Christian? Were you raised a Christian?"

"No sir, I wasn't."

"I ain't go' try to convert you. I know how hard it is to play in this dadgum league. Believe me. But you go' find something, Mouse. You go' find something so you won't have to…do that to yourself."

"Yes, sir."

"I thought hard about turning you in, son. I thought hard about letting the league know right then, when I found out. I know it wasn't right to wait this long, to wait until the season was over. That was my mistake and my weakness, because I needed you so bad. I'm go' tell you, I'm ashamed of that."

My stomach bottoms out.

"And now it's too late. So here's what we're go' do. You-all will be suspended for four games at the start of next year. You'll get your pay, but you can't practice and you can't play. Nobody but you and me's go' know why. And then we're go' welcome you-all back with open arms."

"…"

"You don't need it. I promise you that. I been coaching, what, thirty years. I know 'em when I see 'em."

This isn't true. It just isn't true. He cut me. He watched me run around this summer and then chopped off my head.

"I know you're not a Christian, Mouse. I'm just at the beginning of thinking about this, but I know there's got to be a way to ignore every other voice you hear, and only listen to God's. Imagine if you had a group of men, and they did that. You could find 53 men who did that. I don't need you-all to listen to us coaches, not really. We'll tell you what play you go' run. But can you imagine if you shut everything else out? Purity of focus, for just one cause. Mistakes would get made. You-all are human. Maybe we'd even lose. But there'd be glory in it."

My eyes follow the big-screen game without seeing it.

Fond says, "I keep thinking maybe because I waited, I was too old. Maybe there's something wrong in my genes…maybe that's why he got sick." Now his throat catches a bit.

I say, "Sir, I'm sure that's not why he—"

"He liked meeting you, Mouse. He sure enough told me that."

CHAPTER 28

Townsel calls. "Aggie and me are over at the park. Bring a football."

It's a few days after my talk with Fond, ten days since our season ended. I've slept a bunch and thought about going away, or visiting my parents. My joints ache, a condition that's maybe as much about HGH as football; I'm still taking injections, but tapering the doses. I haven't been back to the team complex, haven't really seen anyone. Townsel has stopped by a few times, to see if I'm really okay with him taking Aggie to Houston in a couple days. It breaks my heart, but I am. Henny has phoned several times, too, but I haven't answered.

It's been me and Dilgo Khyentse locked up together alone.

Have I come to any great revelation? Perhaps only this: stop aiming for a great revelation. Maybe this is excuse-making. I don't know, but if a game is what stirs in you feelings of selflessness and integration and *happiness*, then play that game. Do I regret illegal drug use? It was and is an extortionate, indispensable ladder. I can never go back.

At the baseball fields, Aggie gallops over to say hello. He kisses my hand then pads back through fresh snow to stand (and subsequently piss) by Townsel. I toss my teammate the ball, and he zings it back.

Townsel. Even if I did see Shugarts and Hoverman with Ronnie the K, he couldn't offer those multimillionaires enough cash to make participation in his schemes worth their while. No, it would have to be minimum-salary guys like me.

And like Townsel.

I think about his easy missed interception against Chicago. I think about his game-clinching kickoff fumble, the one that sealed the final margin at ten points.

Maybe the main reason I haven't called Gasper yet is I don't want to know.

*

We play catch in our heavy clothes. Townsel's phone rings. It's Kade Gregory, another practice-squadder, who has Marcus Schenk with him at the team complex, and they're bored and say they'll come on by. The four of us fling around the rock for a while, then start running plays two-on-two, two-hand-touch, one blitz per series. Schenk is on my team, and I ask him to take off his ski hat so I can look at "Hand with Reflecting Sphere" again, but it turns out his hair has started to grow in over the tattoo, giving the whole affair a stubbly, through-the-weeds aspect that's disconcerting.

During a break in the action, Schenk calls Conrad King, who's also supposedly still in town. Sure enough, King wants to play. This gives me the idea of mass-texting most everyone on the team. While many of the big names have taken off for parts unknown, it turns out there are still some guys hanging around Detroit, healing up or else waiting for their kids to get through the school year. Brohammer shows up with Ruvell Underwood and Ahmad Custance. Yates and Maynor arrive at the same time. Bolduan calls to tell me he's in Costa Rica, but wishes he could play. Scoggins, the punter, appears with two 24-packs of not-so-premium beer. Soon there are a dozen of us flinging the ball around. We choose teams and start playing. The linemen all get to run as quarterbacks and receivers, while Schenk, King and I are blockers. Brohammer wants to get rid of the touch football rules and play tackle, but common sense prevails.

Have I ever laughed so much? Underwood catches a bomb from Custance and is about to score when he loses his footing and flips into the air, landing face first in a soft pile of blown snow, so that his head, arms and torso are momentarily lost, and only his kicking legs are visible. A pass goes right through Tommy Way's hands and hits him squarely in the forehead, causing him to fall backwards into Meleki Faafeu and they crash to the ground while the football bounds straight up and lands directly on Way's belly for a completion. I "block" Calcaterra with what I consider to be classic offensive lineman technique—hands up, butt low, feet stomping hard side to side—and he doubles over with hilarity. Faafeu, one of the biggest men in professional sports, makes a circus catch in the end zone and tries turning a cartwheel by way of celebration, but only succeeds in kicking off one of his boots, which flies over the park fence. Nobody keeps score.

We play until dusk and wonder if the park lights will come on. And they do! Everyone's sweating and shivering, but nobody wants to stop.

My phone rings again. It's not another teammate. It's Henny.

"Hello," I say.

"You answered."

"True."

"Why'd you answer this time? And why are you breathing like that?"

"..."

"I went back to California. But now I'm back. I'm here. Doesn't that tell you something?"

"Only that you freaked yourself out almost committing to another member of my gender."

"I love you I love you I love you I love you I love you I

love you. Okay?"

"..."

"Can I come see you? Are you at your hotel? I had a revelation, all right? I finally understand what you were trying to tell me all those times."

"Henny, *I* don't even know what I was trying to tell you all those times. I don't even know what times you're talking about."

"I'm sorry your team lost. You played really well. I bet you're beating yourself up over fumbling, but when you ran that long one. Wow."

"..."

"You think I don't know. You think I wasn't paying attention. But I know: I know you wanted to stop living by what other people say." Her tone is lawyerly. "Well, you lose. Too bad. It's never gonna happen. Maybe there are people out there better than us who can do that, who can just try their best and smile a lot and feel really good and *integrated* and let the fucking chips fall where they fucking may. But not you and me. Not you and me, my friend. We're only happy when someone pats us on the head and gives us a cookie and says, 'Good boy. Good girl.' And how can you undo that? You can't, that's how. But there's good news. There's good news, Nick. Do you wanna hear what it is? The good news is after all this time we've known each other, when I finally got to watch you play again, it turns out I get a cookie when you get a cookie. I get a cookie when you get a cookie, Nick. If that's not love, tell me what it is."

I look at the guys, who are puffing smoke on each exhalation. The semidarkness has widened my pupils, so when the headlights of early commuters scud down Allen Road, I feel the ocular equivalent of an ice-cream headache, and blind spots arise. The calf, old tormentor, has started complaining, and I think: *maybe it'll never heal properly* followed quickly by *I won't be able to do this next year without those shots.* These giants standing around me, these beasts. If only I could shrink them down and send them punching and kicking inside my brain, laying waste to these thoughts, maybe to all thoughts. I look at another bypassing car, stare at its headlights, savor the rampaging distraction in my head. "I gotta go," I tell Henny.

"I'm sorry," she says. "That's all I really wanted to tell you. I'm just really really sorry."

I blow snot out through one nostril, then the other. "DeLuca Field. About six blocks from my place." It's impossible to tell if I say this out of weakness or out of strength.

ABOUT THE AUTHOR

Christopher Harris is the author of four novels, *Slotback Rhapsody*, *The Big Clear*, *War On Sound* and *Tulsa*. He lives in Amherst, MA, and Los Angeles, CA, USA.